"I want to know who you are,"

Mercy said stubbornly. "And who shot you."

"That's not important," he stated flatly.

"You could have died," she said. "Another inch higher and I wouldn't have been able to just slap a bandage on, you know." She paused. "You came here because you didn't want your wound reported. If I'm going to protect you, the least you can do is tell me your name." She looked at him expectantly. "I've got all day."

He shrugged his shoulders in defeat. "My name is Rio Barrigan. That's all you need to know, and that's *all* you're getting." Then he spoke more softly. "You don't want to know more about me. So don't ask any more questions. They'll only bring you trouble."

"It's too late," she said coolly, looking into his chilling eyes. "I've already got it."

Dear Reader,

It's summertime, and the livin' may or may not be easy—but the reading is great. Just check out Naomi Horton's *Wild Blood*, the first in her new WILD HEARTS miniseries. In Jett Kendrick you'll find a hero to take to heart and never let go, and you'll understand why memories of their brief, long-ago loving have stayed with Kathy Patterson for sixteen years. Now she's back in Burnt River, back in Jett's life—and about to discover a secret that will change *three* lives forever.

We feature two more great miniseries this month, too. Cathryn Clare's ASSIGNMENT: ROMANCE brings you *The Baby Assignment*, the exciting conclusion to the Cotter brothers' search for love, while Alicia Scott's THE GUINESS GANG continues with *The One Who Almost Got Away*, featuring brother Jake Guiness. And there's still more great reading you won't want to miss. Patricia Coughlin's *Borrowed Bride* features a bride who's kidnapped—right out from under the groom's nose. Of course, it's her kidnapper who turns out to be Mr. Right. And by the way, both Alicia and Patricia had earlier books that were made into CBS TV movies last year. In *Unbroken Vows*, Frances Williams sends her hero and heroine on a search for the heroine's ex-fiancé, a man hero David Reid is increasingly uninterested in finding. Finally, check out Kay David's *Hero in Hiding*, featuring aptly named Mercy Hamilton and enigmatic Rio Barrigan, a man who is far more than he seems.

Then join us again next month and every month, as we bring you more of the best romantic reading around—only in Silhouette Intimate Moments.

Yours,

Leslie Wainger,
Senior Editor and Editorial Coordinator

Please address questions and book requests to:
Silhouette Reader Service
U.S.: 3010 Walden Ave., P.O. Box 1325, Buffalo, NY 14269
Canadian: P.O. Box 609, Fort Erie, Ont. L2A 5X3

HERO IN HIDING

KAY DAVID

Silhouette®
INTIMATE™MOMENTS®

Published by Silhouette Books

America's Publisher of Contemporary Romance

LANG LIT
FIC PB

SILHOUE

ISBN 0-373-07725-4

HERO IN HIDING

Copyright © 1996 by Carla Luan

Books by Kay David

Silhouette Intimate Moments

Desperate #624
Baby of the Bride #706
Hero in Hiding #725

KAY DAVID

is a native Texan who currently resides in the Patagonia region of Argentina, along with her husband of twenty-one years, Pieter, and their cat, Leroy. She holds undergraduate degrees in English literature and computer science, as well as a graduate degree in behavioral science. Her careers have varied from designing jewelry to building homes, but her first love has always been writing. She has also been published under the name Cay David.

To PDL—*te amo, querido.*

Prologue

"It's happening again."

"Are you sure?"

"*Sái.* There is no question about it— unfortunately."

"And it's him?"

"Oh, yes. Sister Lydia was sitting up with the mother superior—she's ill, you know—and she heard a scream from the river. When she got to the window, she saw it all. It was...ugly."

"*¡Diga me!* Tell me everything."

"There was only one man. He'd just crossed the river, his trousers were still wet. Sister Lydia said two men in uniforms forced him on his knees, then hit him across the face. When he fell down, they took the wallet he'd hidden around his waist. They laughed when he begged them to leave him enough money to get back home."

"Did they kill him?"

"*No, no*—not this time—but I'm afraid, Rio. It could happen so easily—"

"But it won't."

"Then you'll come?"

"Yes, Sister, I'll come. But this time, I'm not leaving until the job is done."

Chapter 1

His aim was flawless, and his arm was strong. He could have easily pierced the man's throat with a single throw.

Rio Barrigan's fingers trembled as they curled around the hard rubber handle of the twelve-inch serrated knife.

He'd never wanted to kill someone this badly.

The desire scared him as it coursed through his veins. He'd felt passion plenty of times in his forty-year life—passion for women, passion for power, passion for money—but he'd wanted nothing as badly as he wanted, right now, to feel the muscles in his arm tighten and release in a pitch of perfect precision.

His tongue snaked out and moistened dry lips, then he wriggled closer to the dry brush that shielded him from view. Fifty feet below, Rick Greenwood—*Sheriff* Greenwood—paused, a clutch of bills in his hand, blood gleaming obscenely on the money. The Spanish pleas of the man he'd been beating whimpered into the silence as

Greenwood stopped and looked straight up the mountainside.

For a heartbeat, Rio held his breath, but Greenwood's pale eyes slipped through him and into the night. The sheriff didn't see him—he never saw him—not even when they passed each other on the street. Greenwood ignored people with skin as dark as Rio's—unless, of course, he wanted something from them.

But that was going to change, Rio thought with blind determination. *He* would make it change. Twenty-five years ago, when he'd been a half-breed kid, he didn't have the power to make Greenwood look him in the eyes, but now Rio did. He not only had the power, but he also had the means, even though Greenwood didn't know it yet.

Rio's hand tightened on the knife. Returning to the Rio Grande valley of Texas was the last thing he'd wanted to do, but when he'd heard the sister's voice on the telephone, he'd known he would come. He owed her that much—and she'd known it, too—counted on it. Briefly, he wondered what she would think if he paid his debt to her by killing the man below.

Before he could be tempted any more, Rio's murderous thoughts froze. And so did his body. Against his neck, a more urgent demand presented itself—the cold twin barrels of a sawed-off shotgun. The voice that spoke was as chilling as the weapon. "Get up, you sneaking pepper-belly, or I'll blow your damn head off."

Rio didn't stop to think, didn't stop to plan. As always, he simply reacted. In a flash of movement and rage—at the deputy holding the gun and at himself for being caught—he rose, knocked the gun from the uniformed man's hand, then sliced his knife across the soft arm exposed in the white moonlight. Dark blood welled as the deputy screamed. Rio ran.

But not fast enough.

The hot, sticky air hovered over the desert in an expectant breath. For twenty-four hours, the temperature had been over one hundred degrees. In a few more hours, the desert floor might cool off, but now, at midnight, the ground still held the heat of the sun.

Rio hardly noticed.

He was too busy watching the woman as she walked from the isolated cabin into her front yard.

The full moon hung over the horizon, watching with him. Using his knife, Rio flicked away an advancing scorpion, then winced in pain and stifled his curse.

If the light had been any brighter, or the deputy more careful with his aim, Rio wouldn't be worrying about finding a doctor. He'd be in a body bag, and the sheriff would be dancing on his grave. As it was, Rio had been lucky—the sisters must have been praying. All he needed was a bandage and some time, two things for which he wouldn't endanger the convent. Thank God Sister Rosa had mentioned the clinic—now it was his only answer.

And the woman—the doctor—was his only hope.

Rio's eyes never left her figure. She was standing in the middle of her front yard, her eyes facing the river—somewhere out in the darkness where Texas ended and Mexico began. *What in the hell was she doing?* A flash of stinging pain shot through Rio's lower back, and his hand tightened on the rubber grip of his knife. Whatever it was, he wished she would hurry up and get it over with—he couldn't approach until she'd turned her back. They were so isolated, no one would hear her scream, but you never knew whose eyes were looking in the darkness. Besides, if he didn't have the benefit of surprise, he'd never be able to take her. He was getting weaker by the minute.

She tilted her head, the moonlight caressing the slim column of her throat. Wavy, thick hair tumbled down her back. As Rio watched, she lifted up the heavy strands and let the baking desert air blow over the nape of her neck. For a second, she paused, her hands on top of her head, her hair curling around her face. In another time and place, Rio would have appreciated the curve of her breasts, the turn of her hips, the graceful way she stood, but right now, hot stabs of pain were streaking down his lower back and into his legs. If he didn't move soon, he wasn't going to move at all.

As if she'd heard his thoughts, she dropped her hands and turned, her narrow shoulders weighed down with an emotion Rio didn't stop to analyze. A second later, he was behind her, one hand covering her gasping mouth, his knife pressing against her throat.

Instinctively she began to fight him, her feet kicking out at him, her hands going into fists. One foot connected painfully with his shin, but Rio was a big man, and it was a simple matter for him to subdue her. The one thing he hadn't counted on, however, was his reaction to her. His shirt hung open, and as he pulled her roughly against him, his feverish chest attracted the long strands of her hair like shavings to a magnet. The curls were silver blond and silky, and their sweet smell surprised him.

Ignoring the sensations, both painful and pleasant, he concentrated on the moment and forced his voice into a coarse demand. "Keep quiet and you'll be fine." He pressed the tip of the knife to the soft spot under her jaw, and finally she froze. "Talk and you die."

The respite lasted only a second. To Rio's surprise, as soon as the words were finished, as soon as their meaning had died in the hot air of the desert, the woman renewed her movements against him. Ineffectually, she tried to hit his side, to lash out in his direction, but all her efforts were for nothing. Disregarding her squirming and her fists, Rio managed to pick her up, one arm around her waist, the other hand holding the knife rock steady at her throat. Her trembling body was supple and delicate under his harsh embrace, but the harder she fought, the tighter he held on. He shook her slightly. "Stay still, damn it."

At length, she slumped against him and nodded once, a low moan of fear escaping from the back of her throat. Her soft, full lips warmed the palm of his hand, and even in his pain, Rio wondered what it would be like to kiss a mouth that generous, that sensual. The heat of her heavy breasts lay across his other arm, and his body automatically responded to hers. Obviously sensing the change, the woman quivered with fear, reminding Rio of a rabbit that had picked up his blood scent earlier in the arroyo.

A flicker of sympathy for her came over him. Putting the image—and the emotion—away from his mind, he jerked her again, hot pain racing down his back. "I've never forced a woman, and I don't intend to start with you. Relax."

It was as if he hadn't spoken. Once more, he heard that tiny simper of frustration and fear. He started toward her cabin. The sooner they started, the sooner he could leave.

She wasn't a short woman, but in his grip, her feet dangled at least six inches off the ground. He strode up her front porch and kicked open the screen door, keeping one arm around her waist and his other hand at her mouth. His eyes took in the scene with automatic precision. They were in a small living room, and the draperies had already been pulled against the darkness of the night. One dim light glowed in the corner. The air-conditioning was off, and the curtains blew in with hot, sticky air.

"I'm going to take my hand from your mouth, but if you scream, you'll regret it." To emphasize his point, Rio pressed the tip of his knife against her skin. He had no intention of cutting her, of course, but she had no idea of that. He stopped way short of breaking her delicate skin. "*¿Comprende?*" She nodded again, her body shuddering against him.

The blade just under the woman's chin, Rio eased her down, her body dragging against his as her feet reached the floor. The movement pulled up her T-shirt, and the contact was instantaneous, her bare back against his bare chest. Slowly, his fingers left her lips and trailed downward, splaying across her throat. Under his touch, her fluttering pulse beat out a rhythm of fright. With his right arm, he pressed her into him, the steel of his arm against the suppleness of her breasts, the knife blade hard at her jaw.

Despite his plans to the contrary, for one short second, Rio allowed himself the luxury of the contact. She was a beautiful woman. His eyelids swept down, and he indulged himself in the fine texture of her skin, the sweet scent rising from her hair, the soft pressure of her body against his. How long had it been since he'd been this close to a good woman? How long since he'd touched someone with gentleness instead of anger? Automatically, his hand contracted on her throat as he realized the answer—too damn long.

In the mirror over the sofa, Mercy Hamilton watched as her captor's eyes closed, terror pouring through her veins. Her breath came in quick, short gasps, and the fear that had taken her in the yard grew to monstrous proportions. Her hands slick with fright, Mercy flicked her own eyes over her living room, desperate for a weapon, a way out, anything.

She bit back a sob of frustration. She'd been in Ciudad Bravo for exactly three days, and she hadn't even had the phone service turned on yet. They were miles, absolutely miles, from any other residence. In the clinic out back, she had scalpels, but what good would they do her out there? They might as well have been on the moon. If only she had a neighbor—only one! But there was no one.

Earlier, the vast stretch of desert had delighted her; now it bound her, as closely as a rope, to the dangerous man behind her.

In a second's consideration, Mercy realized her options were slim. Nothing in medical school had prepared her for this, but she wasn't going to stand still and simply let this stranger cut her throat. She was too far from home to die all alone. She had to fight back; there was nothing else she could do. Heedless of the blade, she tensed and prepared to spring.

A second before she moved, she must have signaled her intent. His eyes flew open, and he reached out to stop her.

But he was too slow.

She swirled, then threw every ounce of her 110 pounds against him. He caught her full weight against his chest, staggered and went down. The knife flew from his hand and fell to the rag rug, bouncing once, a soft thud that went unheard in the heavy grunt of his surprise and the desperate panting of her efforts. Mercy reached out and grabbed the black rubber handle, the heavy blade glinting obscenely in the low light of her living-room lamps.

She was still on top of him when she sat up, her shaking legs straddling his wide chest, the knife clutched between both her damp palms. The point rested against the dark triangle of hair at his throat. "Don't move, or I'll do a quick tracheotomy—without the anesthetic."

Mercy's false bravado worked, and beneath her, the man grew instantly still. Her heart slowed enough for her to get her first good look at him. In the mirror, she'd seen only a shadowy figure. Now she saw reality, and like two trains racing for the same track, her mind split. On one side, logic maintained her fear. On the other track, a gut reaction rocked her. The man beneath her was without a doubt the most striking individual she'd ever laid eyes on.

His entire face was a study of contrast, of lines and angles, darkness and light, from the straight, narrow slope of his nose to the full, sensual pull of his mouth. His hair—so black it shone blue in the dim lights—was held in check by a red bandanna across his forehead, and an equally dark stubble shadowed his jawline. His skin was bronzed—either by genes or by the sun, she couldn't tell—but a thin, white line creased one black eyebrow. It was his eyes, however, that paralyzed Mercy.

They were the lightest shade of gray she'd ever seen, so light, in fact, that she first thought they held no color at all. She shivered involuntarily. Their paleness was totally out of place in the darkness of his features, but something about their very lightness intrigued her. Despite the situation, or maybe because of it, Mercy's heart skidded.

She ignored her reaction, her hand squeezing the knife even harder. "Who are you?"

He blinked once, but other than that, he looked as if he had chosen to lie on the floor with her sitting on his chest. She pressed the tip of the knife into his throat, the skin dimpling slightly. "I asked you a question," she said. "Answer me."

His face remained impassive, but behind the mask, Mercy saw a glimmer of something—she couldn't quite tell what. She swallowed against her fear, a heavy knot that was lodged in the back of her throat. In an instant, she could slice open his throat.

But she wouldn't. Couldn't.

He seemed to read the truth in her eyes. A second later, lightning fast, he rose, flipped her over and pinned her hand to the ground, the knife clattering uselessly to the wooden floor behind her. Stunned by the rapid reversal, Mercy could do nothing but stare at him hopelessly, her chest rising and falling with the surprise of his move. Straddling *her* body, he leaned over to retrieve the weapon, his chest pressing against her face. She got a quick whiff of soap and water, of lime and tequila and an odor that no doctor can ever ignore—blood. Her fear exploded, and she began to struggle once more.

With his knife in his hand, Rio captured both her wrists and pulled them above her head. *God, she was a fighter!* He was shocked that she'd even managed to get the upper hand, and he didn't think he could last much longer. The pain was getting to him. He'd lost blood, and past experience told him he was going to be in serious trouble soon. He jerked her arms.

"What do you want?" she snapped, her blue eyes sparking in the dim lights.

"I got in the way of a shotgun slug, and I need a doctor." He paused. "Can you bandage me up and keep your mouth shut?"

For a second, she looked almost relieved, then her eyes flashed as his question sunk in. "Gunshot wounds are supposed to be reported."

A trickle of sweat escaped the band across his head and ran into his eyes, stinging and burning. He blinked it back. "I'm well aware of that."

"So what makes you think I won't report you?"

"What makes you think you'll live to do it?"

Beneath the tip of his knife, her pulse jumped, but she looked him straight in the eyes with a bravado he had to admire. At the very same time, his appreciation turned into misgiving, however. He felt as though she were looking into his heart.

Her jaw locked. "The sheriff comes by here all the time, you know. He'll find you."

His pain was growing, stinging as the heat of the night rolled over him, but Rio forced his face into a mask of indifference. "And are you friends with the sheriff?"

She looked startled at his question. "Friends? I wouldn't exactly say we're friends, but—"

"That makes two of us, then." Beads of sweat broke across Rio's brow, the effort of talking taking its toll. An involuntary groan escaped his lips. Instantly, the doctor's expression changed into concern, her fear clearly becoming secondary. She bucked underneath him.

"This is ridiculous. Get off me, and let me look at you before you pass out."

She lifted her hips once more, and this time, the muscular man couldn't stop her. He fell heavily to one side, then rolled over. Mercy jumped up, her breath coming in with a sharp intake, her feet ready to take flight. In-

stantly, however, she was halted by the sight of his back. Blood drenched his shirt.

Without thinking, she fell to her knees beside him, her fingers touching his burning skin. Her hands searched out his wound while her mind jumped ahead.

This was her chance. He was weak and growing weaker. If she *was* going to run, now was the time to do it. As she stared at his stretched-out form, Mercy's mind jumbled with the choices. He'd held a knife to her throat, for God's sake. How could she have compassion for someone like that? The instant she had the thought, however, Mercy had the answer. He *wasn't* a killer. If he'd wanted to murder her, he would have already done it.

He groaned and moved against her touch, and Mercy made up her mind. She couldn't leave him here to bleed to death on her living-room floor. She'd treat him first, *then* go for help. She rose to get her black bag and took one step before a hand of iron snaked out and circled her ankle.

''Wh-where are you going?''

He was so weak, he could hardly speak, but his fingers held on to her ankle with mesmerizing strength. As the muscles along his arms bulged with the effort, the veins popped up. She shook her leg, but he wouldn't turn her loose. Bending down beside him, she touched her fingers to his dark hair, brushing it back from his furrowed brow.

The startling gray eyes stared back at her with fearsome determination. ''Where are you going?'' he repeated.

''I have to get my bag,'' she said gently. ''Let me go.''

''You'll help me?''

The words were blurred, but Mercy understood. "Yes," she answered. "I promise—I'm going to help you. Now, let me go."

"You'll come back?"

Her throat closed at the poignant tone in his words. As if he realized what he'd done, he tightened his grip on her ankle. With strength of will more than strength of muscles, he held on to her.

"Trust me," she said, using all her effort to pry his hand from her leg. "I never break a promise."

In the light of day, the strange man seemed even more of a threat, but Mercy kept her promise. She took care of him and never left his side.

Despite what she'd told the injured man, she didn't even know the sheriff. In the days since she'd taken over the clinic, every time he'd stopped by, she'd kept the doors shut and locked, and not just because of the tales of her predecessor, Dr. Ruben, had told her. She hadn't liked the way the tall, uniformed sheriff had looked, standing on her porch, his gaze impassively taking in his surroundings. Sooner or later, she'd have to meet him, but *she* would pick the time and the place.

For twenty-four hours, she tended the stranger—just as she'd been tending to people since she was a child—wiping his brow, changing his bandages, spooning medicine into his dry, cracked lips. Under the cool calmness of her hands, his fever eased, and by late morning on the second day, he was sleeping so peacefully, she decided to sneak a nap herself.

She was dozing in the rocking chair when she heard him fall.

Years of training brought her to instant awareness, and her eyes popped open just in time to see him crash to the floor. Mercy jumped from the chair, but he was already struggling to his hands and knees, his bronze skin gleaming with effort by the time she took the two short steps to his side.

"What are you doing?" she cried, bending down beside him. "You shouldn't have gotten out of bed."

He shook his head, dark shaggy hair hanging almost to his shoulder, the muscles of his back straining with the obviously painful effort. The medicine had made his tongue thick, but Mercy had no trouble interpreting.

"I . . . can't stay here. Have to leave."

He rose slowly to his knees and swayed. Mercy slipped one arm around his waist in an attempt to steady him, her hand sliding over his slippery skin. "You're not going anywhere," she answered with a snap. "Unless you want to crawl."

"Cr-crawled to get here," he mumbled. "Can crawl to get away. . ."

"Forget it," she barked in her best no-nonsense doctor's voice. "You're getting back into bed."

He wasn't a small man, six feet plus and at least 220 pounds, she figured. She grunted and tried to stand, but getting him to his feet was even more difficult now than it had been the first night. At least then he'd had the incentive of pain to goad him up—now he was drugged and half out of it.

"Come on," she snapped, "you're getting back into that bed right now. I don't tend to patients on the floor."

He refused to budge, choosing instead to wobble on his knees, his light eyes fluttering shut. Mercy took a deep breath and tried to pull him up, but her fingers found no grip at his trim waist. There wasn't an ounce of fat on him, and even if there had been, she couldn't have lifted him by herself.

She paused and raised her head, biting her tongue with indecision, her eyes flickering over her shoulder and about the room as if she was looking for help. Instead of finding assistance, however, her gaze shuddered to a stop as it hit the mirror over her dresser.

The murky reflection showed her everything—everything she'd been trying not to see since the night he'd arrived and she'd pulled off the man's soiled and torn clothes. When she'd told herself a thousand times that he was like any other naked man she'd ever seen. When she had forced her eyes away from him and had covered his magnificent body with the sheet as quickly as possible. When she'd wondered how it would feel to have him touch her with desire instead of desperation.

Her eyes had a life of their own as they stared into the mirror. The contrast of the white bandage across his nut brown skin, the taut muscles of his buttocks, the wide stretch of his hard shoulders—the glass showed it all to her in mocking detail, and Mercy couldn't contain her sharp intake of breath. Over his shoulder, she watched herself in the mirror, her hands slipping up from his waist, crossing the white dressing and stroking over his smooth muscles. His head dropped to her shoulder.

Inside her gut, a slow curl of heat unfurled. She tried to douse it with reality—this man was a patient, a stranger, probably a criminal, but the fire refused to go out. In fact, it danced higher as his arms went around her slight form and tightened. Her eyes never left the mirror.

"So good," he murmured, his rough chin abrading her cheek. "Feel so good, smell so good."

Mercy closed her eyes against the erotic reflection. She had to get him into bed. That was her only task, and she concentrated on it once more with the zealousness of a crusader. "Come on," she said roughly. "Stand up."

The strain of her voice must have penetrated his consciousness, because he struggled to rise, moving one leg to stand halfway. Mercy grappled to her own feet and pulled him up with her. They tottered together for two long heartbeats, then his legs gave way and hers collapsed under the weight. Together, they tumbled to the mattress behind them.

Instantly, his gray eyes fluttered open, and his cold, steady glare pinned her against the mattress—pinned her as securely as his hard body did, now stretching out against hers. "You're very pretty," he said slowly, pronouncing the words carefully. *"Muy bonita."*

Mercy's breath quickened, her heart skittering in her chest like a trapped bird. She was sure he was going to kiss her, to put those warm, full lips against hers and thoroughly kiss her. She had the feeling that it would be a kiss she would never, ever forget. Before she knew what she was doing, her tongue came out and moistened her lips.

His gaze rested on the movement of her tongue, then his sensuous mouth curled up at the corners, the movement transforming his entire face. The angles softened into curves, the darkness lightened and even his chillingly gray eyes grew warmer, a touch of pewter coming into their depths. As soon as the expression came, however, it fled, his consciousness going with it. His eyelids fluttered down, and he passed out again.

As quickly as possible, Mercy extracted herself from the tangle of his arms and legs, straightened him in the bed and pulled the pale pink sheet up to his chin. With her chest heaving from the effort and her mind still dazed by her flash of desire, Mercy looked down at the virile strength of his face.

Who was he? Where had he come from? What did he want?

Her hands went to the tumble of hair at her neck, and she pulled it to tighten the rubber band containing the wild curls.

She hadn't expected the peace and quiet of the desert to be shattered quite like this, but then again, that's why she'd taken this assignment in Texas, wasn't it? To help the poor people along the border. To right the wrongs perpetuated by the system. To help those who couldn't help themselves.

Her eyes focused once more on the now-quiet man in her bed. Something told her he wasn't one of the downtrodden.

Rio woke instantly, but he didn't move—a habit born of necessity more than desire. Instead, he lay perfectly still, like a waiting cat, and absorbed the awakening of his senses, the unfamiliar smells, sounds and feelings penetrating his consciousness with razorlike stabs.

A wide white bandage wrapped around his chest and lower back, the gauze tight with tape. The rest of his muscles were sore and aching, but when he tested his strength by curling his fingers and tensing, he was reassured. As long as he could make a fist, he could use his knife. That's all he needed.

Encouraged, Rio let his eyes sweep open. He knew where he was—the woman's bedroom—but beyond that, the details were hazy. How he'd gotten there, where his clothes were, how much time had passed, he had no idea. A memory of incredibly cool hands and gleaming

blond hair came to him, but it fluttered through his mind, then disappeared. When he turned his head slowly, the scent of her perfume rose from the pillow beneath his head, and he thought of soft shoulders and even softer breasts.

He took a deep breath and forced his mind away from her. The mouth-watering aroma of bacon wafted over him, the delicious scent backed up by the sound of sizzling heat. Underlying it all was the temptation of coffee—rich, hot black coffee—the kind the nuns used to drink, but only on Saturday morning when the priest dropped by to visit. Automatically, Rio's mouth began to water. He couldn't remember the last time he'd woken to such exquisite smells.

He heard the muted clanging of utensils hitting plates, a skillet scraping across a burner, the refrigerator opening, then closing—all the sounds of a home, he supposed. He wasn't too sure, actually—it had been a long time since he'd lived anywhere that deserved that label.

Before he had longer to reflect, the bedroom door swung open, and the owner of the cool hands and long hair entered, carrying a wooden tray, his breakfast covering its top.

Her gaze swept over him. He struggled into a sitting position, hiding a wince of pain from his face. By the time his back rested against the headboard, a sheen of perspiration had broken out on his forehead.

She stopped at the edge of the bed, her perfume washing over him like a cool breeze. "I want some answers—and I want them now."

Chapter 2

Silence stretched between them like a fine, thin wire. One false move, and Rio knew it would snap and ensnarl them both—possibly already had.

From the bed, he stared at her impassively. He'd thought she might be different, but why, he didn't know. Maybe it'd been her hands. His gaze went to them as they curled around the breakfast tray. They were large hands for a woman, and the nails were blunt and short. Had he just imagined their coolness across his brow? Their warmth across his shoulders? His voice turned flat and heavy. "Did you report me to the sheriff?"

Her blue eyes flickered, then she moved forward and put the tray across his lap. Rio's hand whipped out and grabbed her wrist. She pulled back, but he refused to let go, and when her gaze met his, he read the fear even before she spoke. He could do that with some people—look into their eyes and see the truth.

"What do you think you're doing?"

"Answer me," he growled. "Did you report me?"

"Not yet."

Rio knew instantly that something wasn't right. After she spoke, her expression wavered, like a light on the horizon at midnight. Obviously aware of it, she immediately recomposed herself, shutting her expression down and closing herself to him. Her efforts came too late, however, Within his mind, Rio cursed.

He released her wrist, and she yanked her arm back, rubbing the skin as if it had been burned, moving quickly to the window on the other side of the room.

"How long have I been here?"

With her back still to him, she answered. "Two days."

This time his oath echoed in the still room. Two days! What kind of misery could Greenwood have wrought in the past two days? Rio hesitated. Then the aroma of the food reached him, and his mouth began to water. Greenwood had been at it for years—another hour wouldn't hurt, Rio suddenly decided. Besides, he was still weak. If he had to run for it, the food would fuel him for a little longer. For a moment more, he stared at the woman's back, then he turned his attention to the tray in front of him.

The coffee was as hot and strong as he'd thought.

For five minutes, an uneasy silence ruled, then finally, as Rio's fork bit into the last of the scrambled eggs, the woman turned, her wrist still cradled in her other hand. Her face wore an expression of weary frustration. "I told you that you could trust me. I took off your clothes. I cared for you. I let you sleep in my bed. I think the least you can do for me is tell me your name."

He looked up from a clean plate. "You don't want to know my name, *Dr.* Hamilton," he said harshly.

"But you know mine. How?"

He nodded toward the clinic, then lied. "It's on the sign."

She didn't look convinced. Across the room, their gazes met and sparked. Rio suddenly knew this was a woman who would never give up.

"I want to know who you are," she said stubbornly, proving his point. "And who shot you."

"That's not important."

"You could have died," she cried. "Another inch higher, and I wouldn't have been able to just slap a bandage on that, you know." She put her hands on her hips. "Someone tried to *kill* you, and from the blood on that knife you held to my throat, I'd say you got in a few licks yourself. I want to know who you are."

Surprise arched his black eyebrows. "You saw blood on my knife?"

"Yes."

"And you still took care of me?"

Her anger shot across the room. "My job is to take care of anyone who comes through that door, but if you recall, I didn't have a choice with you."

"I didn't have one, either."

"There's a hospital in Brownsville."

"Brownsville is hours away." Rio's eyes slid over her face, down her body, then back up again. The slow perusal left a flush on the blonde's cheeks, red and hot as if she'd been running. "And the doctors there aren't nearly as good-looking as you."

Her mouth pursed into a straight line of obstinate denial. "You came here because you didn't want your wound reported, and you think you can bully me into not saying anything." She paused for a second, then spoke again, her voice as hard as the baked land outside the window. "If I'm going to protect you, the least you can do is tell me your name." She sat down in the rocker at the foot of the bed, folded her hands, then looked at him expectantly. "I've got all day."

Rio hadn't encountered such obvious determination since he'd met Sister Rosa. He thought a little longer about trying to stall the blonde, but shrugged his shoulders in defeat. It didn't really matter anyway. "My name is Rio Barrigan. That's all you need to know, and that's *all* you're getting."

Gingerly, he lifted one hand and pulled his long hair out from behind his back, then picked up the mug of coffee she'd brought him and held it out to her, the hard muscles of his arm flexing. "Why don't you fill this up?"

Mercy stared at him, her heart thumping in her chest. Somehow, she'd known he would tell her nothing, but she'd had to try. He was so totally foreign compared to any man she'd ever laid eyes on that she didn't know how to handle him, couldn't predict him. Another person might have given in, but not Mercy. Challenges like this only made her more determined.

She stood and reached for the cup he held in his outstretched hand. As she took it from him, he unexpectedly whipped out his arm and circled her waist, his fingers digging into her hip. The intimacy of the touch shocked her. The steel in it scared her.

She'd seen him naked, bandaged his skin and bathed his brow, but this single, heated contact took her world and turned it upside down.

"You don't want to know more about me." He spoke softly, his slight accent lilting in the heat of the room. "So don't ask any more questions. They'll only bring you trouble."

She swallowed against the swell of her attraction, but something about the tall, dark stranger reached inside of her and pulled out an almost primal reaction. When she'd seen his nude body in her bedroom mirror, she'd acknowledged her feelings, and this morning, she couldn't tidy that up and lock it away—the sensation was real. As real as the strong fingers that rested on the curve of her hip.

She took her hand and gently pried off his grip, looking into his chilling eyes. "It's too late," she said coolly. "I've already got it."

Rio watched Mercy's slim back disappear into the other room, her tennis shoes squeaking on the hard-surfaced floor.

His grip tightened on the sheets, pulling the polished cotton into a tangled knot beneath his fingers. He had to leave. Right now.

She could cause him more trouble than the sheriff.

He'd known women like her before, and nothing good had ever come from the stormy relationships they'd shared. They looked at you because they liked something dangerous, then they always tried to tame you. To Rio, it made no sense at all.

The doctor came back into the room, and Rio took in her hesitation as she paused by the door. She was a beautiful woman—blond hair barely tamed by a clasp at her neck, shocking blue eyes, skin the color of white clouds that drifted over the desert. She reminded him of every mother's daughter he'd wanted to ask out in high school and later in college. Sister Rosa had warned him about them all. He hadn't listened then, either.

Mercy stepped closer to the bed and handed him the coffee cup, then she ran her cool hands against his shoulders and his bandage. If she saw the flare of interest in his eyes, she ignored it. "Turn around," she said in a stern voice, her delicate touch contradicting her tone. "I want to check your wound."

Suddenly, he didn't want soothing hands—he wanted anxious hands, clutching hands, hands that seized his and wouldn't let go. It had been a long time since he'd even allowed himself to acknowledge that need, in fact *any* kind of need, and as the painful realization washed over him, he realized why. It was an impossible dream. A man like him never had a family, never had one woman. Especially someone like *this* woman. She was the kind who would demand payment, and her currency would be more dear than dollars.

She would want his heart, and Rio didn't have enough of that left to buy anything.

Pulling the sheet from the bed and wrapping it around him, he stood abruptly, ignoring her objection and the sickening dizziness that overcame him. "I have to leave," he said thickly.

She stood before him, her head barely reaching his chin. "You can't go anywhere. You're still too weak—"

Pushing her out of the way, he took two shaky steps toward what he assumed was the bathroom. "Where are my clothes?"

"Mr. Barrigan, I must protest. You are going to reinjure yourself, and I cannot be responsible."

Reaching the wall, he placed one hand against the door frame, then looked over his shoulder at the stubborn woman—just in time to catch her eyes slipping over his naked back. Two bright spots of red darkened her cheeks, and when she spoke, her voice was defensive.

"You lost a lot of blood. If I hadn't given you those antibiotics, you might have—"

"*Where* are my clothes?"

She hesitated, then finally nodded toward the door where he stood. "Your pants are in there. I . . . I had to throw away your shirt."

Ten minutes later, he came back into the room, pale beneath the stubble of his cheeks. Unconsciously, Mercy's mouth tightened with disapproval, but as her eyes slid over his face and bare chest, another emotion took over.

He'd slicked back his hair, but in the heat, it was already springing around his face, the heavy black strands gleaming in the morning sunshine. The bandage was shockingly white against his wide bronze chest, the gauze pulled tightly in opposition to his muscles. As she watched, he took a tentative step toward the bed and sat down heavily.

Across the bedroom, her eyes met his. He was too weak to move and too stubborn to admit it. But in a strange way, she almost had to respect him. In the society hospitals where she'd done her training, she'd seen patients with hangnails who acted as if they were dying. This man was tough.

And that very attitude—despite her professional misgivings—made her curiosity grow even more. In the silence, the ticking of her grandfather clock sounded unnaturally loud. "Tell me what you're doing here, Rio Barrigan," she said at length. "Who shot you?"

He picked up the sheathed knife from beside the bed and pulled the wicked blade from the leather cover. The lightness of his eyes flickered over her as he tested the blade with his thumb. "If I told you, you wouldn't believe me."

Behind his mocking words, she heard a lifetime of bitterness. A second later, he stood up and slipped the knife back into the sheath. Tucking it into the back of his pants, he walked toward the rocking chair. "It's best if you just forget I ever came here."

She stood as he approached. "I don't think I can do that." She could smell the scent of her own soap on him, and she blinked in the heavy tenseness, her chest rising and falling with her quickened breath.

Rio met her gaze, every muscle in his body screaming for him to keep his hands off her. Like every other piece of good advice he'd ever heard, however, he ignored it. He reached out toward her cheek. *Just a touch,* he thought with confusion, *just one finger across her skin, then I'll leave and never look back.*

She stood her ground and stared at him, her tongue snaking out to cross her full lips. Unconsciously, Rio mimicked her movement, bowing his head to hers. With the index finger of his right hand, he gently traced a line from her jaw to her cheek, then down the curve of her neck to the base of her throat. At the point of contact, her pulse jumped in an unnatural rhythm.

He slipped his hand around her neck. Under the curtain of her hair, her skin was even warmer, the texture fine and silky. "So what are you going to do about me, *Doctora?* Are you going to call the sheriff and tell him I was here? Will you describe me? Tell him about the wound? Ask him what I did before coming here?" He rubbed his thumb up and down the ridge of her neck and stared at her.

Her eyes widened with fear, but behind that, Rio saw a flicker of something else. Interest? Desire? The irony of an uptight, upper-class doctor finding him attractive was too much to accept, and he found himself almost amused. "What are you going to do?" he asked again.

"I . . . I don't know."

"Why not call your friend? The sheriff?"

The muscles in her neck tensed, and something shifted in the bright blue eyes. She hesitated then spoke, reluctantly, it seemed. "I . . . I've heard stories . . ."

Rio felt his nerves take an uneasy jump. "Stories? What kinds of stories?"

She opened her mouth, then snapped it shut as if hearing the word from his lips invalidated it. "You were hurt. I thought—"

They both froze at the sound of a car's engine, but Rio recovered first, his hand squeezing her neck, his curse breaking the silence. He stepped to the window and hid behind the curtain, pulling Mercy with him. When he saw the dusty brown Bronco with its cherry lights on top and dirty gold shield on the side, anger exploded within him—and with it, strangely enough—an odd sense of betrayal. He didn't even know the woman standing beside him, but for some crazy reason he'd instinctively trusted her.

And this was what it'd got him.

With blazing eyes, he turned to her and shook her slightly, his fingers unyielding against her. "When did you call him, damn it?"

She stared at him, false shock darkening those beguiling blue eyes. "I didn't," she protested. "I swear to God, I—"

She was the first woman he'd misread in a very long time. He cut off her lie with another shake of his hand, then thrust her toward the closet. "Find me a shirt," he ordered, "then get back over here."

For a second, she looked as though she would refuse, then her eyes grew wide as his hand snaked back to the knife at his waist. "Do as I say, Mercy," he commanded softly. "Or we're all going to regret it."

Her face was pale with fear, but her hands went into two fists at her sides. "I *didn't* call him," she said. "My phone doesn't even work, for God's sake."

Rio nodded grimly. "Just find me that shirt."

She hesitated for one more heartbeat, then swirled and threw open the closet door, her hands frantically searching through the clothes. Just as the knock sounded on the front door, she pulled out a paint-splattered man's shirt and threw it at him. Rio caught it, slipped it on with a grimace of pain and buttoned it up far enough for the bandage to be covered. Mercy stood in the center of the room like a frozen statue and watched him. When a second knock sounded, he grabbed her and blasted her with a single freezing look. "You never saw me. Remember that." He paused. "Remember that."

She met his gaze with a head-on stare, never flinching, never quivering. "I won't ever forget it."

A third knock sounded, and the sheriff's voice spoke out. "Dr. Hamilton? You in there?"

Mercy's head whipped toward the door. This was her chance. She could break away before Rio could even bring out the knife. As soon as she had the thought, though, Mercy knew she wouldn't. In some strange way, she'd already bonded with the wild, dangerous man at her side. She'd held him in her arms, comforted him, healed him.

And despite his words, she knew he could never hurt her. Not with the knife, anyway.

Rio's fingers dug into her arm. "Do whatever it takes, but get rid of him." His stormy eyes pierced her with a single chilling glare. "I'll be listening."

When he released her, Mercy stumbled backward, fear weakening her knees. The door shook again as the sheriff pounded on it, and she turned and ran to the living room, breaking her stare with Rio. Behind her, she heard the bedroom door ease shut.

She threw the door open, and the uniformed sheriff stepped back. "Dr. Hamilton?"

He was a tall man, beefy and muscular under a layer of extra weight. Twenty years ago, he would have been as lean and muscular as Rio, but time had claimed its due. Time and Jim Beam, she speculated with a prejudiced eye.

Praying that her voice was strong, she answered, slightly out of breath. "I'm Dr. Hamilton. What can I do for you?"

Under a wide-brimmed hat, dark sunglasses tinted his eyes. She still felt their gaze, however, and she had to hold back a shiver. The man emanated intimidation from the top of his dark brown hat, with its sweat-edged brim, to the bottom of his lizard-skin boots, covered in dust and wrinkled with age.

He didn't move, but his thin lips pressed into a straight line as though he disapproved of her already. He stuck out one enormous hand and engulfed hers in a hard handshake "My name's Rick Greenwood. I'm the sheriff."

Mercy never flinched, but inside she was quivering. Where was Rio? Could he hear what they were saying? What would he do if the sheriff came in? The last thought frightened her so much, she was sure the tall man in front of her could hear her pulse thundering.

As if he'd read her mind, the uniformed man ducked his head and threw a glance toward her living room. "Could I come in? I'd like to ask you some questions."

A lump of fear lodged in the back of Mercy's throat, and for a moment, she couldn't even speak. Finally, her hand groped behind her for the doorknob. "I haven't exactly got my house straight yet—"

"I don't mind—"

"No, no," she said with a false smile of apology. "I couldn't possibly let you see it. I'd be too embarrassed." She stepped out to the porch, the screen banging behind her. "Why don't we visit here?"

The excuse sounded flimsy, even to her. He looked as if he didn't believe her, either, but Mercy didn't care. She couldn't let him go inside—Rio was a bomb waiting to go off, and the man standing before her could well be the only match that was needed.

He hesitated for a second longer, then stepped reluctantly backward and removed his hat. "All right," he said reluctantly. "I guess it'll do."

"Thanks," she said quickly. "The house is bad, but the clinic's worse. I have even more work out there."

He tilted his head slightly and took in the small stucco building at the rear of her house. Finally, he refocused on her. His face was like a granite mask, no emotion, no expression. His lips barely moved when he spoke. She wondered if he practiced the look at home in front of the mirror.

"I need to ask you a few questions about that *clinic* of yours."

His note of derision didn't faze her. "Is there a problem?"

He lifted one broad finger and tilted his hat back with it. "That depends."

She refused to be cowed by him. "On what?" she asked, her voice sharp.

"On you." The dark lenses went up and down, and Mercy fought back a tremble of disquiet. "Frankly, Dr. Hamilton, I don't think having you here is a good idea."

A slow burn started inside her stomach, and Mercy's hands went into two tight fists. "I'm not exactly sure I understand you, Sheriff."

"This is not a good place for a woman." He tilted his head toward the river. "In fact, it's not safe for anyone."

Fear dried her mouth until she didn't think she could speak. Her mind filled with the image of the man waiting for her in her bedroom. "Wh-why is that?"

He lifted one hand and waved it behind him, his gaze never leaving her face. "That's the Rio Grande. When the sun goes down, the laws change." He paused for a second, obviously giving her time to understand his message. When she didn't speak, he continued. "It's a free-for-all. Dopers, wets, killers—you name it, and they're out there. Trying to cross, trying to run, trying to get away from something—usually me." Pausing, he looked toward the sluggishly moving water, then back at her. "Not many of them are successful."

If a steady stare could be physical, Greenwood's would have been choking her. Mercy didn't flinch, however. She looked him right in the eyes. She couldn't see what color they were, and that bothered her, too. "I'll be careful."

"Do you know what a *coyote* is?"

His abrupt change in topic threw her off, and it took Mercy a second to understand what he was saying, especially since he gave the term its Spanish pronunciation. When she finally recognized the word, she still didn't know what he meant, though. "A coyote? It's kinda like a wolf, isn't it?"

He laughed, a harsh, quick sound that held no humor at all. "That's not a bad description, but I'm not talking about that kind of animal. I'm talking about the one with two legs—the yellow-bellied kind.''

Mercy frowned in confusion. "I don't—"

"A *coyote* is a man who leads wets across the river. For a fee." He reached up to his shirt pocket, shook out a cigarette from the pack, then lit it in the bright sunlight. Blowing smoke up to the peeling ceiling of the porch, he stared at her. "They're called *coyotes* because of their predatory habits—they're bloodthirsty scavengers, and if anyone gets in their way, they kill."

She barely had the breath to speak. Thoughts of the savage man in her bedroom crowded out everything else. She opened her mouth, but an image flashed into her mind that stopped her. An image of a naked man leaning on her, whispering against her hair, telling her she smelled good. An image that changed the words coming from her lips.

"What has this got to do with me?" she managed to ask.

The man in the uniform looked as if he knew she'd been going to say something else, but all he did was tilt his head back toward the river. "You're in a prime crossing spot. At this point, the water's low, and you've got that small canyon behind you where they can run after they cross." He drew deeply on the cigarette. "And you're isolated." He paused, the smoke curling up between them. "Very isolated."

Mercy's heart hammered, and the trickle of moisture down her shoulder blades could no longer be attributed to the heat. "I'm sure these people would probably avoid me as much as I would avoid them."

"Don't count on it." He took another long drag on the cigarette, then threw the butt to the porch and ground it out with the heel of his cowboy boot, staring at her the whole time. "These *coyotes* are trash, that's all. No morals, no ethics. They sneak over the river, then around the arroyos, dodging the border patrol and tearing up the countryside. Hell, half of them are bringing in a load of dope along with their *pollitos*."

Mercy licked her lips and surreptitiously wiped her sweaty hands against her shirt. "*¿Pollitos?*"

He hooked one thumb over his gun. "Chicks—that's what we call the illegals, the wets, that the *coyotes* bring over." He let his thumb roll over the handle of the pistol, and Mercy's stomach tightened. "They're nasty criminals, Dr. Hamilton, and they'd be real interested in a pretty lady like yourself. Do you understand?"

Mercy looked into the reflection of his glasses and thought about the man hiding in her bedroom. "Yes," she said with a fear she didn't have to pretend to have. "And I'll be careful, I assure you."

"Good." He reached into his other pocket and removed a business card. Taking it from his proffered fingers, Mercy prayed her hand wouldn't shake. "I want you to call me if you see anything suspicious, anything at all." He pulled his hat down lower on his forehead. "We had a little run-in the other night with a particularly nasty *coyote*. I guess you could say it was a draw— no one was hurt, but the son of a bitch got away." He stepped down off her porch, the hot sun landing on his metal badge and bouncing onto the porch in a bright circle. "I'll expect you to call me if you see him."

The minute the Bronco pulled out of her yard, Mercy turned and went into the house, forcing herself not to hurry. Greenwood had frightened her—with his warnings and with his attitude. On legs that shook, she went back into the bedroom, knowing Rio had heard every word.

He was gone.

He had left the same way he came—silently and without her even knowing what was going on. Except for the tangled sheets, except for the lingering aura of his power, she'd never have known he was even there.

She sunk to the bed and closed her eyes, taking a deep breath. There was no question in her mind that Rio Barrigan was the man Greenwood had been hunting. Why in God's name hadn't she said something?

Opening her eyes, she shook her head at her question. It made no sense at all, and if she was nothing else, Mercy Hamilton was sensible. That's how her parents had raised her, that's how she'd made it through medical school, that's how her life had been—until forty-eight hours ago. She lifted her hand out before her face and watched her fingers tremble. Nothing like this had ever happened to her before.

For the rest of the day, she felt unsettled and almost angry. Even if she never saw him again, she knew Rio would disturb her nights for a long time to come. The polished muscles, the shaggy black hair, the mysterious attitude—something about the man spoke to her, and against her better judgment, she wanted to know more. But she never would, of course.

Putting thoughts of the dark stranger—and the sheriff who was hunting him—out of her mind, she concentrated on making the small cabin her home. Dr. Ruben was single, and she was sure the floor hadn't seen a mop in at least a year. It calmed her to attend to the mundane tasks, however, and by noon, she was exhausted, the heat, the labor and the anxiety taking over.

After eating a quick sandwich on the porch, she stood up resolutely. The clinic wasn't much better than the house, and she still had a lot to do there.

Forcing herself to step into the blinding sunlight, Mercy headed out to the tiny building. She wasn't accustomed to this kind of temperature. When she unlocked the door, the knob almost seared her fingers.

Flipping on the lights, she quickly entered the waiting room. When she'd accepted the position as the free clinic's doctor, she hadn't expected much. She'd known the facilities would be poor and the medical equipment less than what she was accustomed to. A quick look into the examining rooms a few days ago had confirmed her worst suspicions. She'd hurried through the waiting area then because she'd been more concerned about the equipment or lack thereof. Now, in the bright afternoon sunlight, she wished she'd looked closer. Things were even worse in here than she'd first thought.

Peeling green paint covered walls that needed sanding and refinishing, and the plastic chairs lining the perimeter of the room looked as sad as the fake ficus plant that drooped in one corner. A single, forlorn *National Geographic,* five years old and with half the cover missing, rested in dusty splendor on a rickety table in the middle of the room. There was no other furniture. No desk, no reception area, nothing.

To get the building looking halfway decent, she'd need supplies, and not just Windex. After turning on the overhead fan, Mercy pulled out the small notebook she'd brought with her and began to make a list. In short order, she'd filled two pages, half of her mind concentrating on the task at hand, the other half excited about the possibilities before her.

Dr. Ruben had told her the population had no pre-natal care, poor diets, no other place for health care but the hospital in Brownsville—two hundred miles away. If an emergency arose, the locals simply did the best they could—airlifted the patient or prayed. Mercy would be the only source of medical care for three counties.

She finished her list, then headed for the back of the building. The only other room was an examination area—there were no beds, no overnight facilities. Step-ping into the tiny room that held only a sink and one examining table, she started to tidy up around the counter. Her dash to get bandages and drugs for Rio had been a harried one, and she'd left the place in a mess. Now she repackaged everything and returned the un-used bandages to their proper places. Taking a few min-utes, she added several more items to her shopping list.

She finished in a few seconds. Putting the notebook down on the counter, she turned and crossed her arms over her chest to stare out the small square window in the back of the breathless room.

The hot, stuffy air reminded her of how she'd felt when Rio had been in her bedroom—her chest tight and heavy as if there weren't enough oxygen for both of them. For days, she'd been trying not to think of those cool gray eyes, those viselike hands, that mocking voice... but in a single strained breath, she managed to evoke his powerful image.

Where was he right now? What was he doing? Was he really a *coyote?* In the stifling room, she shivered sud-denly and asked herself one more question—the most obvious one of all.

Why did she even care?

Chapter 3

On Saturday, Mercy revved up the battered pickup Dr. Ruben had left behind in a generous moment and headed toward town.

The trip was short.

In twenty minutes, she was driving down the main street of Ciudad Bravo. If she'd kept going another two minutes, she would have been on the other side of town.

She stopped in the middle of the second block, the pickup sputtering to a halt in front of the drugstore. The tiny pharmacy wasn't too impressive, but she went inside and purchased replacement bandages for the ones she'd used on Rio and as many of the other items on her list as she could find. There were still quite a few things she'd have to send off for, she realized as she stuffed the list back in her pocket, but that was one of the things Dr. Ruben had warned her about, and she didn't mind. Five minutes later, she was out on the street again.

She put her bag through the open window of the truck and deposited her purchases on the blistering-hot seat. A moment later, she was crossing the street at her usual clip, the small Mexican café on the corner her destination.

Opening the door of the restaurant, Mercy stepped inside, a welcome blast of air-conditioning hitting her the minute she walked in. For a second, she closed her eyes and let the delicious cold run over her, then a soft voice spoke at her side.

"*Buenas tardes, Doctora.* Would you like a table?"

Mercy's eyes flew open, and she smiled at the young Mexican girl waiting to seat her. She wore the typical teenager's uniform—a T-shirt advertising a rock group and a pair of baggy jeans. Her dark eyes and raven hair, worn long and plaited in twin braids over her shoulders, gave away her heritage, though. They could have just as easily been on the other side of the river.

"Yes, please," Mercy answered. "One close to the air conditioner if it's not already taken."

"*Sí.* It is very hot today." The girl led Mercy to a table in the back, then paused as she sat down. Handing her a menu, the girl leaned closer and spoke hesitantly.

"You . . . you *are* the new *doctora,* aren't you?"

"Yes, I am," Mercy answered. "At the clinic—out on the highway."

"Then I would like to come see you, *señorita.* My grandmother, she's *muy enferma.*" The girl pointed to her chest and made a face. "She has trouble breathing and she's very weak. When she cooks dinner, she has to stop and rest before she can finish it all." She let her gaze go down, then it came back to Mercy's face. "I . . . I notice these things. Some day, maybe, I'd like to be a nurse."

"Well, it sounds as though you'd make a good one if you're already catching details like that." Mercy tried to smile encouragingly. "What's your name?"

The young girl glanced over her shoulder, then looked shyly back at Mercy. "Mary. Mary Hernandez."

"Well, Mary, why don't you bring your grandmother out to the clinic? I'll look her over. It could be her heart, but..." Instantly, the young girl's face contorted with concern, and Mercy couldn't help but reach out and pat her. "But it could just as easily be indigestion, who knows? Bring her out, and I'll be happy to check her over." Mercy waited until the young girl looked at her again. "You can even help me with her," she said with a smile. "Get some experience."

Mary returned Mercy's smile, but then the expression faded slowly. "I work here until midnight, but maybe next week we could make it by then. I've been saving my money—I'll pay you as much as I can."

It took Mercy a moment for the words to register. "Pay me?" Her forehead tightened and wrinkled. "The clinic is free, Mary. No one has to pay."

The young girl's eyes grew huge with disbelief. *"Gratis?"*

"Yes." Mercy nodded. "It's free—no charge." Her hands grew tense on the menu. "The doctor who was here before me—he didn't charge you, did he?"

"Oh, no. no. He never charged, but when he left..." Mary shrugged her shoulders and glanced once more behind her. "We were told the new doctor would make us pay."

Mercy's stomach turned over in anger. These people had so little already—what kind of person would want to take away free medical care from them? Her voice was tight. "Who said that?"

The young girl's brown eyes flickered once more, and Mercy could only have described her expression as fearful. "I have to go," she said suddenly. "Your waitress will be here in a minute." She turned and fled to the front of the café, leaving Mercy in an even greater state of confusion.

For a full five minutes, Mercy sat and stared out the window at her side. It made no sense at all. The clinic was supported by government funds and private donations—that's one of the things that had attracted her to the post in the first place. She wanted to tend to people who really needed her services—not executives with headaches. When the agency taking her application had realized she spoke Spanish, the decision was cinched.

The other reason she was in Ciudad was tradition. For generations in her family, every doctor gave their first year out of medical school to charity work. It was a ritual expressing the deep-seated feelings of the Hamiltons that one should always help those who, for whatever reason, were unable to help themselves. She'd been looking forward to this year since she'd been old enough to know what the word *doctor* meant.

No one was going to come between her and her patients.

The waitress came, took Mercy's order, then returned with a huge glass of iced tea. Mercy's fingers tightened around the drink. Ciudad was a tiny town, but already she'd run into more trouble than she'd ever bargained for.

Why did she have such a strong suspicion that Rio Barrigan was behind most of it?

* * *

The hat Rio wore low on his forehead shadowed his face, but not his view of the small Mexican town square just across the river from Ciudad. As the late-afternoon sun baked the empty park, Rio waited patiently for his contact. He was accustomed to waiting, almost liked it, in fact. He used the slow hours to think, to plan . . . to remember.

Today, however, he shifted uneasily against the hard park bench and held back a groan. His back was still tender, and it pained him. He probably should have taken advantage of the doctor's hospitality a little longer, but he couldn't . . . not with Greenwood nosing around. The sheriff wasn't the only danger, though, and with a sigh, Rio finally acknowledged the vision he'd been trying to stifle for days now.

Mercy Hamilton. *Dr.* Mercy Hamilton.

She'd bandaged him with care, then had lied for him. He'd stuck around long enough to hear her do it, then he'd fled through her bedroom window while she was still talking to Greenwood.

Why?

Why had she done that for him . . . a total stranger?

Rio didn't have any answers; he only knew one thing. He could have no more contact with the beautiful doctor. Even if she knew the truth, she wouldn't approve of who or what he was, and she certainly wouldn't understand what he was there to do. Getting involved with her was the last thing he should do.

Making up his mind to put Mercy aside, Rio forced himself to concentrate on the moment, to let his eyes search the square. The man he was waiting for was late, but then that wasn't news. He was always late. Rio's annoyance evaporated, however, as his gaze raked over and returned to the figure of a woman getting out of a battered pickup across the way. *Damn—it was as if his thoughts had conjured her.*

She strolled into the small park, her blond hair catching the sunshine, her long legs bare and tanned beneath crisp white shorts. A light blue T-shirt molded to full breasts, and Rio cursed himself as he remembered their heavy weight against his arm. His body hardened. What was Mercy Hamilton doing on this side of the border?

The park had only one sidewalk, and regardless of which way she went, Mercy would eventually come upon him. For a second, Rio thought of leaving. Avoidance was how he usually dealt with things like this, but he had to wait for his connection. It was too important to miss. He drew his lips into a thin line of resignation and settled back onto the bench.

But even as he cursed her arrival, his eyes never left her figure. Slowly, she circumvented the little green square, every step of her walk bringing her closer and closer to him. She was still too far away for him to really smell her perfume, but Rio was already imagining it in his mind. Just as he was recalling the way they'd tumbled to her bed and the soft curves he'd felt when he landed on top of her.

As she rounded the last bend of the park's sidewalk, her Sunday-afternoon stroll almost complete, Mercy was the picture of relaxation. Rio was exactly the opposite, his body a coil of rigid tension. He had to forcibly pry his fingers from the metal arms of the bench.

She bent down to smile at a baby in a stroller, then as he watched, she straightened, glanced around and froze. Her expression changed slowly, a metamorphosis that triggered a corresponding reaction in Rio. It had been a long time since he'd had a woman look at him like that, and instantly his blood heated.

Still, though, he didn't move, and like a robot, she covered the distance between them. Stopping before his stretched-out legs, she spoke, her voice a husky invitation. "What are you doing here?"

Rio let his eyes go up and down her body—slowly, sensuously. "Waiting for you," he finally replied.

The answer seemed to fluster her, just as he knew it would. He'd said it to throw her off, to make her stop before she asked more questions he couldn't answer, but suddenly, Rio wished his words had been the truth. For once, he longed for that simple kind of assignation—a man waiting for his sweetheart in a park on Sunday afternoon.

For him, however, those days were past.

Ignorant of his yearning, she recovered quickly and sat down beside him, the now-familiar scent of her light perfume teasing him from the other end of the bench. Rio tried to ignore it.

"How do you feel?" she asked.

"I'm fine," he lied. "But then I had a great doctor."

"You didn't think that the last time I saw you." Her blue eyes searched his. "In fact, you accused me of siccing the sheriff on you."

Rio pulled down the brim of his hat and let his eyes lazily roam the park. "I was wrong," he said simply.

She settled against the park bench, apparently satisfied, but Rio felt his own agitation grow. He couldn't decide what bothered him more—her closeness or the possibility that she'd be there when the man he waited for arrived. As she crossed one long leg over the other, he decided it was the former.

"It's a beautiful park, isn't it?" she said conversationally.

"Yes."

"Do you come here every Sunday?"

"No."

"There's a small one in Ciudad, but I prefer this one, don't you?"

The breeze picked up a curl from the side of her face and brushed her cheek with it. Rio instantly wondered how it would feel to take the wind's place, to lift that silken ribbon of hair and tease it across his own bare skin. A second later, he blanked out the thought. "What are you doing here, Doctor?" He returned to his casual surveillance, still speaking as he surveyed the park. "It's a little far from home for you, isn't it?"

"I wanted to see where the people live."

"What people?"

"The ones you bring over the border."

Rio's breath caught in his throat, and he was glad he wasn't facing her. She could have read the surprise in his eyes. To gain time, he flicked an imaginary speck of dust from the leg of his jeans, then readjusted the brim of his hat. "What are you talking about?"

"The sheriff told me everything. I know what you do, Rio."

Slowly, deliberately, he turned to face her, abandoning his pretense of no interest. "And what exactly did Sheriff Greenwood say?"

She blinked—at his cold tone or at the bright sunshine, she didn't know which. "Enough for me to figure out that you're a *coyote*—that you bring people illegally into the States for money."

This was the confirmation Rio had been waiting for, and a small thrill of triumph rippled over him. The look in her eyes, however, almost extinguished it. Fear had replaced the desire of a few moments before. "Is it true?" she pressed.

Rio didn't hesitate. He had to stop the questions before they went too far. He leaned over and cupped her jaw in his left hand, his thumb caressing the smoothness of her skin. The shock of his touch widened her eyes, but she didn't pull away. He made his voice low and sexy. "You're too inquisitive, Mercy," he said slowly, his fingers stroking her cheek. "I told you not to worry about that."

She held his gaze. "I make it a point to make my own decisions."

He smiled slowly. "A woman who likes to be on top... of things, huh?"

An apricot blush darkened the satin skin under his thumb, but she showed no other emotion. "I like to know the truth," she said tightly. "It's very important to me."

From the corner of his eye, Rio caught a sudden movement across the park. A powerfully built man dressed in typical Mexican peasant clothing stood under the shade of a giant Formosa tree. He'd removed a large straw hat, and underneath it, he wore a red bandanna to cover his hair. With an almost invisible tipping of his head, he acknowledged Rio's gaze, then settled to the dusty sidewalk to wait.

Rio turned back to Mercy. The whole exchange had taken no more than a second, and she'd no idea what had transpired. As he continued to ignore her words, her full lips pursed into a line of blatant disapproval, and Rio's eyes skimmed them. For one quick second, he thought about kissing her, remembering how tempted he'd been before to taste their sweetness. At the last minute, though, he dropped his fingers and stood. Her surprise forced her mouth slightly open.

"People always say they want the truth, Doctor," he said finally with a tight smile, "but in my experience, it's not what it's cracked up to be."

Like a bevy of south-Texas quails, the small group of nuns halted their efforts in their garden and eyed Mercy as she rounded the corner. They seemed somewhat uneasy with her, and Mercy wasn't sure if it was her white medical coat or her brown bare legs. One way or the other, it didn't matter. The clinic had been contracted by the diocese to provide medical care, so here she was.

She stopped at the edge of the tiny plot and shielded her eyes with one hand. "I'm looking for Sister Rosa," she called out. "Is she here?"

A tall, angular woman handed her rake to one of the other women, then walked toward Mercy. Despite the devastating heat, the woman wore a black skirt that hit her midcalf and a long-sleeved white blouse neatly tucked into the waistband. On her head—the only apparent concession to the temperatures—a wide-brimmed straw hat shaded her face. She was a plain woman, but she walked with grace and beauty, her carriage erect, her head thrown back.

She stopped in front of Mercy, her right hand extended. "I'm Sister Rosa," she said in a forceful voice. "And you must be Dr. Hamilton."

Mercy's hand was enveloped in a steely grip, then pumped once. She barely managed to conceal the wince. "Yes," she answered gingerly. "But please call me Mercy."

The nun's face broke into a smile. "What a lovely name for a doctor," she said. "Your parents must have known what you would do."

"They were both physicians themselves," she answered. "But it's what I always wanted to be, anyway." She smiled almost apologetically. "I was one of those kids who always brought home birds with broken wings and cats that had been in fights."

"A born healer." Sister Rosa smiled again, then held her hand out toward a bench on a nearby covered patio. "Let's sit for a moment. We'll have some fresh lemonade and gingerbread."

Mercy followed the black-skirted woman to the shade. They sat down, and the nun poured out two glasses, passing one to Mercy. For a moment, they didn't speak, content to sip their drinks and watch the other women work in the broiling sun, their energy apparently boundless. *No heart problems here,* Mercy thought, *or they'd be dropping like flies.*

Sister Rosa turned to her and smiled once more. "I'm so glad to finally meet you. I was thrilled to hear a woman was replacing Dr. Ruben. It will save us so much time."

Mercy lifted her eyebrows and stared at the nun over the rim of her glass.

"The older sisters never cared for Dr. Ruben," the nun explained. "They felt more comfortable with a female physician, so we had to drive them into Brownsville whenever they needed something. With you across the way, our lives will be much simpler. Especially with the mother superior as ill as she is."

The diocesan priest had explained the illness of the nun in charge. She was seriously ill; Mercy would have her hands full, she knew. "I'm glad that I can help," she answered, setting her glass down. She knew she was taking a risk, but the nun's open and friendly manner encouraged her. "Maybe you can do something for me in return."

"Gladly. Tell me how."

Mercy leaned across the table. "Earlier this week, I met a young girl in town—her name was Mary—and she said the people think that I'll charge them for my services. Have you heard this rumor?"

The nun's gaze fell to her glass, and for a moment, Mercy didn't think she'd answer. Finally, her dark brown eyes met Mercy's. "Yes," she said. "I have."

"But it's a lie! You've got to tell them—"

The nun held up her hand to stop Mercy's protest. "I told them it was not true, but my word against the other meant little."

"Who would spread such a lie? Who wouldn't want me to help these people?"

The nun pulled her lips in, as if she didn't want to speak. Moments passed, and she still didn't answer. Reaching across the table, Mercy put her hand on the nun's warm arm and asked the question she'd been too afraid to ask at the park on Sunday. "I've also met a man named Rio Barrigan. Does he have anything to do with this?"

Her eyes jerked to Mercy's. "Why would you think that?"

The nun's reaction told her that her suspicions were probably on target. "Just a guess," she said with a shrug, leaning back into the chair.

Now it was Sister Rosa's turn to lean forward. "Rio Barrigan is not a man to be trifled with, Dr. Hamilton. He's dangerous, in fact."

Their gazes locked over the table. "I've been told there are a lot of dangerous men here, Sister."

"But some are more so than others." The nun's expression was tense, and in her lap, her fingers nervously turned a small silver crucifix. "We've had some terrible things happen here lately," she said abruptly. "Illegals—they come to the door in the middle of the night, confused, beat-up, their money gone." She hesitated. "The women—well, they haven't said for sure—but I think perhaps..."

"Sexual assaults?" Mercy supplied softly.

The nun shook her head. "I...I'm not sure." Her fingers moved even faster. "I think you've come at the right time to help, but you must be careful." She leaned a little closer. "This is not an easy place to live, Doctor. There are snakes of many colors."

She rose unexpectedly and motioned for Mercy to follow her, the conversation obviously finished. The cryptic answer made Mercy think even more of Rio, but she held her silence. From the steel in the nun's posture, she knew any more questions she had would go unanswered.

For the next few hours, she busied herself with taking medical histories and examining the eldest of the sisters, including the mother superior. She was as bad as the priest had indicated, in her eighties and already bedridden with a failing heart. The younger nuns scheduled appointments and promised to come to the clinic, where the checkups would be easier to conduct.

Mercy was closing her bag and preparing to depart when Sister Rosa stopped by the tiny room. "Thank you again, Mercy, for stopping here. It was very kind of you."

Mercy stepped into the hallway and smiled. "I enjoy making house calls, actually. If I had my way, that's all I'd do."

The nun answered her smile. "In the old days, we would have had a much fuller house for you to examine." She waved her hand toward the end of the hall and a closed doorway. "This used to be the local orphanage, you know. At one time, we had more than twenty children. But not anymore, unfortunately."

Mercy stopped, her surprise obvious. "I had no idea. What happened? Why did you stop?"

"The state closed us down. They said we didn't have the proper facilities." The nun shrugged. "I don't know about you, but I think the most important 'facility' would be a loving environment. We could give that to the children—the State of Texas certainly can't."

They reached the door, and Mercy shook her head, her hand on the doorknob. "I couldn't agree with you more, Sister. The state-run organizations I've seen are *not* places a child would want to be. It makes no sense."

The nun lifted her hands and shrugged once more. "There are a lot of things in the valley that make no sense, Mercy." Her eyes drifted out to the desert, then back to Mercy's face. "That will change soon, though. God has sent us someone to help."

A week later, the clinic opened on Monday morning, and by midafternoon, Mercy had seen only one patient—a small boy with a cat that had the mange. Mercy hadn't had the heart to turn them away, so she doctored the cat the best she could and sent them on their way, the boy grasping one of the fruit pops she kept on hand for her younger patients, the cat hissing and spitting. Determined to keep the clinic open its full posted hours, she read medical journals until 9:00 p.m., but she didn't see another soul. At nine-thirty, she finally gave up, locked the doors and walked to her cabin, disappointment swamping her.

She knew there were people who needed her help, so why didn't they come? As she crossed the yard, Mercy worried especially about Mary's grandmother. A potential heart condition was nothing to ignore, and wiping her brow in the heat, Mercy vowed to return to the café as soon as possible. If all else failed, maybe she could convince Mary to take her to her grandmother.

Reaching her back porch a second later, Mercy stepped inside the cabin with a feeling of hopelessness. With extra effort, she could reach Mary's grandmother, but what about the others—the ones Mercy didn't even know about? Surely Sister Rosa had told everyone the truth. After all, she'd plainly thought God had sent them Mercy—had said as much—so why *not* encourage them to come to her?

At her refrigerator, Mercy swung the door open and took out an ice-cold beer, trying to put her problems behind her. Popping the top, she went back to the porch and sat down in the wooden swing. The air-conditioning was still out in the house, and repeated calls to the repairman had done no good. *Mañana* was definitely the key word down here. *Tomorrow,* she thought, putting the frosted bottle against her neck, *it's always tomorrow.*

She let the cold glass chill her skin, a drop of condensation escaping to run down the valley of her breasts. The cool trickle left a sensual path that immediately took her thoughts to Rio. He'd wanted to kiss her Sunday. She'd seen it in his eyes, but something, or someone, had stopped him. Maybe it'd been her with all her questions. Staring out into the black desert, Mercy couldn't help but wonder where he was, what he was doing. Was he safe? Had his wounds healed? Did he think of her?

The thoughts disturbed her, and she shook her head, trying to dislodge them. They were stubborn, however, and refused to leave. In her mind's eye, an angular face formed, shadowed by darkness, surrounded by the night. Gray eyes, black hair, brown skin. A long swallow of beer went down her throat, and she remembered the feel of his hands against her neck. Would she ever see him again?

Despite her education, despite her experience, Mercy was not a woman who'd known a lot of men. She'd dated in college and throughout medical school, but her books had always come first. There were few men who could compete with the demands she faced. But there had never been anyone who'd really interested her. Not like Rio. She didn't even know the man, but something about him stayed with her. No matter what she did, a small part of her thought about him constantly.

It was annoying.

She took another swallow of beer and told herself it was a passing fascination, that's all. He represented all the bad boys she'd ever known—the ones her parents wouldn't let her date in high school, who drove motorcycles and smoked by the high-school fence after lunch. Every woman grew up being oddly attracted to them, to the men they couldn't have, didn't they?

The night was dark, and the quarter moon played hide-and-seek with thick cumulus clouds. When the silver light finally won, the beams fell down on Mercy's arm, contrasting against her skin. Remembering, she suddenly shivered. Rio's hand on her skin, with the same

amount of contrast, had shown her just how different
they really were.

And she wasn't thinking about the color—Mercy
didn't see color.

What Mercy did see was violence. The white scars of
knife fights, the angry wound across his back, traces of
other fights—Rio carried his history on his skin, and it
wasn't a peaceful one. If he was indeed a *coyote,* she
wanted no part of him. Her life had been devoted to
healing. How could she possibly be attracted to a man
who believed in just the opposite?

The desert turned darker when the moonlight shifted
once more, and in the inky blackness, a turtledove
called. As if the bird had summoned the wind, a breeze
rose, and Mercy got a glance of the river, the water
twinkling from behind a ragged stand of pampas grass.
Her eyes readjusted to the lack of light, then the bird's
cry stopped abruptly. Her eyes narrowed, her breath
suddenly catching in her throat. On her beer bottle, her
fingers froze.

Five figures hovered near the edge of the grass. She
could tell by their size and shape that they were men, one
taller and broader than the rest. Other than that, nothing. Her chest immediately closed in misgiving, and
Greenwood's words exploded within her mind. *You're
in a primary crossing zone . . . these people are dangerous . . . killers . . . dopers. . . .*

Despite the beer, Mercy's throat turned dry as she
tried to decide what to do. No lights burned inside her
house. If she stayed perfectly still, the men might not
even see her. They'd obviously already crossed the river.
As she'd told the sheriff, wouldn't they be as anxious to
avoid her as she them?

She blinked, her eyes boring into the tall grass. The figures huddled together, but there was nothing timid about their stance. Four of them handed something to the tallest man, and she watched as he nodded his head, then stuffed whatever they'd given him into his pocket. A second later, the moon came out from behind the clouds and flooded the desert with light. Instantly, the shadows melted into the darkness, and as hard as she stared, Mercy could see nothing. They'd disappeared.

She released the breath she'd been holding and eased her grip on the porch swing's arm, her other fingers cramping on the now-warm beer bottle. The ravine at the back of the clinic ran all the way to the river. Maybe they would find it, then go completely around her house.

For another twenty minutes, Mercy stayed exactly where she was, her eyes glued to the river. Clouds came and went; moonlight advanced, then retreated. As hard as she stared, she saw nothing other than a startled jackrabbit. The men must have left. Finally she stood, rotated her shoulders and took a deep breath, closing her eyes and forcing herself to relax.

That's when the hand fell on her shoulder.

That's when she screamed with all of her might.

That's when she realized why the tallest man had seemed familiar.

Chapter 4

"You!" she gasped. "That was you down by the river?"

She stepped back from his touch, stumbling until she hit the railing of the porch with her back. The moon cleared a large cloud, and for the first time, Rio got a good look at her. Her bloodless face reminded him of the porcelain angels the nuns kept on a high shelf in their sitting room. He'd never been allowed to touch them.

"You *are* a *coyote*."

Her words were a shocked statement, not a question, and Rio stared at her quietly, the irony of the situation mocking him. He said nothing.

Her face was etched with distrust, anger and more than a touch of fear. "I saw you take their money, Rio. Don't try to deny it."

He sat down abruptly in the swing she had vacated, his side aching with heaviness. Nothing he could say would ease her fears. "They need help," he said simply, not explaining further.

"So you provide it—for a fee." Her voice turned contemptuous. "That's how you make a living—off other people's misfortune?"

He ignored the question, choosing instead to let his eyes rake over her. The short denim skirt she wore showed off her legs to their best, and the tank top that outlined her curves left little to the imagination. He'd never seen any other doctor dress like that, but from what he'd seen so far, there was nothing about Mercy that fit a mold.

He stretched one arm along the top of the swing and smiled at her casually. "You charge your patients, don't you? Everyone's got to earn a living."

She answered stiffly. "The services I provide are free, and I'd appreciate it if you didn't tell people otherwise."

He let his puzzlement show, his forehead wrinkling with confusion. "I haven't—"

"Don't bother to lie to me," she interrupted. "I *know* you've been spreading that rumor. You want me to leave, and the best way to do that is to keep my patients away." Her body stiffened. "It won't work."

He watched her chest rise and fall with her quickened breath, then he dragged his eyes back to hers. Silently, they locked gazes, the tension thick between them.

She crossed her arms protectively, her eyes glittering in the bright moonlight. "You take advantage of these people."

Despite his efforts to remain neutral, Rio's jaw tightened. "You don't know what you're talking about."

"*Coyotes* prey on the illegals. It's common knowledge," she responded. "The sheriff said so."

"And he *always* tells the truth." Unconsciously, Rio let his fingers go to the bandage under his shirt.

She frowned immediately and took a step forward before stopping abruptly. "Does it hurt?"

He shrugged. "I've felt worse."

Feeling the heat of her stare, he rose and moved to her side, his eyes searching the desert night. The four men who'd been with him at the river were probably miles away by now. He'd taken as long as he dared getting them over the border in hopes that Greenwood would appear, but nothing had happened. They were bait, albeit willing bait, and Rio would keep using them until he reeled in Greenwood. No matter how long it took, no matter who got hurt in the process. Rio would do whatever was necessary—just as he'd used the woman standing beside him.

Turning his head and looking down at her, he stared, his hands gripping the posts of the porch. "Where are you from?"

Obviously startled by his question, she hesitated, then answered. "Illinois—Edwardsville. It's a small town near St. Louis."

"With friendly people, honest cops and good schools—right?"

She looked uncomfortable. "Yes, but—"

"This isn't Edwardsville, Mercy." He dropped his hands and turned to her. From over his shoulder, bright moonlight illuminated her face—her innocent face. "Here, the people are *not* friendly—they're distrustful and mean because they have to be. The schools aren't good—they're horrible, and the cops—let's just say you should avoid getting arrested, if you can." He paused. "This is Texas, and we live life hard down here in the valley."

"I'm a doctor." Her neck was as stiff as her demeanor. "I treat people from all walks of life."

"I'm sure you do. Then you drive home in your BMW to your nice little house in the suburbs, where your clean-cut friends live and your cat is waiting by the fire." He reached out and twined one lock of her blond hair around his finger. As he spoke, he pulled it gently. "This ain't Kansas, baby."

Her hand came up, and she yanked back her hair, the strands slipping through his fingers like watered silk. "If I'd wanted Kansas, I would have gone there and opened a private practice," she answered sharply. She sat down, crossed her arms and looked up at him defiantly. "The point is—you are a criminal. You take people's money and bring them illegally into the United States. If I'd known that's what you did, I wouldn't have treated you the other night."

Her words echoed in the dark and empty desert, and Rio couldn't dispute them, any more than he could have when he'd seen her in the park. To do so would jeopardize his very life. He told himself he didn't care what she thought—she was like every other pale and beautiful woman he'd had the misfortune to know—but deep down inside, he knew he was deceiving himself. She was different and he cared. Why, he didn't yet know.

His eyes met hers in the blackness of the porch. "You're lying," he said softly. "You would have treated me regardless. You're a doctor *and* you're a woman."

"What does that mean?"

He stepped closer to the swing, then sat down beside her. The seat was small, so small that his thigh pressed against hers, hip to hip, knee to knee. The warmth should have been uncomfortable in the heat of the night, but to Rio it was a siren's call. Turning slightly, he put his arm on the back of the swing. To innocent eyes, they could have been lovers, sharing an evening chat, anticipating the night to come.

Idly, he let his fingers drift over her bare shoulder, the contrast of his skin against hers a sight to which he knew he'd never become inured. Under his touch, her skin was velvet. "That's obvious, isn't it?" he said, his voice deepened. "You're very much a woman, Mercy."

At the base of her throat, Mercy's pulse pounded, the delicate hollow moving rapidly. Rio wondered what it would be like to press his lips against that soft, sweet spot, to smell the perfume now gently teasing him, to taste the silk of her skin.

"Women nurture. You could never have turned me down."

Her eyes glittered as they met his. "I wouldn't bet on that if I were you."

"I already did," he said softly, pausing. "And I won."

"You might not be so lucky the next time."

At her shoulders, his fingers stilled. He dropped his hand against her skin, the palm completely covering the curve of her upper arm. Their eyes locked, and when he spoke again, his voice was husky with desire. "Luck doesn't have anything to do with it, Mercy. Don't you know that by now?"

They came from two different worlds, but Rio couldn't resist. He reached out and took her hand. The cool touch of her skin was like a soothing balm to him, and closing his eyes, Rio brought her fingers to the rough side of his unshaved jaw. For one long second, he stayed that way, then when she spoke, he opened his eyes.

"All I know is that I'm confused," she said softly. "You're a puzzle to me, and puzzles drive me crazy."

Her mouth tempted him with its fullness, and in the heat around them, he could smell her perfume. It lingered in the air like an exotic bouquet of flowers. Without stopping to think, Rio brought his face closer to hers, one hand reaching out to trace the outline of her jaw. "Believe it or not, you probably know more about me right now than anyone I've met in the past twenty years."

Her forehead wrinkled. "But I only know your name—"

"That's right," he said softly. "And most never even hear that." Under his touch, her skin felt like a miracle, soft, sexy, womanly. "I'm a loner, Mercy. By necessity *and* by nature. You've undressed me, you've seen me sleeping, you've cared for me. The last time I let anyone get that close, I was too young to walk across the street by myself."

Surprise darkened her eyes, but as Rio leaned even closer, he wondered. Was it really surprise or something else? Something like passion?

He moved toward her.

The minute their lips touched, Rio knew he'd made a serious mistake.

But by then, it was too late.

Her mouth moved under his, and involuntarily, Rio's hands tightened on her back to bring her closer. Because of everything he was and everything he had to be, Rio had been fighting his attraction, fighting his arousal, but as Mercy moaned under his touch, he wondered why. It was pointless to even try.

For endless seconds, Mercy weathered the onslaught of his passion, her own desire shattering her with its intensity. Rio Barrigan was like no man she'd ever encountered in her life, and his kiss affected her even more than she'd imagined it would. It scared her, it thrilled her, it turned her inside out.

The realization pulled her up short, and she broke the seal of their kiss, her hands pushing against his hard chest.

"Stop," she gasped, pulling back from him. "This is all wrong, all—"

Instantly, he obeyed her, but his eyes—those pale gray eyes—stared at her with a barely checked passion. "Wrong? Nothing that feels like this could be wrong." His hands moved to her arms, and he clasped her with a strength that frightened her. "Tell me you didn't feel anything, Mercy—then it would be wrong."

She shook her head, her eyes refusing to meet his, her hair tumbling over her shoulders. "I don't know you, you don't know me. It's crazy, and—"

"Why don't you just admit the real reason?"

His light gray eyes swept over her like a searchlight, and she felt just as exposed. Mercy heard the blood rush through her veins, felt the pounding of her pulse. She rose swiftly to her feet and moved away from him toward the railing. "I think you'd better leave."

"You don't like my company?" His voice was mocking.

"I don't like your profession."

His fingers gripped the back of the swing until the knuckles turned white, but his expression never changed. "You don't know what you're talking about."

"You said that already," she retorted, "and you're wrong. I spoke with Sister Rosa. She told me about the injured illegals who've come to the convent."

A frown of shock and then confusion darkened his already swarthy brow. "What's that got to do with—"

"They were beaten up, Rio. Crossing the river, trying to get to the United States. Someone is ambushing them, then taking every cent they've got. Someone who knows the crossing routes, someone who knows their ways."

"Someone like a *coyote*."

"Yes." She forced herself to meet his stare. "Someone like a *coyote*. Someone . . . like you."

He stood so quickly that the swing swung out violently behind him, hitting the railing three feet back. In one fluid motion, he was at her side, his face inches from hers, his fingers on her arm. "Let's get one thing straight here, Doctor. It's been years since I went to confession, but beating up innocent people isn't one of the things I'd have to list."

He bent his head down and stared at her, his eyes narrowing into even slits of chilling silvery light. His fingers bit into her arm, but Mercy stayed perfectly still, almost petrified with fright and something else—a strange kind of tingling that made her pulse pound so loudly she could barely hear his words. She stared at the dark triangle of flesh she could see inside his open shirt collar and told herself it wasn't happening. That she wasn't getting excited. That she couldn't be interested. He was too dangerous, too exotic, too masculine—he was a man she wouldn't know what to do with even if she could catch him.

He seemed to agree with her. Suddenly, inexplicably, and without another word, he dropped her arm, swirled off the porch and disappeared into the night—as quickly and as silently as he'd arrived.

The next morning dawned hotter than ever. When Mercy rose from a sleepless bed and stumbled into the bathroom, dark rings of fatigue and confusion shadowed her eyes. Looking in the small mirror above her washbasin, she cursed softly and splashed lukewarm water on her face.

Why did everything have to be so complicated?

Rio Barrigan stood for absolutely everything she despised—violence, crime, intimidation. He'd come to her with a gunshot wound, had held a knife to her throat, lived by a completely foreign set of rules.

And she'd thought of nothing but him since the minute he'd stepped off her porch.

After pulling on a pair of shorts and a T-shirt, she ran a comb through her hair, tied it back, then went into the kitchen. She *had* to get him out of her mind, *had* to put him aside. He was nothing but trouble, and if she hadn't suspected that before, last night had proved it. He was a man who lived off helpless people—a man who deserved the name of a predatory animal, and if she didn't watch out, she was going to get caught in his trap, too.

As she automatically filled up the coffeepot, then carefully measured out the coffee into the filter, Mercy thought about how haywire her life had gone in just a few short weeks. She'd survived the rigors of school, the hours of internship, the stress of simply being in the medical field, but nothing had prepared her for this. For Rio.

When her coffee was ready, she poured a mugful, then went to her back door. Pushing open the screen with her foot, her coffee in one hand, a piece of toast in the other, Mercy stepped outside. The morning air was already hot, and the desert shimmered in the early heat, a blistering wind picking up dust devils and tossing them about the yard. She squinted against the glare, her eyes automatically going to the clinic. Instantly, her heart tripped, and the coffee mug in her hand trembled and threatened to spill.

Five people stood patiently in a line snaking around the front of the clinic. The first was a woman holding a small child in her arms. She was rocking the child back and forth, oblivious to the heat, her concentration focused on trying to calm the agitated child. Next in line was an elderly woman, then a teenager. Bringing up the rear was a young couple, holding hands.

For a moment, all Mercy could do was stare stupidly. Patients? She had patients? After talking to Sister Rosa, she'd assumed she was going to have to go out and find them—and now here they were. Had the nun convinced them otherwise? In the next moment, a pair of pale gray eyes flashed into her mind. Or had Rio changed his mind—and theirs? Suddenly, she didn't care. She had patients, and that was all that mattered.

"I'll be right there," Mercy called out excitedly. *"Un momento, por favor."* Dashing back into the cabin, she threw her toast and the chipped mug into her kitchen sink, then ran to the desk in one corner of the living room. Snatching up a white coat with her name embroidered on the pocket, she poked her arms into it, then reached for her stethoscope with one hand and her bag with the other. In two seconds, she was flying toward the clinic.

Smiling at the waiting patients, Mercy quickly unlocked the door, flipped on the fan and ushered them in. Her Spanish was flawless, and tentative smiles rewarded her instructions for them all to take a seat and give her a few moments to get organized. Continuing to the back of the building, she turned on the light in the examining room, then opened the small, high window to get a draft going. For a moment, she leaned against the table and closed her eyes, her heart clamoring with excitement.

Her first *real* patients in her *own* clinic! How many years had she waited for this? How many times had she dreamed of this moment? The small thrill raced over her, and she smiled to herself, straightening her jacket and clasping her stethoscope around her neck. A second later, she called in the first woman.

By lunchtime, Mercy had seen everyone in the waiting room, except two who'd come in later—Mary and her grandmother. The young girl's eyes were ringed with worry as she ushered in the elderly woman and introduced her to Mercy.

Mercy helped Mrs. Hernandez up to the examining table, the elderly woman's feet not even touching the footrest once she was situated. Her face looked like a dried apple, with wrinkles deep and twisted, but shining out of it were two black-raisin eyes that twinkled with alertness. Her Spanish was rapid-fire, and Mercy didn't even catch everything she said the first time.

Mercy pressed the stethoscope against the woman's mahogany skin. She followed Mercy's instructions to the letter, breathing deeply, then letting the air escape from her lungs. Her heart fluttered more than it beat, and by the time Mercy noted the woman's swollen feet and enlarged neck veins, she knew one thing. Mrs. Hernandez needed more care than Mercy and her little clinic could provide.

After a few seconds, trying to keep her face noncommittal, Mercy helped her climb down from the examining table. With her granddaughter's help, the elderly woman put on the black cotton dress she'd worn into the clinic.

"You need more tests," Mercy said in Spanish. "I obviously don't have the facilities here to do them, but you should go into Brownsville as soon as possible and have them done there. I'll get the name of another doctor for you, a cardiologist—a heart specialist." Reverting to English, she glanced at Mary, whose face had deepened into a frown of concern. "I'm not sure, but she could be in the beginning stages of a possible cardiac problem. But there are medicines available—very powerful, but good. She'd need to stay on a low-salt diet, too. Before we do anything else, however, her heart should be checked thoroughly. By a specialist."

Mrs. Hernandez glanced toward her granddaughter and shot off a question that was simply a blur to Mercy. Mary nodded unhappily, then faced Mercy once more. "She doesn't want to go to Brownsville. She doesn't trust the doctors at the big hospital."

Mercy's forehead knit, and she looked at the older woman. "*¿Por que no?* The physicians in Brownsville are very well trained, very professional."

The grandmother shook her head violently and pulled her black shawl closer to her thin chest. "My friend Carmine went there and never came back. She died at the hospital. I don't want to die."

Mercy moved forward and put her arm around the woman's shoulder. "Hospitals are not bad places, Mrs. Hernandez. Your friend was probably very ill when she went. You aren't." Unconvinced black eyes stared back. "If it would make you feel better, I could go with you. Would that help?"

The woman pursed her narrow lips into a circle of obstinacy. It was a familiar expression to Mercy. She'd thought of specializing in geriatric care at one time and had even done volunteer work in a nursing home while attending college. Anything unfamiliar was automatically suspicious. She tightened her arm and patted Mrs. Hernandez reassuringly, knowing that she needed finessing. "Mary could go with us. We could make a treat of it—maybe do something in Brownsville while we're there. How does that sound?"

The old woman looked at her granddaughter, then fired off another round of Spanish and pulled away from Mercy's touch. Without another glance, she left the room.

Astonished, Mercy stared at her back, her mouth hanging open.

"My grandmother is a very stubborn woman, Doctor. She says she's not going to Brownsville, and that's all there is to it." Mary turned and followed in the old woman's footsteps, but Mercy couldn't allow her to leave. Reaching out, she put her hand on the girl's arm and stopped her.

"She needs an ECG, Mary, an electrocardiogram. That's a test to judge the condition of her heart. I don't have that kind of equipment here. In addition to that, she needs blood and urine workups and a chest X ray, too. You can't just ignore this kind of problem—it can be serious."

Mary's eyes went to the floor.

Mercy tightened her grip. "None of these are painful tests," she said desperately. "And everything may check out just fine. If it doesn't, then there are medicines that can help her. She's got to be looked at, though."

The young girl looked up, her face stricken. "But what can I do? If she doesn't want to go, I can't convince her."

Mercy dropped her hand and released her. "I don't know," she answered truthfully. "But if you'll help me, we'll think of something."

* * *

"You've got to do something, Mercy. Can't you help her?"

Perched on the edge of the mattress, her brown eyes filled with concern, Sister Rosa looked up from the frail body stretched out on the mother superior's bed.

Mercy shook her head and rolled down her sleeves. Tilting her head toward the door, she whispered, "Let's go outside."

Sister Rosa stood and began to tuck the ironed sheets around the almost motionless body. She worked as if she could keep the sickness at bay if only the sheets were straight enough.

Mercy sighed, then stepped into the hallway of the convent and waited. The only windows were fifteen feet above her, and the sunlight that drifted down was, for a change, mercifully filtered. She rubbed her eyes, then looked up into the light. In the silence, the dust motes danced, and a passing whiff of baking bread came to Mercy.

The nun reached her side and took her arm. "Let's go to the kitchen. Sister Lydia said she'd keep lunch for us."

They passed an open door, and Mercy couldn't resist a curious peek. A black-garbed woman was sweeping out a stark room filled with cots of all sizes, mostly small, their mattresses neatly tucked into rolls at the foot of each one. Mercy's feet slowed, then stopped, her heart filling with sudden sympathy.

"Was that where they slept?"

Ahead of her, Sister Rosa stopped and glanced back. Clearly, her mind was on the mother superior as her forehead frowned into a wrinkle of confusion.

"The children," Mercy supplied. "Did they sleep in there when this was an orphanage?"

Sister Rosa's expression cleared. "Yes, all the younger children, the ones under fifteen. If they were any older, they received their own rooms, upstairs. They usually had to share them, but only with one other student." She turned, her thick-soled shoes gliding soundlessly against the floor.

For a few more painful minutes, Mercy stared, then she hurried after the nun. Her bedroom back in Edwardsville had been twice as large, with pearl white carpet and ruffled drapes. There hadn't been a time when it wasn't filled with toys, books, dolls—whatever she wanted. Here she saw chipped linoleum, barren windows, unrelieved austerity. She'd known there were places like that, places where unwanted children spent sad and painful childhoods, but to see one in all its unbending harshness was a shock. What kind of adult would such a child become?

They reached the sun-filled kitchen, and Mercy forced her thoughts away from the forgotten children. In one corner of the industrial-size cooking area, a small table and four chairs awaited. As soon as they sat down, a white-aproned sister bustled over with tall glasses of lemonade and small sandwiches she'd obviously prepared with love, the crusts cut off evenly, the plate decorated with a sprig of fresh mint.

Sister Rosa pushed the plate toward Mercy. "Please, help yourself," she said. "I...I don't think I can eat anything."

Mercy's hand paused over the plate, her eyes going to the nun. Instead of taking a sandwich, she found herself patting the woman's arm.

The nun smiled through her tears and shook her head. "I'll be all right. You eat."

Mercy nodded once and took a sandwich. After a few bites, however, her appetite fled, as well, and she put the food down, then pushed it away, mimicking Sister Rosa's actions.

"She's not going to last much longer, is she?"

When Mercy answered, her voice was regretful. "I don't know what to tell you, Sister," she said, glancing out the window. "She's very, very ill and very, very weak." Outside in the blistering heat, six nuns hoed the garden. Mercy let her eyes return to the woman beside her. "She's in her eighties, Sister Rosa. Bodies break down at that age."

"I'm being selfish, aren't I?"

Mercy smiled gently. "You love her—you don't want to let her go. That's perfectly normal."

"But we're going to have to."

It wasn't a question, and Mercy didn't reply.

The nun swallowed and folded her long, lean hands around the sweating glass of lemonade, her brown eyes blinking rapidly. She was looking out the window, but Mercy doubted that she saw the garden and the toiling women. Her next words confirmed Mercy's suspicions.

"I've never been able to say goodbye gracefully—and this is just like when the children left," she said quietly. "I knew ahead of time. Months before the end, the state had told us they all had to be gone by December. The babies, of course, were usually no problem. They're always so cute, so sweet—it was never difficult to find them a home, no matter what color their skin." She dropped her eyes and stared into the glass of pale yellow liquid. "The older children weren't so lucky. Their personalities had already been warped—by time, by hatred, by prejudice. Some were too young to be on their own. We had to find places at state schools for them. The older ones—we simply turned them out the door.''

Mercy's heart clenched at the image that brought to mind. When she'd been looking forward to high-school dances and crying over skin problems, the kids who had lived here were simply trying to survive.

The nun's voice cracked. ''I never felt right about that, and all these years it's bothered me. I let them down.'' She lifted her face to Mercy's. ''I feel like I'm doing the same for the mother superior.''

Mercy spoke instantly. ''But there's nothing you can do. She's lived a good life, and you should take comfort in that.''

''Oh, I understand that, but there's always something we can do, Mercy. It may not look like a solution at the time, but there's always something.''

Mercy could see the guilt piling up behind the nun's brown eyes. She'd devoted her life to helping other people, but still it wasn't enough. She wanted to save them all. Mercy dropped her voice, the muted sounds of cooking playing like background music to their conversation. ''Sometimes that 'something' is letting go, Sister,'' she said softly. ''You can't rescue everyone— someone's always going to slip through your fingers.''

''Is that what you tell yourself when you can't cure someone?''

The bluntness of her words shocked Mercy into silence, but she recovered quickly. ''We all have coping techniques—but some work better than others.'' She brought her glass of lemonade to her lips and sipped, trying to regain her equilibrium. She *had* lost patients, and it *had* hurt. Had hurt so badly she simply didn't let herself think about it. Slowly, she put the tumbler back to the table, carefully setting it inside the ring of con-

densation that had formed on the scarred top. "I try to focus on the successes," she finally said, her steady gaze meeting the nun's. "Surely you have some of those you can think about."

"Successes?" The nun repeated the word thoughtfully. "There was one young man." She sighed deeply. "I thought he was going to be one of the fortunate ones. He was so bright, so intelligent, so handsome. Except for his attitude and certain circumstances, he had everything—everything but parents, of course. He *could* have done it."

The reminiscing seemed to take the sister's mind away from her dying friend, and Mercy encouraged her gently. "Could have?"

The nun nodded thoughtfully. "He…didn't turn out *exactly* as I would have liked." She glanced down at her hands. "Considering everything, though, I guess he did the best he could."

"Where is he now?"

The sister turned her face to Mercy, her expression a mixture of regret and concern. "You've met him already. His name is Rio Barrigan."

Chapter 5

By the time she finished a lonely salad and flipped through the three television channels that were available in Ciudad Bravo, Mercy knew she had to get out of the tiny house. She'd never been the kind of person who had to have a city to be entertained, but the isolation of the cabin was beginning to put her on edge.

Or so she told herself as she walked out the front door and down toward the river. She didn't want to acknowledge the fact that Rio Barrigan was the real reason behind her tenseness, but she was too honest with herself not to. Her footsteps left impressions in the dust as she conceded the point.

Images of him filled her every waking moment—and her sleeping ones, too. The kiss they shared had taken on a ghostlike quality. The taste of his lips on hers, the heavy warmth of his hands against her skin, the vision of his dark against her light—she couldn't escape the memories, no matter how hard she tried. They haunted

her night and day. While she was seeing patients, while she was trying to sleep, while she was reading—nothing she could do would exorcise those sensations. To find out he'd been an orphan, then learn nothing more, had been torture. Sister Rosa had been adamant, however. She'd refused to say anything else and had sent Mercy on her way abruptly, as if she'd already said too much.

The west Texas sun hung over the horizon like a giant ball of fire. Staring at the still, hot rays as she walked, Mercy frowned and lifted her heavy hair from her neck, the blond curls tangling against her fingers, the breeze sluggish on her skin. She felt frustrated and anxious and vaguely restless.

The wind had dropped, and the humid heat beat on her with damp determination. As she reached the sluggish water, Mercy gave in to temptation and, dropping to a nearby boulder, she slipped out of her tennis shoes and shed her socks. In the more urbane areas, the Rio Grande had turned into a polluted disgrace, but she knew that here in the isolated country, it remained clean, if not clear. In a second, she was in the water, the brown wetness cool against her feverish skin.

For at least ten minutes, Mercy stood in the center of the river, the water barely reaching her knees at the deepest point. Somewhere between her toes, Texas stopped and Mexico started. Turning to her left, she stared across the endless, stretching range. In the distance, the bare bumps of a mountain range caught her eye. The land was desolate, empty, forbidding.

Just like Rio.

On a whim, she moved forward in the water, wading to the other side. Her feet dug into the mud, the soft, oozing smoothness giving way to sharper, rock-filled sand as she reached the shore. She stood there, in Mexico, for several long minutes, the failing sun punishing her, the breeze whipping her hair into her eyes.

When she was a little girl, she'd played outside her grandmother's house, in the dead-end street it faced. There was no traffic in the area, but her grandmother had told her never to cross the tiny road. She wanted Mercy to stay on "their" side.

The temptation had simply been too much for a six-year-old girl, though, and one hot summer afternoon, Mercy had looked back once, then dashed across the fifteen-foot span. For five delicious moments, she'd danced up and down the gravel on the "wrong" side of the road, the feeling of freedom a new and exquisite choice made even sweeter by its prohibition. Her exhilaration had ended abruptly when a bumblebee found her little toe.

She had run back into the frame house, crying and screaming, but she found little sympathy. "You should have stayed on this side, like I told you to," her grandmother had admonished. "You got punished because you disobeyed."

Mercy smiled to herself as she remembered the incident. Her grandmother had never been able to sufficiently explain to her why the bumblebee knew Mercy was on the "wrong" side. Mercy's expression faded, however, as she laid that experience over the transparency of the present. Rio had just as much sting in him as that bee, and she knew she was tempting fate by even thinking of him.

Turning abruptly, she waded back into the muddy water and crossed back to "her" side. During her reverie, the sun had slipped its ties and dropped beneath the horizon, and in the red afterglow Mercy felt her first shiver of alarm. She shouldn't be out here this late.

With the sheriff's warnings echoing in her head, she sat down on the rock, hastily grabbing her shoes. Using her socks, she dried off her feet, then thrust them into the damp tubes of cotton. She was tying her last shoelace when a deep voice broke the silence.

"What in the hell are you doing down here?"

Her surprised face turned pale, while behind her, the river gurgled and mocked her plight. "Rio," she said with a guilty catch in her voice, one hand at the base of her throat. "You startled me. I . . . I didn't expect to see you down here."

He took another step toward her, his boots skidding carelessly down the slight incline. "Who did you expect?" His tone was more belligerent than he would have liked, but seeing her there, dragging her feet through the water, playing in the river like a naive kid, had sent his anger flying.

Hadn't she understood a word of his warning?

Her expression seemed to close in on itself. "I didn't expect anyone," she answered. "This *is* my yard, you know."

With his hands on his hips, Rio stared down at her upturned face. Even in the dim light, he could see the flare in her blue eyes. They looked like twin flames, and he knew that if he got much closer he'd get burned. He turned his heart against their allure.

"Yard?" he said, a mocking tone in his voice. "This isn't Edwardsville, Mercy. Yards have nice green grass and tended borders." He curled his lip and held one hand out to indicate the barren landscape. "I don't see any of that around here."

She pulled her own mouth into a straight line, and the movement forced Rio's stomach to tighten. Her lips weren't made for such strict discontent—they were too soft, too inviting and too sexy for anything but kissing. Instantly, he wanted to press his own mouth against hers and erase that expression of disapproval.

"It was simply a manner of speaking," she replied, her expression turning stormy.

For a second longer, Rio stared at her through the growing darkness, then he squatted down beside her. He didn't trust himself to sit on the rock at her side. Inevitably, they'd touch, and then he'd kiss her and then they'd both want more. And that simply couldn't happen.

He'd been telling himself for days *why* it couldn't happen. His life-style. Her career. His past. Her upbringing. But his feet had still brought him to her doorstep tonight. When he'd seen her lift her hair, as she had the first time he'd laid eyes on her, they'd brought him to her side.

"It's too dangerous for you to be out here," he said gruffly.

"Dangerous?" She chuckled nervously. "That's rich—coming from you." Her perfume drifted toward him. "*You're* the one who was holding a knife to my throat the first time we met."

Rio raised one eyebrow and dipped his head. "I didn't hurt you."

"No, you didn't." She paused. "But somehow I'm not too reassured."

He jerked his head up and stared at her. Her skin was almost luminous, her hair a shining halo of light. He knew he shouldn't, but he reached out and ran his finger up her bare arm. "If you really thought I'd hurt you, you would have turned me in."

"How do you know I haven't?"

In the dusk, his eyes probed hers. Her face was like a song—he didn't know the melody, but the words haunted him night and day. He flipped his finger over and dragged the knuckle side back down her skin. "If you had, the sheriff would have already come after me."

Her voice was a husky whisper. "Maybe you're too fast for him."

"Maybe so." He paused, his finger lying in the crook of her arm. Her skin was warm and slightly damp. "Am I too fast for you?"

Her eyes widened slightly, just as he imagined they would if he made love to her. "Too fast?" She softly repeated the words, then shook her head, the blond hair catching the apricot sun. "I'm not sure *fast* is the right word. Maybe *dangerous* might be better."

He slipped his hand around her elbow, then let his fingers tease the underside of her upper arm. "This is a dangerous place. If you want to survive, that's what you have to be."

"Is that how you made it after the orphanage turned you out?"

Automatically, Rio's fingers tightened into a grip of surprise and anger. He didn't even realize what he was doing until her face blanched, then immediately, he released her and stood up. He faced the river and spoke. "How did you hear about that?"

"I had to go to the convent today. Sister Rosa and I started talking about the orphanage, and she told me."

He heard Mercy rise, then walk toward him, the pebbles along the riverbank announcing her movement. In a second, she stood beside him, her head barely coming to his shoulder. In another second, she laid her hand on his arm, her cool, soothing, healing hand. It made him think of the hours he'd spent in her bed.

"It must have been horrible."

He swung his head around and looked at her. "Horrible would have been growing up on the other side."

"Yes," she answered. "But what you had wasn't so great, either." Her fingers tightened. "It made me feel guilty."

"Why should you feel guilty? You had nothing to do with my childhood."

"That's true." Her fingers knit together. "But I guess hearing about it affected me because I was lucky enough to have the perfect adolescence. There were never any money problems, my parents loved me and each other, we had a nice house . . . very 'Leave It to Beaver' kind of stuff."

"There's always going to be haves and have-nots. You can't change that."

"But I can help—and you should, too."

At her words, anger pumped through Rio like an adrenaline hit. His voice was soft and deadly. "Watch what you're saying."

"Why? Does the truth hurt?" Dropping her hand, she stepped back from him as though she'd realized how close she was. "Frankly, I had a hard enough time understanding before what you did, how you take advantage of these people. But now? Now, I know I'd never understand in a million years." She put her hands on her hips. "You *came* from a terrible environment, and you're perpetuating the hurts."

The accusation was too much. He swirled and faced her, his heart hammering. "You're talking about something you can't comprehend—not with your background—not now, not ever."

"But—"

"Did the sister tell you everything? Give you all the gory details?"

She stared at him speechlessly.

"I didn't think so." He dropped back from her, took a step away as if he couldn't stand to be so close to her. "They found me on the riverbank." He threw his head toward the water. "Just about a mile from here—beside the body of my dead mother. She died crossing the river just so I could be born on this side." He took a deep breath, intending to stop, but somehow going on, the pent-up resentment pouring from him like poison. "In my mother's things, the nuns found a small diary. My..." He paused, seemingly reluctant to even say the word. "My father—an Anglo, by the way—had raped her."

The harsh words hung in the humid night air, expelled by Rio's frustration, suspended by his anger. He'd never told a single soul what he'd just told Mercy, and now that it was done, Rio couldn't believe she was still standing there. But she was. Her blue eyes glimmering, she blinked rapidly and swallowed, her throat moving with a jerk.

"I...I'm sorry."

He turned away. He hadn't wanted sympathy; that's not why he'd told her. To save his life, however, he couldn't say why he *had* told her. His anger dissipated like air from a deflated balloon. "It was a long time ago."

"Where did you get the name? 'Barrigan'?"

He looked at the moon's reflection in the water. "The parish priest." He smiled ironically. "I didn't understand until later why he'd looked so surprised when I asked him if I could use his name. He agreed, though.

In fact, said he'd be honored." Rio dug the tip of his boot into the pebbled sand. "I remember because that was the first time I ever felt good about myself—when he said he'd like me to have his name." He paused, his voice turning softer. "He said he'd never have a son, but if he had, he'd want him to be like me."

The distressed cry of a turtledove filled the silence, then Mercy seemed to recover. "So why do you do what you do?" she said softly. "Why take advantage of people who are trying for the same thing your mother died to give you?"

He jerked his gaze to her face. She was pushing him way too hard, as if she almost *wanted* him to get angry. With an effort, he held himself in check and finally answered, his voice a harsh slash, the words a mixture of truth and fiction. "Because if I don't, someone else will. Someone who will take more than their money—someone who'll take their lives."

Her face blanched, and her fingers went to her arms. She rubbed them as if she were cold. "Are you trying to scare me?"

He swirled and looked at her. "Yes, damn it to hell, I am. You don't belong down here, and if you know what's good for you, you'll leave. Right now. Before it's too late to go."

A lump of fear formed in the back of Mercy's throat as she stared at the tall, dark man in front of her. She hadn't thought he could get much more frightening than he had the night they'd met, but the cold, distant persona he wore now was even more alarming. "I can't leave," she said automatically. "The clinic would close without me."

"Then maybe that's what needs to happen."

"What *needs to happen* is for someone to care about these people. Someone who can help them help themselves." She took a deep breath. "That's not what we're really arguing about, though, is it? You're just bound and determined to run me out of here, aren't you, and that's why you're telling the people not to come to me? I'm in your way."

His pale eyes glittered in the dying light, and before Mercy knew what was going on, he'd moved to her side. His ability to get close to her without warning was uncanny, and suddenly, her pulse accelerated.

"I already told you I'm not the one who's frightening your patients away." He leaned even closer, and she could feel the heat of his skin. "You're right about one thing, though."

His face was inches from hers, so close that she could see where the white scar on his eyebrow started and ended. Momentarily distracted, she blinked at the thought of how close he must have come to losing that eye, then when he spoke, she focused once more on him. Inside her chest, her heart beat as irregularly as Mrs. Hernandez's.

"What . . . what's that?" she asked.

"I *don't* want you around here. Here in Ciudad. Here in the Valley. Here in Texas." His voice flowed over her like cold tequila. "But it's too damn late. Every time I turn around, you're there. In my dreams, in my work . . . in my bed. It's driving me crazy."

They were not touching. No part of Rio's body was in contact with hers, but if he had removed her clothes and was making love to her, Mercy couldn't have felt his intensity more.

"How do you do it?" he asked, his voice angry and questioning. "How have you managed to climb into my head like that? You don't belong there. You belong with some yuppie lawyer who takes you to the country club for dinner and dancing on Saturday night.''

Mercy spoke without thinking. ''You don't dance?''

His lips curled up into a smile that she felt all the way to her muddy toes. ''I dance—I'm just not sure you could keep up.''

''I might surprise you.''

Heat coiled inside Mercy's stomach like a flickering torch. Every nerve ending she had screamed danger, told her to run, but she ignored the warnings as she had her grandmother's advice twenty-plus years ago.

''There's a lot of things about me that might surprise you,'' she said staunchly. ''I'm not the innocent you think I am.''

''Experienced? You?'' His eyes slowly passed sentence on her. ''I'm not talking about losing your virginity in the back seat of a Chevy.''

She felt the blush start at her neck and work its way up to her face as he glared at her with a wicked gleam. When he finally touched her, one finger to her cheek, she held her breath as he spoke. ''That's only the beginning, you know.''

Mercy dropped her eyes, desire pulsing through her in a rush she couldn't ignore. At that one point of contact—where his finger burned on her cheek—the heat started, then radiated out in growing circles of warmth. Another circle had started low in her stomach.

He put his fingers under her chin and lifted her face to his. She knew he was going to kiss her, knew he was going to raise the temperature even more. Moistening her lips in anticipation, Mercy grew breathless.

He dipped his head toward her, his hand tensing on her chin. On his jaw, she could see the stubble that

would be rough against her skin, could feel the minty breath that would be warm against her mouth, could smell the male scent that would linger on her later. She tensed.

"That's only the beginning," he repeated, "but *this*, Dr. Hamilton, is the end."

He dropped his finger, swirled around and disappeared.

Mercy's sheets were tangled and hot.

No matter which way she turned, she couldn't get comfortable. She punched the pillow once more and dropped her head to its crumpled form, burying her face against the softness and moaning. How could one man disrupt her life so thoroughly?

She took a deep breath against the pillow and squeezed her eyes shut. The sheets had been washed twice since Rio's stay, but she'd swear she could still catch a whiff of his presence. Her heart thumped against her chest in a crazy rhythm, and she finally gave a name to the restlessness that possessed her.

Desire.

She was disappointed that he hadn't kissed her, and the more she thought about it, the more she realized that's exactly what she had wanted. She'd needed to feel his lips against hers, the hard pressure of his hand against her back, the insistent demand of his tongue in opposition to hers. She'd wanted him.

Flipping on her back, Mercy gave up and let her eyes pop open. Soft moonlight drifted through the curtains, and as she eased up on the pillows, the reflected movement in the mirror caught her eye. Instantly, she remembered staring at Rio's bare back in that same glass. Against the sheets, her fingers spread.

He was total disaster, no doubt about it.

And she wanted him.

Everything about him spoke of danger, smelled of fire. He broke the law, lived only in the night, appeared, then disappeared. He represented the dark side of life and all it held—everything she'd been taught to avoid. And she wanted him. More than any man she'd ever known before.

She closed her eyes and leaned against the brass headboard of the bed, imagining his muscular silhouette. Yes, his long black hair was smooth and silky, and yes, his chest rippled with the type of muscles that didn't come from a fancy gym. His chiseled face was the kind a woman couldn't get out of her mind, and yes, his long brown legs would feel hard and tight if they stretched on either side of hers.

But wasn't there more?

Mercy's eyes opened slowly, and in the silver light of 3:00 a.m., a woman unknown stared back at her from the mirror. A woman whose moistened lips were slightly parted, whose heavy-lidded eyes gleamed in the heat, whose breasts ached and swelled at the neck of her nightgown...a woman who looked ready for love.

She blinked, and the woman winked seductively. There *was* more to Rio, Mercy argued silently; there had to be, or she wouldn't find him so damn appealing. A trickle of sweat ran down the valley of Mercy's breasts, and the woman staring back at her pursed her lips. *A lot more,* she agreed silkily. *Like danger and heartache and desires you know nothing about. Things you've heard about, always wanted to experience, but didn't know how to.*

Mercy breathed deeply, then closed her eyes and merged with the woman in the mirror, her hands pull-

ing the sheets into a tangled knot at her side. It didn't matter, did it? Rio had said this was the end, and he was right. He wanted nothing to do with her, and she wanted nothing to do with him. Even if he'd been telling the truth and he wasn't the one trying to keep everyone from her clinic, she didn't need a man like him.

She didn't need him at all.

Mercy's eyes fluttered open, and the sexy woman in the mirror brought her hands up to the column of her throat, the skin hot and slick beneath her fingers. Under her touch, her pulse beat with a tingling rhythm that she hadn't felt since she'd been a young girl just discovering her own sensuality. Eyes that seared in their intensity stared back at Mercy from the mirror. They mocked her with their want. She didn't need him at all, she repeated to herself. Not at all.

"And how old is your baby?" Mercy looked up from the clipboard she held and into the eyes of the young girl standing before her. The girl herself couldn't have been much more than sixteen, but she held an infant in her arms, and a toddler, his mouth ringed with something red and sticky, clutched her skirt.

"The baby, she's six months," the girl said in Spanish, "and Juan—" she tilted her head toward the older child "—he's two years."

Mercy smiled at the one named Juan and said hello, but instead of answering her, he buried his face into his mother's skirts and began to howl. A simple smile wasn't going to win him over... he knew Mercy had a box of syringes hidden behind the desk where she sat.

With school beginning in a month or so, Mercy had decided to do an all-day Saturday immunization clinic. She'd loaded up the truck and come to town. Under signs in both Spanish and English, she'd attracted a surprisingly steady line of customers all morning long.

Mercy finished asking the rest of her questions, then looked over at Mary Hernandez. When her shift at the café had ended, the teenager had volunteered to help Mercy.

"I'll need a DTP and one Hib," Mercy told the girl, then turning to the young mother, Mercy indicated the folding metal chair beside her. "Why don't you sit here," she said, "and hold Juan on your lap? Mary can hold the baby, then we'll switch and do her next."

It was easier said than done, but a few moments later, the baby was in Mary's arms, the syringe was in Mercy's hands and Juan couldn't escape his haemophilus B conjugate vaccine. With the older child still screaming, the three women quickly exchanged armfuls, and seconds afterward, the baby was crying, too, her diphtheria/tetanus/pertussis shot finished. The mother looked as if she wanted to cry, as well, when Mercy asked her about her own shot record. By the time she was finished, Mercy had handed over two red fruit pops. Holding the baby, the mother walked away with Juan, both she and her son sucking on their treats and rubbing various parts of their bodies.

Five more customers arrived in short order—two who howled over more DTP's, and two who grinned when all they needed were oral polio vaccines. They finished up with one more customer, then Mercy turned back to the teenager by her side.

"Have you had a chance to talk to your grandmother?" she asked the young girl. "She really needs to get to that specialist in Brownsville."

Mary straightened the paper-wrapped syringes on the folding metal table they'd set up on the sidewalk, then

she looked up at Mercy with concern in her dark eyes. "She says she's feeling better. That she doesn't need to go."

"She *does* need to go," Mercy said. "Heart problems don't just disappear, and at her age..."

Mary's expression turned even more serious. "I know, *Doctora,* I know. I just can't seem to convince her, though. She's...she's scared."

"I understand." Mercy nodded thoughtfully. "When I was doing my residency, I worked with older patients a lot, and things like this *are* frightening to them. Heck—medical tests are scary even if you *do* know what's going on." She paused, then continued. "You know, if you want someone who's scared to do something, though, the best approach is the same one you use with kids. I should have thought of this earlier."

"What's that?"

"Make them buy in to the situation. Appeal to their best side." Mercy tilted her head with a questioning attitude. "You've always lived with your grandmother, haven't you?"

The teenager nodded shyly. "My mother left Ciudad right after I was born. Grandmother raised me."

"Then I bet she'd do anything if it was for you. Am I right?"

Mary nodded again.

Mercy leaned across the table toward the teenager. "Why don't you tell her *you* want to go? Tell her you helped me today, and that you really enjoyed it. She already knows you have some interest in medicine, right? Why not tell her you'd like to see a big hospital, that you've been wanting to see what it's like, then once she gets used to that idea, you can say 'since we're going to be there...why don't you see the doctor, too?'"

Mary looked unconvinced. "Do you think that would work?"

"Maybe, maybe not." Mercy shrugged. "I don't know, but it's worth a try, isn't it?"

"But . . . it's dishonest, isn't it?"

"No, I don't think so. You *are* interested in medicine," Mercy countered. "You told me when I first got here that you might be interested in nursing, didn't you?"

"Well, yes, but . . ."

"Then seeing the hospital in Brownsville would be good for you, Mary, and if nursing is something you're interested in, then I'm sure your grandmother would want to encourage you."

"Do you think *I* could do that, though? I mean, really be a nurse?" The teenager's eyes shone with the possibility. "Most of the girls around here—they just talk about getting married, having babies. I . . . I'd really like to do something else, you know?"

"And you can. You can be anything you want to, Mary. You just have to work hard, that's all." Mercy reached over and squeezed the young girl's arm. "Don't let anyone tell you any different, either."

At that moment, another mother arrived, her face an expression of exhaustion, five children hanging on to her arms, her skirts, her legs. She couldn't have been more than twenty-two.

Mercy looked at the young mother, then back at Mary, her own expression pointed as she reached for her clipboard.

"Think about it," she said. "You could help yourself *and* your grandmother." With a smile, Mercy turned and greeted the woman. "How old is your baby? . . ."

* * *

Rio slithered deeper into the pampas grass. Above his head, the tall spikes swayed with the night breeze, but lower, at his level in the thick of the damp greenness, there wasn't a single breath of air. He'd been lying in the heat for so long that his entire body was soaked. Stinging drops of moisture escaped the red bandanna he'd tied around his forehead and slid into his eyes. He was miserable from efforts of staying quiet and staying alive.

Nearby, he could hear the river current as it moved over the rocks and gravel. The night was so hot that even the sluggish Rio Grande looked good, and Rio paused for just a second, remembering how Mercy had looked last week, standing in the middle of the water, her blond hair clinging to her neck, her legs wet, her T-shirt molded against her breasts. The image did nothing to cool him off, and cursing, he slid farther into the grass, his mission the last thing on his mind. Why did she have to look so damn good? And why, in heaven's name, couldn't he get her out of his mind?

Passing his hand over his forehead, Rio grunted and continued through the grass. He was running out of time—and so were the people who had the bad luck of trying to cross at Ciudad. The body he'd found in the desert last week was proof of that. He couldn't even tell how long the poor son of a bitch had been dead. All Rio could do was dig a shallow grave and say a quick prayer. Anything more and he might have joined him. Rio had marked the spot for later, but when it was all said and done, did it matter?

Pausing to catch his breath, Rio let his head drop. He'd been in Ciudad for weeks now, and all he'd seen was the one incident that had occurred the night he'd been shot. If he hadn't known better, he'd almost think that Greenwood was lying low, but why? Did he know Rio was back? *Had* Mercy said something?

As soon as he had the thought, Rio dismissed it. She hadn't told anyone, and she wasn't going to. She was the kind of woman who survived, who stood on her own two feet, who depended on herself more than anyone else— fortunately *and* unfortunately.

And he *had* to stay a million miles away from her.

He pulled forward into the grass, then froze, his legs and arms instantly motionless, his chest tight with a breath he couldn't release. Ahead, he heard a babble of voices, and they were all raised in excitement.

With renewed caution, Rio inched forward. He'd been hoping to catch Greenwood, but a sixth sense told him this was one party to which the sheriff hadn't been in- vited. The words that Rio could make out were all in Spanish, and from their tones, he knew something was very, very wrong.

Noiselessly, he reached the edge of his cover, and as he did, he held back a cry of surprise. In a small clearing, near the water, three men stood in close proximity, a fourth at their feet. One man gripped a gun, the barrel pointing at the prostrate figure. The other two men were arguing with him, holding his arm and obviously trying to convince him not to shoot.

In an instant, Rio took in the situation and developed a plan. Using the cover of the running water, he circled the men until he was at their backs, crouching in back of a low rock. The man with the gun was directly in front of him. Like a sleek, black panther, Rio tensed, then lunged.

It was over in a second. With his knife at the man's throat, Rio spoke roughly in Spanish. A heartbeat later, the pistol dropped uselessly to the desert floor.

When they saw what was happening, the gunman's two companions each took a quick look at Rio, then disappeared. They obviously didn't want to know the man's fate—or become a part of it.

"Some friends you've got," Rio said in Spanish. "Or are they *pollitos?* Scared little chicks whose money you've already taken?"

The man's curse split the air, a classic indictment against Rio's heritage. Rio jerked his arm against his neck and laughed coldly. "My mother is dead, and I've been calling my father that myself for years." He pressed harder. "You've got to try harder than that to impress me, my friend."

The man's gurgled voice came back with something unintelligible, and that's when the figure at their feet moaned and twisted in the sand, grabbing his leg with his hand. Rio looked down then, and a shaft of shock pierced what little of his sensibilities he had left. What he had thought was a man was a boy—a young boy. Rio's grip jerked once more as he realized the man he held had been about to kill in cold blood a kid no more than ten or twelve.

"You son of a bitch," he growled. "I ought to stick you right now and throw you in the river." He let the point of his knife nick the man's throat. "What happened? Your chick get hurt making the run?"

The man nodded, his fingers clawing at Rio's arm. In one fluid motion, Rio kicked the gun into the river, released his arm and pushed his captive down to the ground beside the boy. The man fell to his knees, gasping and clutching his throat.

Rio stood over him with a menacing stance, his long legs parted, his knife still clutched in his hand. He could do nothing with the *coyote* but kill him, and for just a moment, he seriously considered the idea. When he realized what he was thinking, however, he forced his fingers to relax on the hilt of his knife. "Get out of here," he said with one last disgusted look. "You're not even worth the effort."

The man scrambled away, half running, half falling, but never looking back. Already forgetting him, Rio sheathed his knife, bent down and laid two fingers on the young Mexican boy's neck. A fluttering pulse answered Rio's touch. The child's bruised and battered face gave mute testimony to the cruel nature of the man he'd paid to help him, and against one side of his lanky left leg, a long open cut gleamed obscenely. He groaned against Rio's tender touch.

He was no expert, but it seemed to Rio the child would never make it to Brownsville. He deliberated for only a moment, then scooped up the boy and strode into the darkness.

Chapter 6

She hadn't seen him in two weeks.

Mercy wasn't counting the days, of course, but as she glanced at her appointment book, she couldn't help but realize that it'd been two weeks. Fourteen days. One half of a month since Rio had almost kissed her and told her their relationship was ending—before it had even begun.

She sat at the small desk in one corner of her living room and gnawed at the end of a battered pencil. The scattered papers in front of her fluttered in the air spitting from the air conditioner. Why she bothered to have the machine repaired, she didn't know. It was almost cooler with the windows open—and certainly a lot quieter.

Throwing the pencil to the top of the scarred desk, Mercy stood up, then reached over and snapped off the window unit. Blessed silence filled the tiny cabin, and as she went to each window and raised it, the quiet night-time breeze filtered in, blowing the gauzy curtains with it and bringing a scent of moisture from the river. Standing by the last window, Mercy paused to watch and listen as a streak of lightning split the sky, a crash of thunder following it. Rubbing her arms, bare under the short-sleeved T-shirt she wore, she stepped outside on the porch, then shivered slightly in the cooler air. With the ancient air conditioner rattling, she hadn't even known it was about to storm.

She scanned the thunderous horizon as another streak of lightning seared the sky. The wild landscape here did something for her that home never could. It gave her a sense of freedom, a sense of latitude, and the woman she'd always wanted to be—less encumbered, more feeling—was having an opportunity to grow and expand as she never would have back in Illinois. Something about the untamed land, living so close to foreign territory, was changing Mercy.

As if sensing her thoughts, the wind picked up. From her porch, Mercy could hear the tall grasses down by the river. They whispered and sang to each other, their fronds tossing in the stormy weather. Another strip of lightning peeled back the darkness from the sky, and Mercy blinked as the bright light momentarily blinded her. In an instant, huge raindrops began to fall, splattering the dry ground and exploding puffs of baked sand like miniature bombs.

She backed away from the railing of the porch to the sheltered area by the door, her arms crossed in front of her, her hands massaging her goose-pimpled skin. Just as the old screen door bumped against her legs, a huge crack of thunder rumbled out of the foothills, lightning right on its tail. A second blast followed, a reverberation of noise and illumination that split the sky open with dazzling light. The stark radiance revealed a snapshot image, a mental negative of black and white that burned into her eyes with instant deliberation.

Like the frozen reflection, her heart seemed to stop. Seconds ticked. She didn't move. She didn't breathe. She didn't blink.

Instantly, the night was plunged back into darkness, but Mercy no longer needed light to see. She could close her eyes and envision the figure emerging from the clump of pampas grass closest to the river. A tall approaching figure.

She opened her eyes once more and leaned forward, her heart hammering against the inside of her chest. All she could see now, however, were the vivid after-spots from the streak of lightning.

She rested weakly against the door, her trembling right hand pulling a strand of hair away from her face. Was she thinking about Rio so much that she'd begun to hallucinate? The small porch shook as another eruption of thunder sounded, and Mercy fumbled for the handle of the screen door. Even Rio wouldn't be near the river with a storm like this taking place.

And if it wasn't Rio, Mercy didn't want to know who it was.

Before her fingers could find the rusted metal, another fire bolt shattered the night, this time so close she could smell the distinctive ozone odor. For endless seconds, the surrounding desert was bathed in an uncanny rippling sheet of light. For miles, Mercy could see every rock, every hill, every stunted tree, and she froze against the door, paralyzed by fear and disbelief at the scene that jumped into her vision. It couldn't be, but when she blinked her eyes and looked again, she knew her vision wasn't lying.

Like a devil delivered by the weather, Rio strode up the rutted path, his faded jeans molded to his hips, rivulets of water streaming off his hair and over his sinewy bare chest. He looked like something from a dream, bronze muscles swelling, wild hair cascading around his face, his eyes blazing in the storm. Mercy's heart hammered in her chest, then her eyes widened incredulously as her sight took in what it hadn't before.

In Rio's arms, he held a body—a dead body.

Rio ignored the shocked expression on Mercy's face. "Get out of the way and open the door," he demanded. "I don't even know if he's still breathing." Shaking his wet head like a dog, Rio splattered the stupefied woman as she stood silently in front of him. "Open the door!"

Instantly, she obeyed, and the second they were inside, she led him through the familiar living room and into her bedroom. She grabbed her black bag from the closet and indicated the bed with a toss of her head. "Lay him down there," she called out. "I've got to wash my hands."

As she stepped into the bath, Rio carefully lowered the filthy child to the bed. He glanced toward the half-open door, then allowed himself to awkwardly smooth a dark lock of hair from the boy's forehead. He was so young, so helpless. With a vengeance that stopped his breath and left him shaking, emotion overtook Rio. He stepped away from the bed, but he couldn't escape the long-held anger that instantly attacked him. There was always someone ready to take advantage, he thought savagely—always.

As Mercy began her examination, Rio took another halting pace backward, his anger slowly fading into concern. He stared at the thin, bloody youngster while something clutched at Rio's heart, making it difficult to breathe. To deliberately force the pain into the place where he kept such feelings, Rio made his voice harsher than usual. "Will he die?"

Mercy's answer was a typical doctor's noncommittal grunt. Ignoring him, she proceeded to unwrap Rio's bloody T-shirt from the boy's body.

Despite himself, Rio's emotions intensified as he watched Mercy's fingers glide over the boy's chest, then legs. A soothing woman's touch, he thought distractedly, a mother's touch, a lover's touch, a wife's touch. The sight of it curled within him, then stabbed him with a sense of longing so intense that it stole his breath away. Stumbling, he turned toward her bedroom window and leaned against the open pane, his fingers clutching the sill for the support his legs refused to provide.

Memories of another time and place swamped him. Even when he'd needed it the most, when he'd been a few years older and a hundred times wiser than the child stretched out behind him, Rio hadn't had that kind of love and attention. All he'd gotten was the hardest life had to give, softened only by what little comfort the nuns could deliver.

Behind him, Rio heard the bedsprings squeak and then release. When he turned, Mercy was staring at him, her hands on her hips, her pale face flushed. Her expression nailed Rio's heart to the floor. At his side, his fingers clenched into useless fists of frustration. Obviously, his efforts had been useless—the kid was already dead.

Mercy's blue eyes were the color of a desert sky at its hottest, and their heat was turned straight on Rio. "I hope you're happy." She paused, her chest heaving with an obvious effort to keep her emotions intact. "That child is barely alive."

Alive? Alive? The words echoed in Rio's mind like twin gunshots. He closed his eyes as relief flooded over him, none of Mercy's words registering except the last. *Alive!*

A second later, his smile vanished as Mercy's hand connected with his wet face. Rio's eyes flew open, and his hand automatically went to hers. More surprised than angry, he captured her wrist before it could fall to her side. "What the hell—?"

"That was for him." She tossed her head toward the boy on the bed and jerked her arm, but Rio only held on tighter, the silky skin turning red under his grip. "It's certainly less than you deserve, but for the moment, it'll have to do since he can't do it for himself."

"You think *I* did that to him?"

Her ivory skin flushed with anger. "That slash across his leg didn't get there by itself."

He wouldn't allow himself to feel the hurt that her distrust ignited. Instead, he channeled his emotions into anger, rage infusing him with a deadly calm. His voice turned low and icy. "I'm lots of things, Mercy, but stupid isn't one of them. Why in the hell would I bring a kid to you that I had cut?"

"I don't know—I'm not a psychic—but I can recognize a knife wound when I see one." Her jaw clenched. "And that *is* your weapon of choice, as I recall."

His fingers automatically tightened on her arm, and she winced. "I don't hurt kids," he repeated.

She yanked against him once more, and this time he released his grip. Staring at him with open distrust, she rubbed the reddened flesh and shot him a question.

"Then what happened to him? He didn't do that to himself."

Rio felt like leaving without even answering her. Her skepticism wasn't unexpected, but the pain it caused was—and he didn't like it. It had been a long time since mistrust like hers had hurt. Finally, he spoke. "I found him down by the river. A *coyote* was about to shoot him in the head, if you want to know the truth. He probably sliced his leg in the river—it's full of glass. My guess is he was slowing the rest of them down, so the *coyote* was going to solve the problem. With a bullet."

Her expression went to shock, then reverted to skepticism, but it took a long time. When she spoke, she sounded as if she were trying to convince herself as much as him. "You really expect me to believe that?"

He took a step toward her, intending to intimidate but finding that it was his own heart that suddenly started to beat faster. Her blue eyes stared up at him, the lighter centers of azure ringed by a darker navy. She didn't back down from his stare, and she didn't step back when he moved even closer. His hand shot up, and he twined his fingers in her hair. The contrast of the curls' paleness against his skin, their smoothness against his rough palm, their perfume against his nose, coiled deep inside of him, in a private place where no other woman had ever touched him. He gently tugged the heavy hair back, exposing her throat to him and lifting her face to his. "I don't give a damn what you believe," he lied.

Despite her obvious efforts to appear unaffected, Mercy's eyes widened automatically, the dark centers taking over. In passion, he knew they'd grow even more—grow until they made her eyes dark with desire. The need to effect that change almost overwhelmed him. He forced it down with a costly effort, and he put the thought aside. Over Mercy's shoulder, he took one last look at the kid on the bed. The boy was still, his eyes closed.

Rio brought his gaze back to Mercy. She was waiting, her mouth slightly parted, her hair a wild tumble of curls. Rio's body responded with a vengeance, but all he could do was pull his hands from her hair, swirl and head for the door. He stopped and turned at the opening, searing her with his eyes. "You take good care of him," he said, his voice almost cracking. "And don't let the sheriff know he's here."

Mercy stared at Rio's chiseled back as he fled into her living room. A second later, she heard the screen door slam shut behind him. Rushing to the window, she watched the night and the rain envelop him in their misty curtain. He disappeared as a crack of thunder rolled over the arroyo and reverberated in the tiny cabin.

She let her head fall against the windowpane as she took a ragged breath, her knees trembling. He scared her—and he intrigued her. He seemed to almost hum with power, with sensuality... with temptation.

Her distrust warred with her attraction. He *wouldn't* have brought her someone he'd cut—it made no sense. On the other hand, he *was* a *coyote*. She'd seen the proof with her own eyes. Anyone who could take advantage of people like that wouldn't hesitate to injure whoever got in his way. She had proof of that, too. Or did she? A tiny voice reminded her that he'd never hurt her. The knife had been close, but that was all.

On the bed, the boy moaned, and Mercy turned back to him, her anger at Rio evaporating. He hadn't hurt the boy, and she knew it.

So why had she accused him?

She was just surprised, she told herself as she started to work on the youngster. She'd been so shocked to see Rio materialize from the storm that her sense of reality had seemed to suffer. That was no excuse, though; in fact, it didn't even make sense. She was a trained physician—had been taught to react quickly and logically to emergencies. No—she'd wanted to push him away, pure and simple.

What was she so scared of?

Rio or herself?

For the rest of the night, Mercy felt as though she were watching a movie she'd already seen.

The boy tossed and turned in her bed just as Rio had done, his moans filling the tiny room with the sound of tortured memories. Even the painkiller she'd given him couldn't release him from the nightmares she feared were based in reality. Whatever had happened during that crossing had given the child an image that only years would erase, and Mercy's mouth drew into a line of anger each time he groaned.

The logical side of her had finally accepted the fact that Rio hadn't done this—couldn't have done this—but the emotional side of her responded with the reality of his profession. He *was* a *coyote.* He held the same power over others that someone had used to abuse this boy. It wasn't right.

On the other hand, Rio had brought the child to her, and only a blind man would have missed the expression of empathy on that hardened face when he'd stared at the boy on her bed. Rio identified with this kid, and Mercy knew why. The child obviously had a rough life, a poor life, and from the look on his face, even in pain—

ful sleep, the young boy told the tale of every other kid
trying to improve his life.

Through the night, she dozed in the chair by the bed,
managing a few hours' sleep but rising every hour or so
to check the child's temperature and bandages. After a
while, he slept soundly through her gentle touches and
concerned looks, and seemed completely ignorant of her
ministrations. By the morning, he came to long enough
for her to spoon soup through his cracked lips for
breakfast, then went right back to sleep. He didn't say a
word.

Mercy held her regular clinic hours, but she had only
two patients, and one was the little boy with the cat. His
pet was fine now, but Mercy had the sneaking suspicion
that the child had decided she was a good supplier of
treats. She didn't mind. He was a cute little thing, with
enormous eyes and sweet, plump lips ringed by the
candy she gave him—the kind of child the one in her bed
would have been under different circumstances.

Every hour, she looked in on the boy in the bed, but
he continued to rest quietly. By the evening, when she
returned to the cabin, he was awake but hadn't moved.

Mercy stepped to the bed and spoke in Spanish. "How
are you feeling?"

He stared at her with dark, suspicious eyes and said
nothing.

She sat down on the edge of the mattress, her hands
moving to his bandaged leg. "You've been here almost
two days. You were brought in from down by the river.
Do you remember?"

He blinked and lay perfectly still. His only change in
expression came when she pulled the tape holding down
his bandage. He grimaced slightly.

She switched to English but got the same response. Nothing. His eyes followed her every move, however, and Mercy knew he understood her. For some reason, he wasn't going to talk. He was in shock possibly; maybe he was mute. But more likely he was holding his cards to his chest, she finally decided. From where he came, silence was probably the best defense he had.

She finished changing his bandage and stood. "Do you know the man who brought you in? Rio Barrigan?"

For the first time, a flicker came into his eyes. Of fear? Of respect? She couldn't tell. He *did* recognize the name, though. "He carried you here," she said, "in his arms during a terrible storm." She turned and threw the old bandages into a plastic garbage bag. "You need to thank him. He saved your life."

She stepped into the bath and washed her hands. Toweling them dry, she walked back to the edge of the bed. "In a few days, you'll be back up. The cut on your leg is shallow, and your face will heal fast." She reached out to touch his cheek, and he drew back sharply. "Whoa, there—I'm not going to hurt you."

His eyebrows drew into a single distrustful line, but then he held still. Her fingers brushed across the scraped bruise. "In a few more days, it'll look fine." She drew in her bottom lip. "Who did this to you?"

She hadn't expected an answer, so she wasn't disappointed by his silence. He turned his head to avoid her eyes, choosing instead to focus on a point outside the window. She was clearly dismissed.

"Have it your way," she said in a noncommittal voice. "But sooner or later, you're going to have to talk. Either to me—or to the sheriff."

* * *

When she got in from the clinic the next evening, Mercy went straight into the bedroom to check on the child. Intensely focused, she didn't even see the shadows move until a darker one detached itself from the rest and moved to her side. She gasped, her hand at her throat, as Rio materialized.

"My God," she said in a strangled voice. "Don't you ever knock like normal people? Why do you always sneak up on me?"

Waiting for his answer in the dim light, Mercy let her eyes slide over Rio. Poised by the bed, he wore a pair of jeans slung low on his hips and a white cotton shirt that contrasted sharply with his bronzed skin. The sleeves had been rolled once, as far as his biceps would allow. The material puckered slightly across his chest, strained by the width of his muscles. His gleaming black hair, framing the planes of his face, picked up highlights from the lamp nearby. Mercy found herself breathing faster.

His smile was sardonic. "Why do you think they call us *coyotes?*"

His words soaked in and made her remember their last encounter, and her blush deepened even more. She had to apologize for slapping him, for jumping to conclusions, for everything else, but she didn't yet know how she was going to do it. One thing was for certain, though. She wasn't going to say what she had to say in front of the boy. She tilted her head toward the door. "Outside" was all she said. Immediately, she headed toward the door, then stopped and turned when she realized Rio was not with her.

He had halted beside the bed and was talking softly with the boy. Mercy couldn't catch all the words, but to her surprise, the youngster was actually speaking. Rio nodded his head, then briefly touched the young boy's arm. A second later, Rio was by her side and guiding her out the bedroom door, his fingers warm on the inside of her elbow.

As soon as the bedroom door closed, Mercy stepped out from Rio's grip, went straight into the kitchen, opened the refrigerator and removed two cold beers. His hand was no longer on her skin, but she felt the imprint as though it were. Taking a deep breath, she popped open the drinks, then turned and found Rio directly behind her.

His proximity set off warning bells, and in her chest, Mercy's heart kept up the rhythm. In the inches between them, she lifted one hand and held out one of the cold amber bottles.

"How about a peace offering?" she said, her voice stronger than she felt.

His gray eyes roamed over her face, and if looks could touch, she would have felt his stare for the hot invitation it was. She shivered, the bottles still between them. For a second, she didn't think he'd take the drink, then he reached out slowly and wrapped his fingers around the chilled bottle, enveloping her hand with his.

His voice was low and throaty. "Does this mean I've been found innocent?"

Innocent was the very last word Mercy would have ever used to describe Rio. Dangerous, deadly, tempting—anything but innocent. She swallowed and forced herself to meet his gaze. "Let's just say I called a mistrial," she answered. "Lack of evidence."

He released her hand, brought the beer to his lips and drained half the bottle. When he lowered it again, his hard lips turned upward in a mockery of a smile. "So you're the judge *and* the jury? Sounds rigged to me."

Her breath had disappeared, trapped somewhere between her throat and her chest. "I'm learning the Texas way," Mercy finally answered. "Aren't you the one who told me things are done differently down here?"

His eyes lightened another shade, then he took a second swallow of beer to finish the bottle. She couldn't help but stare as the brown column of his throat moved in sensual deliberation. When he finished, his tongue came out and slowly licked his mouth.

"You're a smart woman," he said in a measured voice. "You learn fast." He reached behind her and set the empty bottle on the kitchen counter. As he brushed past her, Mercy felt her heart accelerate once again. When he straightened back up, he left his hands on the counter, trapping her between the hard Formica and his hard body. "Would you like to learn some more about Texas?"

Tension coiled between them like a snake in the desert, and suddenly, Mercy realized her apology had taken on a dimension for which she hadn't planned.

"One lesson a day is all I can handle," she finally managed to say. Looking toward the refrigerator, she blinked, then faced him once more. "Let me get you another beer."

The calculation in his eyes told her he knew what she was doing. The tenseness in his body told her he wouldn't let her get away with it. Mercy held her breath, then after three more hurried heartbeats, she sighed with relief when he finally moved away.

"Sure," he said carelessly. "That'd be fine."

She stumbled to the corner, then belatedly realized she still held her own beer. She handed it to him, then, grabbing another bottle from the fridge, she pried the top off and turned and motioned toward the porch.

"Let's go outside," she said. "I think it's cooler out there."

In another few minutes, they were settled in the porch swing, but Mercy's heart was far from calm. Her pulse continued to beat as if she'd had five cups of coffee instead of one swallow of beer. She searched her mind for something to say—anything that would take them away from the undercurrents that had connected them in the kitchen. As her eyes caught the light from the bedroom, she realized they *did* have something to discuss. The boy. She tilted her head toward the bedroom. "What did he say to you? I haven't been able to get a word out of him."

Rio pursed his lips into a smile that made Mercy weak. "He wanted to know if we were married."

Shocked, Mercy stared at Rio. "Married? Why on earth would he think that?"

Rio looked at her with amused eyes. "You find the thought that staggering?"

"Well…no…it's just that I'm surprised, that's all." She tried to recover her equilibrium. "I haven't been able to get him to speak. I need to know about his family, his situation."

Rio grunted, then tipped the beer bottle up. "Don't bother," he answered a second later. "If he had a family, he wouldn't have been out there in the desert. He's on his own."

"Then he'll have to stay here until he's completely well."

Rio's expression shifted in a way she couldn't decipher. "Forget that, too," he snapped. "You wouldn't be doing him any favors."

"But he's only a kid—you can't expect him to take care of himself."

"I had to—and I was a hell of a lot younger than him."

"Maybe that happened, but it doesn't mean it's good." Her fingers clutched the slippery bottle of beer. "He needs some rest, someone to look after him."

Rio turned to Mercy and hardened himself to the pull of her bright blue eyes. Since the minute he'd arrived, he'd been struggling with himself—struggling to keep his hands off her, his lips away from her, his body at a distance from hers. It was proving an almost impossible task.

She wore peach-colored shorts that emphasized her long, firm legs and a halter top that must have been cool for her but was causing him to burn every time he looked at her. He tore his eyes away from her open stare and forced himself to think about the boy in her bedroom.

"He can't stay here, Mercy," he explained again as patiently as he could. "If Greenwood comes through here and sees him, he'll grab him and ship him to a holding pen somewhere. Is that what you want?"

Her face took an an expression of appropriate horror. "A holding pen? My God, no, of course not. That can't happen." She shook her head, the blond braid hitting against her bare back. "But it's too soon to move him. Just a few more days, please."

Rio stared down into her eyes and felt the jolt all the way to his boots. The level of her caring was incredible, and not for the first time, he found himself wondering what it would be like to have her care for him—really care.

Initially, he'd been attracted to her blond beauty, but now, Rio was beginning to see past that basic temptation. Besides being the sexiest woman he'd ever known, Mercy was gentle and kind and loving—everything he'd never had in his life. She *was* different from the other women he'd known, and it scared the hell out of him.

Just as her apology had. For whatever reason, she *did* believe him now, it was clear to see, and that was almost harder to take than her skepticism had been. He didn't know how to handle that kind of reaction.

"Please, Rio," she repeated, her voice as slow and sweet as farmers' honey. "Let him stay a few more days."

"You're putting yourself at risk."

"I don't care." She turned toward him in the seat, her leg resting on the cushion between them. "He needs the time."

The bedroom lamp spilled out an ivory glow from the window beside them and washed her face with tenderness. Her skin gleamed with it, as though lit from within, and Rio couldn't control his hand as it went up to touch her softly planed face. He let his fingers spread over her cheek, then slip under her braid, the nape of her neck warming his hand. "Why do you care so much?" he asked.

"I'm a doctor."

He shook his head. "Not good enough. Try again."

Her eyelids brushed down, the soft lashes painting shadows across her cheeks. For a second, she sat there quietly, obviously thinking about her answer. Rio's heart constricted against the warmth he felt for her. Everything in him screamed at him to jump up and leave her alone... but he couldn't. She was addictive.

When she finally looked up at him, her eyes held his and refused to let go. "Because that's who I am," she said. "I've always cared for people—it's what makes me

be me." Her full lips curved into a gentle smile that made
Rio's gut twist. "Does that make any sense?"

He nodded once. "We all have a destiny to fulfill."

She leaned forward and gazed into his eyes, searching them as if she could read the answer to her next
question in their light gray depths. "And what about
you, Rio? Do you have a destiny?"

"Of course."

"What is it?"

Closing the distance between them, he lifted his other
hand to her face and cradled the line of her jaw in his
fingers, the touch so light he could barely feel the heat
of her skin. He couldn't tell her the whole truth, so he
gave her the part he thought she wanted to hear. "At the
moment," he said, his gaze piercing her, "this."

He brought his face closer to hers until he could smell
her light perfume and feel her breath upon his cheek.
Her eyes didn't close until Rio brought his lips to hers,
then they fluttered down, and she frowned as though in
concentration.

Rio tasted her lips slowly, carefully, holding himself
in check. They were moist and soft, and they reminded
him of a different time in his life—a time when things
were simpler and better. He bit gently on the bottom
one, then pulled it into his mouth and sucked it for a
second, as a child would a sweet. When he reluctantly
released it, he heard her catch her breath. He started to
pull back, but she reached forward and brought her
mouth back to his. With light, feathery strokes, her
tongue stroked across his lips.

Their first kiss had been passion, explosive, uncon-
trollable passion, but this one was different. This one
was the slow give-and-take between two people who realize something important is happening between them—

something fragile and rare that one false move could destroy.

Rio pulled her closer to him, a gentle persuasion he made with his hands upon her neck. She answered instantly, never breaking the seal of their touch, but moving into his arms naturally, as if she'd practiced the move.

He covered her lips with his once more, then deepened the kiss, his tongue slowly caressing her lips, then delving into the warmth of her mouth. He tasted the tang of the beer they'd shared, the smoothness of her hidden places, the promise of what they could share. Upon her back, his hands spread out, then tightened. His fingers stroked bare skin, skin as smooth and soft as a Texas morning.

Her arms contracted around his neck, and she moaned softly into his mouth. Arching her neck, she pulled away slightly and exposed the long column of her throat. Rio's mouth trailed down it, Mercy to meet him. With his teeth, he lightly nipped her skin. "God," he murmured against her, "you taste so good, so sweet."

Her fingers tangled in his hair as his lips traveled lower. When he reached the base of her throat, he could feel her pulse with his mouth. The beat was as fast and irregular as his own.

Enjoying that erotic pounding, that heat, that flowing life, was the most sensual experience he'd ever had, and the last of Rio's control began to seep away. It wasn't an explosion; it wasn't a fireball. It was a slow eroding of force, an inevitable release that had been set into motion the first time he'd seen this woman.

He groaned against her fevered skin and raised his hands to her neck. With one quick tug, the two halves of her top slipped down, exposing her breasts to him. Her breath stopped, then expelled in a rush as he cupped her fullness in both of his hands, his thumbs circling their sides with the barest of touches. Her breasts were ivory satin, smoother and softer than anything he'd ever touched before.

In the dim light flowing over them, Rio raised his head and looked into her face. "You're so beautiful," he said almost reverently. "So perfect."

Her eyes opened for a moment, then closed halfway as she swayed closer to him. "Kiss me, Rio," she whispered. "Kiss me right now, hard and sweet like you did that very first time."

She didn't have to ask again.

Rio dragged her to him, her bare breasts flattening against his shirt. Through the thin material, he could feel her nipples harden, and his body responded in kind. Without a second's hesitation, he brought his lips to hers, his arms wrapping around her.

The explosion came then, lightning fast.

Rio was shocked by the depth of his response. Never had a woman brought him to such instant awareness, and he felt his body harden and respond to hers as if he'd taken her already. She pulled him closer, her fingers clutching at him, taking as much as he wanted to give. Against his chest, her breasts turned warm and taut with erotic intensity. His hands were everywhere at once—on her back, on her shoulders, drifting over her arms. The feel, taste and smell of Mercy was everywhere—and still he wanted more.

His lips covered hers, demanding that "more." He wasn't going to let off, wasn't going to release her. Like a hungry spider with a trapped fly, he was going to devour her—and she was his willing victim.

For as long as he dared, Rio allowed the inevitable to take place, allowed his torture, his mouth trailing over her face, her neck, her shoulders. As his head dropped to her breasts, he rounded their fullness with his tongue, cupping them in his hands, brushing the nipples. His breath was hot and urgent, but when Rio lifted his mouth from her breast and saw his fingers still against her softness, he froze in the heat of the moment.

Even in the darkness of the porch, the contrast in their skin was remarkable. His hands were spread over the ivory of her breasts, brown against white, rough against smooth, big against small. That one sight seemed to epitomize everything that was different between them, and it stopped Rio as surely as a sniper's bullet.

Instantly, his hands stilled, and he found himself holding his breath. Mercy's voice came to him from a distance, as though she were traveling backward at a high speed. In reality, Rio had been the one to move, and in his mind, he'd retreated behind a fence that was a thousand miles high.

"What is it?" she said softly, her hand cupping his face. "What's wrong?"

Her tenderness made the barrier go even higher, and Rio hated himself for building it even as he added another strand of wire to it. This was the perfect example of their differences—she knew something was wrong and she wanted to fix it. He knew something was wrong— and he wanted to run.

When he didn't answer, she reached for the straps of her top and started to cover herself, but Rio's hands stopped her. Taking the length of cotton from her, he paused, then motioned for her to turn around. As she lifted her braid off her neck and exposed her back to him, he tried to regain his equanimity. He should go—go now—as fast and as far as possible. He found it impossible, however. As surely as his fingers tied the ends of her halter together, he found himself bound to her.

He finished and she turned around, her blue eyes as inquisitive and determined as he'd ever seen them. She caught his hands between hers. "What is it, Rio?"

He was tempted, tempted sorely, but what could he tell her? The truth would only separate them more, and a lie would bind them tighter. He did the only thing he could. He shook off her touch and stood.

"I think it's time for me to leave." Abruptly, he moved to the railing, his back to her waiting silence. "Tell the boy I'll be back later."

She jumped up, and he heard the porch swing flying out. In a moment, she was by his side. "What are you doing?" she said in a voice filled with amazement. "You can't touch me like that—kiss me like that—then leave as if nothing has happened."

Rio felt the words as much as heard them, and they struck against his back like rocks thrown against a glass wall. His defenses shuddered but held. Slowly, he turned around and faced her. "I can do anything I please, Mercy, and I usually do. It might serve you well to remember that fact."

For a moment, she looked stunned, as if he had slapped her, then she seemed to regain her balance. When she spoke, her voice held an almost taunting quality. "You aren't who you seem, are you, Rio Barrigan?"

Rio's heart stopped, but he recovered instantly. "What in the hell does that mean?" he growled.

She stepped back from him as though she needed the physical space between them. It was her way of countering his emotional space. "I don't take chances, Rio.

I'm a doctor—I'm trained to go *with* the odds, not against them." She shook her head, the heavy braid falling against her back. "But you—I thought you were different. I thought you liked danger, liked putting money on the dark horse."

The wind picked up his dark, shaggy hair and blew it into his eyes. With it, Rio felt his anger grow. In a second, however, he'd snatched the strands back, and his stare pinpointed her like a spotlight illuminating prey.

"I'll take a chance as well as the next guy, but you shouldn't. In fact, if you know what's good for you, you'll stay as far away from me as you can get."

"I don't believe you." She shook her head casually, then crossed her arms and leaned against the railing. They could have been discussing the weather for all the concern she showed. *"In fact,"* she repeated tauntingly, "I think you'd like to take a chance on me, but you're too scared to try."

Rio felt his eyes narrow, and the hair along the back of his neck rose. How in the hell could one woman make him want her so badly one minute, then anger him so deeply the next? He let his irritation simmer, let the adrenaline pump, until it had lost some of its strength and he could control it once again.

"Scared?" he repeated finally. He lifted his hand and put one finger at the base of her throat, right on top of her pulse point. It beat rapidly—very rapidly. "I've always heard that we accuse others of what we feel." He paused to press against the rhythm of her pulse. "From the looks of things, I'd say *you're* the one who's scared, *Dr.* Hamilton."

She stared at him mutely as he drew his finger down the V of her halter, then in the blink of an eye, she grabbed his finger and stopped its natural progression. "If either one of us had any sense, we'd both run." Her breathy voice sent a liquid heat into his belly. "But we can't—can we?"

Chapter 7

Hot sunlight bounced off the sheriff's badge and hit Mercy squarely in the eyes. Two days had passed since Rio had kissed her and left her trembling, but her knees were shaking now as if it had just happened. But this time, the cause was fear—not passion. She raised one hand and shielded her eyes from the sun's glare, praying Greenwood wouldn't notice the flutter in her fingers.

"What can I do for you, Sheriff?"

"I need to talk to you, Dr. Hamilton." His voice was blunt, the words cold in the heat.

"All right," she said reluctantly. She pulled open the screen door and stepped back, forcing herself not to look toward the bedroom door. She knew it was closed, knew the boy was asleep, but it took every ounce of her willpower not to turn around to make sure. "I have to be back at the clinic in twenty minutes, though. I keep regular hours, you know."

He nodded once, then advanced into the living room from the porch. Still wearing his sunglasses, he swung his head around and took in the cabin with one spare glance. Nervously, Mercy folded her hands in front of her and nodded toward the couch. "Have a seat," she said. Automatically, the manners her mother had instilled in her took over. "Would you like something to drink?"

He shook his head once. "I didn't come to socialize." With that, he sat down heavily on her sofa, removed his hat and pulled a thin book from his pocket. Like the last time, he did not take off his sunglasses. Mercy still couldn't see the color of his eyes, and that small detail unnerved her as much as it had before.

Glancing once at his notes, he pursed his lips, then spoke without preamble. "I have it on good authority, Dr. Hamilton, that you are harboring an illegal alien here." He looked directly at her, or so she felt. "A wetback."

Her fingers found the back of the nearest chair, and she pulled it out, sitting down quickly. A lump formed in her throat that blocked everything but a scream. She kept the sound in check by sheer willpower, and a second later, she swallowed and spoke. "What on earth do you mean?" she managed to say.

The dark lenses moved up and down her. "I'm the sheriff, Doctor. I know what's going on in every inch of this county. You've been treating Mexicans and even going across the border to help the ones who can't come here. I know—I have lots of eyes."

The palms of her hands turned instantly wet, not just moist but wet, with anxiety. "And you're saying these eyes have reported to you—"

"That you have an illegal living here—with you."

Mercy's heart dropped into her stomach. "That's ridiculous." She managed a fake laugh. "This place is hardly big enough for one, much less two. Who would tell you such a thing?"

Ignoring her question, he flipped the notebook shut and crammed it into his pocket. "Is it true?"

"Of course not."

"Then you wouldn't mind if I look around?"

"Actually, I would mind," she said tightly. "After all, this *is* my home. I'm sure you understand, don't you? You wouldn't want a stranger going through your house, your things." She forced herself to laugh lightly again as though the matter weren't that important. "Besides— there's no reason for you to do so, anyway."

Outside in the heat, the cicadas chirped to a stop, as if they had sensed the tension building within the tiny house. Moisture gathered under Mercy's blouse, between her shoulder blades. She had to force her hands to stay steady.

Greenwood slowly leaned forward and put his elbows on his knees, steepling his hands together. He didn't wear a wedding band, but on the fourth finger of his right hand, an enormous gold ring with a chunk of onyx winked at Mercy like a *mal de ojo*. She ordered herself to meet his mirrored gaze.

"I think there *is* a reason," he said in a voice that rumbled like the river after a heavy rain. "And if you don't let me, I'll just get a search warrant and do it anyway." His fingers suddenly gripped each other as if he were strangling something.

Mercy dragged her eyes from his hands back to his face and ignored the quiver in her stomach. "No judge in his right mind would give you a search warrant to look in my house, Sheriff. You simply don't have good cause."

"I disagree, and I'm sure I could convince the local judiciary of that." He stood up, towering over her. "In fact, I have the *full* cooperation of the judges in this area, and I wouldn't have to do any convincing at all. They back me in everything I do." He paused and looked over her shoulder at her bedroom door. "If I wanted to walk over there right now and bust that door down, nobody in three counties would care."

Instantly, Mercy jumped to her feet. "Well, I would," she said, her strained voice revealing her anger. "Where I come from, that sort of thing is illegal."

His smile was oily. "This is Texas, Doctor, and more importantly, it's the Valley. We have our own way of doing things here. Hasn't anyone told you that yet?"

She crossed her arms and spoke stiffly. "Yes. I have been told that—several times already—but I'm not your average citizen, either. I'm educated, and I know the law." She took a deep breath, then continued, her voice a lot braver than she actually felt. "If you do an unlawful search on this house, you'll regret it."

His mouth lost its amusement and drew into a narrow line, his hand going automatically to the gun at his hip. He didn't draw the weapon, of course, but the threat was explicit. He was trying to intimidate her. Unfortunately for the sheriff, it had exactly the opposite effect on Mercy. Her resolve grew even stronger.

She strode past him and held open her door. "You're wasting my time, Sheriff." Glaring at him, she looked pointedly through the screen door and out her porch toward his Bronco. "I need to get to my clinic."

He stared at her for a full minute, as if taking her measure, then he walked slowly to the screen door. At the opening, he paused and looked down at her, his close proximity stiffening her spine. "I know you've got someone back there, and I intend to find out who it is. In the meantime, you might want to consider this fact." He paused, and in the quiet, Mercy heard a trapped fly buzzing against the screen door, screaming to escape. Her throat turned dry.

"I don't take kindly to people challenging my authority." His voice was cold and calculating. "I *am* the law around here, and the ones who forget that find themselves in the kind of trouble they don't want."

Greenwood drove off, and as soon as Mercy's knees could support her, she turned and went toward the bedroom. When she quietly twisted the doorknob, however, her gasp of surprise could have been heard in the next county. Not only was her patient awake and dressed, but Rio was standing beside the bed, helping him. The boy's face was pale and clammy, and an immediate rush of anger and concern overtook Mercy's fear of a moment before.

"What in the hell do you think you're doing?"

Rio looked at her with faint amusement. "Hello to you, too."

"Do you know who was just here?" She stormed into the room and took the boy's arm. "Get back into bed," she said sternly. "You're not going anywhere."

He resisted briefly, then his small store of energy gave out. Sitting down on the bed, he turned his eyes to Rio, beseeching him silently for help.

She glared at Rio, her heart thumping. "Greenwood was in my living room—*my living room*—" she repeated, "not two seconds ago. If he'd come in here and found you—"

"But he didn't." Rio's fingers went around her elbow, their light touch setting her senses on fire. Mercy tried to ignore the heat even this single contact seemed to bring with it, but it was hard—very hard—especially with Rio looking down at her as he was, his gray eyes taking in every detail of her face, his palm hot against the tender skin of her upper arm.

Her resistance began to melt, and she struggled to regain it. "The boy is too—"

"Come into the living room," Rio said, his grip turning harder, the amusement leaving his voice. Turning once toward the boy, he spoke. "I'll be right back, don't worry."

When the door was closed, she jerked away from him, her face dark with anger. "Didn't you hear me? Greenwood was just here—*right here.* He could have caught both of you." She swung her braid over her shoulder and looked toward the bedroom. "And that boy is not going anywhere, either. He's still too weak."

Rio's eyes flashed at her tone and her words. "Damn it to hell, Mercy, what is it going to take to make you understand? I *have* to get that kid out of here. I would think Greenwood being here would make even you see why."

Her back stiffened. "*I* am the doctor here, Rio. *I* am the one who discharges patients, and I am the one who's in charge. When I say that child is not ready to travel, that's what I mean. He's *not* going anywhere, Greenwood or no Greenwood."

"Oh, yes, he is." Rio's voice was grim. "One way or the other, he's leaving. If not with me, then with your friend, the sheriff. I heard the whole conversation you had with him, so which one of us would you prefer?"

"Neither," she answered. "The child's not ready."

"Do you really think the sheriff cares about that?"

"He's not coming back," she said with more confidence than she felt. "No judge in his right mind would give him a search warrant."

Rio shook his head in an exasperated movement, then ran his hands through the tumble of his dark hair. Mercy's stomach tightened as she remembered how soft and silky it had felt beneath her fingers two nights before.

"Greenwood was telling you the truth, Mercy. He has every official in three counties in his back pocket. They'll do whatever he asks—and if they aren't around, he'll come back with his idiot deputy and his sawed-off shotgun. *That* will be your warrant, goddamn it."

"But that's illegal."

Rio's voice turned desperate, and he spit out his answer as though it tasted bad. "That's right—it *is* illegal, and so are a lot of other things Greenwood does." He broke off abruptly as if he'd said more than he wanted. Turning away from her, he took two strides toward the screen door, then stopped, stretching his arms over his head and filling the doorway with his frame. Visibly shaken, he breathed deeply and stared out into the desert. Behind him, Mercy stood uncertainly, her eyes skimming over the imposing silhouette he made against the hot morning sun.

He stood there for at least two full minutes as Mercy thought about his words. Obviously, Rio was scared, and that thought frightened her beyond belief. If Greenwood scared Rio...what could the sheriff do to the boy lying in her bed?

The answer was obvious. Anything he damn well pleased.

She moved to Rio's side and put her hand on one bicep. Beneath her fingers, the muscles were silken steel, and for a second, she lost her concentration. His aura had the power to reach out and confuse her, whatever the situation, and no man had ever been able to do that to her. She forced herself to concentrate by closing her eyes and taking a deep breath. When she reopened them, he was staring at her.

"I brought more than just my stethoscope with me when I came here, Rio. I brought my ethics, my background, my childhood, my responsibilities . . . and all of that is so different from this reality that I'm not sure how to act sometimes."

She looked down, then back up to his striking face. His expression was at once tender and fierce, protective and threatening, sensual and chilling. Inside of her, a thin line of desire stretched, then broke. She ignored it and continued. "I don't like it, but I guess I have no choice. If you say the sheriff is going to come back, then I'm going to have to let you take the child with you." Her fingers clenched his arm. "But take care of him, please."

He turned and dropped his arms, putting his hands on her shoulders. For a second, his eyes searched hers, their light gray depths washing over her, then he wrapped his arms around her and spoke against her hair. "I promise you, Mercy, I will do everything in my power to keep him safe." He tightened his arms, and underneath her cheek, the firmness of his chest grew even harder. "There is a place—a secret place—that I will take him, and where he will be cared for." He spoke, and she felt the sound as much as heard it. An instant heat spread throughout her lower body. "He won't get as good care as you offer, but he'll be hidden from Greenwood and looked after, I promise."

"All right," she said reluctantly. "But—"

He shook his head and brought his hands up the curve of her neck to her face, where he cradled it between his fingers. "You have to forget him now," he said huskily. "*I* am taking him away, just like I brought him. Your only job at this point is to see that Greenwood finds nothing. Okay?"

She nodded slowly, then Rio dipped his head to hers. His breath was warm against her cheek as he brushed his lips over her face. Every inch of her skin he seemed to touch, to kiss, to caress, and Mercy found herself wishing, once more, that nothing stood between them. Nothing.

"You are such a beautiful woman," he said quietly. "You're beautiful inside *and* out. How can this be?"

She smiled at the compliment. "You can say that even after I held a knife to your throat?"

His eyes lightened, then twinkled unexpectedly. "I held it to yours first." His fingers ran down her neck, tickling her sensually. "And what a perfect throat it is, too."

She leaned against him, her arms going around his trim waist, her legs feeling the hardness of his thighs. "Would you have used it?"

"What do you think?" His voice was a silken thread of desire that wound around and around her, tying them together in a carnal trap. "Do I look like the kind of man who would do that to a woman?"

She moistened her lips. "You look like the kind of man," she said, a husky catch in her voice, "who could do whatever he wanted to a woman."

His fingers closed gently around her throat, their strength and pressure both exciting and sensual. "And would you let me do whatever to you?"

A liquid warmth built and spread deep within Mercy as she stared into the paleness of his eyes. Her hands gripped his back, and her breath quickened, her breasts rising and falling against his chest. "I think you already have."

He smiled slowly and released his hold. Turning over his hand, he rubbed the knuckles of his fingers against her skin, then dropped them down the neckline of her blouse to the tops of her breasts. "Once again, you are mistaken, dear Mercy. I haven't even started yet."

An hour later, Rio and Paco departed. He'd told her his name, then said nothing more but a mumbled thanks—and that came at Rio's urging. As she watched the young boy's shaky departure, Mercy's heart clutched. Would he make it all right? Who would change his bandages? Who would see that he took the antibiotics she'd thrust into his pocket?

Rio's attentions left her with trembling knees and a quivering stomach. Paco's departure left her with guilt and concern. As she watched them both disappear into the tall grass near the river, the boy leaning against Rio's tall form, Mercy squeezed her eyes shut against the threatening tears. She *had* to let the child go, but it was one of the most difficult things she'd ever done.

Resting against the porch railing now, Mercy sipped from her coffee cup and thought about Rio's hands on her. Every time they got together, tension stretched between them like a fine wire, and the kisses they were sharing only drew it tighter. Pretty soon, the wire was going to snap and ensnarl them both. She knew it was inevitable, but when it finally happened, someone was going to get hurt.

* * *

"And he came back?"

Mercy snapped her black bag shut and looked up at Sister Rosa. "Of course," she answered. "Greenwood was there two hours later, a search warrant in hand. It looked authentic, so I had to let him in. He looked over the entire house, but of course he found nothing."

The nun nodded curtly. "He's a dangerous man."

Mercy looked at her sharply. "You said that before, Sister. What exactly do you mean?"

The nun glanced toward the bed that sat between them. On it, the frail mother superior barely raised the sheet with her thin frame, her shallow breaths a flutter more than anything else. Mercy followed Sister Rosa's glance. Today had been a bad day for the older woman, and she hadn't spoken a word. As if she wanted to protect the woman from any more pain, Sister Rosa tilted her head toward the hall and indicated they should leave.

Two seconds later, they were outside the bedroom and heading down the length of the corridor toward the deserted nursery. Mercy followed the black-skirted woman into the cot-filled room.

"We'll have some privacy in here," the nun said. "And what I have to tell you should never be repeated." Sister Rosa patted the blanketed cot where she sat. "Sit here."

Puzzled by the clandestine air, Mercy sat down. "Greenwood's not a nice man, I can see that, but—"

"Not nice?" The nun snorted derisively. "That doesn't begin to cover it." She glanced over her shoulder, then back at Mercy. "Things go on around here that you wouldn't believe—things I can never tell you or anyone else. But there was one incident—it happened a long time ago—that is a perfect example of how power corrupts."

The nun's brown eyes grew suddenly troubled. "You must promise me you won't tell anyone."

Mercy nodded instantly. "Of course," she said. "Consider this patient-doctor confidentiality."

The nun didn't look too reassured, and Mercy wondered if she would continue. Obviously, she decided it was worth the risk, however, and she went on. "Rio Barrigan has a very special reason for hiding Paco. He doesn't want what happened to him to happen to anyone else." She paused and took a deep breath. "When Rio was twelve, Rick Greenwood tried to kill him."

Mercy's breath blocked her throat, and she could feel her eyes grow huge with disbelief. "Greenwood tried to kill Rio? But... but the man's a sheriff. He's supposed to uphold the law, not break it!"

"You're right, of course," the nun answered grimly. "But that's in other places, not here in the Valley."

"It doesn't matter," Mercy gasped. "This is the United States. Law officials are supposed to—"

"What they're supposed to do and what they *do* do are two different things here, Mercy. Greenwood considers himself the law, the absolute law. He does whatever he wants, whenever he wants." For a second, her brown eyes focused on a point Mercy couldn't see. "Considering everything, you'd think that even he wouldn't do that, but..."

The puzzling comment only fueled Mercy's questioning. "What happened?"

Sister Rosa's lips compressed into a line. "I never got all of the details. Rio refused to talk too much after it happened, but apparently, Greenwood caught him down by the river with some other boys. They were throwing rocks and acting mischievously, like all young boys, and Greenwood tried to run them off. Told them to cross the river and go back to where they belonged. Rio stood up to him and said that he was a U.S. citizen, but Greenwood wouldn't listen. As an example to the other children, he put Rio in the back of his truck and drove off." Her fingers picked at the worn cotton blanket on the cot, then grew still. "If the other boys hadn't come to tell me, we might never have known."

Mercy swallowed past the lump in her throat. "Where did the sheriff take him?"

The nun's eyes met hers. "To the desert. Greenwood drove to the middle of nowhere, then kicked Rio out of the truck." She paused. "He left him out there all alone, Mercy, and he was only twelve years old. He could have died. If God hadn't had plans for him . . ."

Against her chest, Mercy could feel her heart expand, then contract. "How did you locate him?"

"We called the INS office and told them what happened. One of their patrols got extremely lucky and found him and brought him in. It took them a while, though. Rio was already dehydrated and suffering from heat exhaustion. A few more hours, and he would have been dead."

Mercy closed her eyes against the mental image, but it refused to leave. All she could see was a twelve-year-old kid, alone in a desert with no way to turn, nowhere to go. When she finally opened her eyes, she had to fight to keep the tears back. "Couldn't you do something to the sheriff?"

"What?" The nun shrugged her shoulders helplessly. "The only witnesses were a bunch of little boys—little boys who shouldn't have even been where they were to begin with. It was their word against the word of the powerful law official. There was no other proof, and Rio refused to talk about the incident himself. What could we do?''

Mercy shook her head and leaned against the wall at one end of the cot. "That's unbelievable, Sister Rosa. Think about how that must have affected Rio.''

"It has, that's for sure. I'm positive that's why he's a—"

"A *coyote?*''

The nun looked startled for a moment, and Mercy suddenly wondered if she'd revealed something new to Sister Rosa. She recovered instantly, however, and nodded her head. "Oh, yes," the sister answered. "I'm sure that's why Rio does what he does. It's his way of trying to right a wrong.''

Mercy licked her lips, a tangle of emotions swirling inside her. "But what he does is wrong.''

The nun frowned. "Not everyone sees it that way, Mercy.''

"He takes advantage—"

The nun held up her hand. "You see the meager savings of these people, and you think when they give it to a *coyote,* spend it all on coming to the United States, that they're being taken advantage of." She shook her head. "That's not always the case.''

Shocked, Mercy stared at the nun. "Then you condone what he does?''

The sister answered calmly. "I am trying to point out to you that different people have different priorities. I'm sure you've had patients who would spend their last penny to obtain good health. These people are just like that. They think that by coming to the United States, all of their troubles will be over. They see the *coyotes* as saviors. Without them, their journey would be even more perilous.''

Mercy's emotions tangled deeper. There was some truth to the nun's answer, but it was a mixed-up truth, and the confusion upset Mercy even more. Everything about Rio was a contradiction—was nothing simple? She dropped her eyes to the cracked linoleum floor and mentally shook her head.

Only one thing was simple—her attraction to him.

And the more she got to know him, the stronger that pull became.

An hour later, Mercy had seen the rest of the nuns and shared a delicious lunch of tortilla soup and hot tamales at Sister Lydia's kitchen table. The women talked of nothing but the upcoming fiesta to be held across the border in a few days. By the time Mercy had finished eating, they had made her promise to come to the outdoor party. She had to admit to herself that the idea of returning to the village square where she'd talked to Rio a few weeks ago made the idea even more appealing, as well.

An hour later, when she headed toward the front door, Sister Rosa caught up with Mercy once more, stopping her with a hand on her arm. The nun's fingers were rough but warm, her eyes full of concern.

"Please, Mercy. Remember that what I told you should never be repeated. I know you and Rio have, well, have seen each other, and I would hate for him to think that I've carried tales about him."

Mercy tried to smile reassuringly, but surprise made it difficult. "I'll say nothing, I promise. How did you know about Rio and me, though?"

The nun's face turned flustered. "Well, Rio told me."

Mercy raised her eyebrows. "When? How?"

Sister Rosa looked as though she didn't want to explain, but was in too far not to. Her guilty expression made Mercy think one thing, though. Was the convent the "secret place" where Rio had brought Paco? The pieces fell together inside Mercy's brain as she gave the idea some thought. It made perfect sense, really. The place was huge, the women would protect the child and Mercy doubted that even Greenwood could get past Sister Rosa without a huge fight.

Picking up the beads and crucifix hanging off her belt, the nun fingered them nervously, then finally spoke. "Well, uh, Rio stops by on occasion and sits with the mother superior. When he was here as a child, she took a great interest in him, and I think he's trying to repay that in some small way now."

Mercy digested this new bit of information slowly. Another contradiction. A man who could pull a knife on her *and* care about a dying nun *and* take the risk of hiding a wounded child—it all seemed strange, but she was learning that Rio was a strange man. Whether he was hiding the child here or not, Mercy didn't doubt Sister Rosa's words.

"He usually comes at night, of course, after the other sisters have gone to bed, but I think she knows when he's here. She seems to grow more calm. He stays for hours and holds her hand."

"And he told you we had met?"

"Yes."

Mercy didn't know what to say. Her relationship with Rio was so highly charged that she felt uncomfortable even discussing it with the nun. If Sister Rosa noticed Mercy's unease, she didn't let on. All she did was drop her beads, then reach out and put her fingers on Mercy's arm again. Her eyes seemed to hold even more concern than before, their brown depths filled with something that Mercy couldn't quite define even as she studied it.

"Be careful," the nun said quietly. "Rio is a complicated man, Mercy. And he's not at all what he seems to be."

Chapter 8

Mercy washed her hands, dried them then turned around from the sink to look at the young boy squirming on the edge of her examining table. He was the fifth child she'd seen this week who'd sat on the table and done the exact same thing.

With a miserable expression, he scratched behind his ear, then plowed his fingernails up and down the back of his scalp. In quick succession, the fingers then went from his arm to his right knee, down to his left ankle and back to his ear again. His parents stood on either side of him, their own faces wearing lines of deep concern. Before Mercy could speak, the father did.

"Will he be all right? This medicine you're going to give him, it will cure him?"

"Nothing cures the chicken pox," Mercy said, "but time. Do you have any idea where he got it?" She'd asked every parent of every sick child she'd seen in hopes of nailing down the source of the virus, but so far, she'd had no luck. At this point, it didn't really matter anymore, though.

The parents exchanged a look, then the mother spoke. "We went to see our cousins in Refugio about two weeks ago. Their little girl—she was scratching, but we thought she'd got into some ants after the children had broken the piñata."

"She had red spots? Some fever?"

The mother nodded.

"I don't think it was bugs," Mercy said. "But just for the record . . . were there a lot of people there? At your cousin's?"

"Oh, *si,*" the mother said, her mouth curling into a big smile. "It was little Angie's birthday." She glanced toward her husband. "There were at least thirty kids there, right?" She turned back to Mercy. "It was a great party."

Mercy hid her dismay and made a mental note to order more antihistamine. Everyone in Ciudad was related to everyone in Refugio. She would bet her first year's salary that in the next few weeks, she'd be seeing at least twenty-five or more miserable, scratching children.

Her expression turning serious once more, the mother reached out and smoothed the little boy's hair. "He'll be okay, won't he?"

"Absolutely. He'll be fine within ten to fourteen days. It's not a terribly serious disease for most children, although it can be serious for adults." Mercy reached into the drawer beside her and pulled out a prescription pad. "Mainly, it just makes the poor kids miserable." Scribbling a few lines across it, she signed her name, ripped the paper off and handed it to the mother. "This lotion will help calm the itching."

She turned around and opened one of the cabinets behind her. Removing what she needed, she turned around. "I want to give him an antihistamine shot, too. It will make him feel better."

The child took one look at what Mercy held and immediately began to scream.

"It's okay, it's okay," she said, keeping up a flow of conversation as she directed the mother to hold on to the child's tiny arm. "Just a little pinprick—" in one deft motion, Mercy swabbed, stabbed and injected "—and then it's all over."

Removing the needle while the little one continued to scream, Mercy quickly dumped the syringe into the sharps container by the sink and turned back around, this time a red fruit pop in one hand and a sheaf of *ninja* stickers in the other. "Take your pick."

The child blinked his eyes and swiped at his face, a suspicious disbelief still darkening his gaze.

"Come on," she said with a smile. "Which one would you like? Sugar or spice?"

He snubbed once as his parents looked on and smiled, then he reached out with one grubby hand and snatched the red treat out of her fingers.

"Good choice," Mercy said, smiling her own approval. "I go for food myself every time."

The mother reached out and picked the child up. "Thank you so much, *Doctora*. He's felt so bad. I didn't know what it was."

Mercy nodded. "Anyone with chicken pox is pretty uncomfortable. Just continue to bathe him and use the lotion. He'll be okay in a few more weeks." The young couple thanked Mercy once more, then picked up their child and walked out.

Mercy washed her hands again, then looked out into the waiting room. Finally, it was empty. She took a deep breath, then began to tidy up. Like clockwork, her mind turned to Rio. He would probably be at the fiesta. She glanced down at her watch as she wiped off one of the counters in the examining room. The party would start in another few hours.

The sisters were expecting her.

A night out might be nice.

She made up her mind with a final swipe of the sponge. Flinging her white coat into the laundry basket, Mercy left the clinic and all her thoughts of chicken pox.

The evening sky had yet to turn completely dark, but through the truck's windshield, Mercy saw stars dotting the peach and purple horizon. They spilled across the desert night like glitter that someone had carelessly tossed. In contrast, the mountain peaks in the distance provided a dark silhouette. As she pulled into the small village across the river and cut the engine, however, Mercy's eyes were drawn from Mother Nature's finery to the town's.

She wouldn't have recognized the sorry little hamlet if she hadn't known where she was. Colored lights swung from wires over the square, and underneath them a mad confusion of children, animals and adults milled about, seemingly aimless. A variety of stands ringed the area where people were selling everything from *enchiladas mole* to *pan dulce*. Even the nuns had a booth stocked with Sister Lydia's famous lemon bread, Sister Rosa's fine squash and handmade linens that would, Mercy could tell even from a distance, rival Porthaults any day of the week.

Off to one side, the men circled a large keg of beer, and in another corner, the young mothers had improvised a giant temporary playpen from cases of soft drinks. Mercy was suddenly glad she'd decided to come; it seemed as though everyone from six counties had turned out.

Everyone but Rio.

She let her eyes search and her heart hope, but she didn't see him anywhere. He obviously wasn't there, or she would have spotted him—his tall form would have towered over everyone. In one way, she was glad, but in the back of her mind, she felt a stab of disappointment that she immediately squashed.

Opening the truck's door, she climbed down from the cab, smoothing her skirt and blouse with nervous hands. Despite her affluent upbringing, her parents had entertained little. They were serious people, their conversation consisting of patient talk and hospital problems. Consequently, Mercy always felt a little uncomfortable at parties. She didn't know how to make small talk and generally stayed away from affairs like this. The other woman inside of her, however, had brought her to the fiesta. To her, it had sounded like fun. Now that Mercy was here, she wished she hadn't listened.

She moved toward the mirror at the side of the truck, her multicolored cotton skirt tickling her calves, the fullness giving her a feminine feeling that years of white coats and tailored dresses had forbidden. Glancing into the reflection, Mercy swallowed and pulled up the elastic on the neckline of her blouse. The lace refused to move another inch, though, and her full cleavage shadowed the valley of her breasts. She hadn't realized how low the collar dipped until now.

Raising her eyebrows, she brought her eyes to her face. The other, freer Mercy had dressed her tonight, and in addition to the festive clothing, she'd applied the smoky gray shadow and pale pink blush to Mercy's face. Looking back at her was that woman, and along with her apprehension, Mercy felt an irrepressible tug of excitement.

Leaning closer to the mirror, she raised one finger to her lips to correct the line of her lipstick, then froze as a deep, instantly recognizable voice spoke behind her.

"You look perfect already. Don't change a thing."

Mercy turned slowly, and as she did, Rio's heart dropped to the sandy sidewalk beneath his feet. He hadn't lied—she *was* perfection.

He let his eyes roam over her, and like a hungry cat with a bowl of cream, he lapped up the sight with slow, greedy gulps. From the tip of her coral toenails to the silver blond hair that she'd pulled into an elegant braid, Mercy Hamilton looked like a misplaced angel—one that was ready and willing to fall.

Did he want to be her Satan?

Her startled blue eyes met his. "You're here!"

He lifted his lips slightly. "So are you."

In the small space he'd allotted her, she squirmed slightly, but he didn't move. In the closeness between them, her perfume rose.

"I . . . I looked around, but I didn't see you," she said in way of explanation. "I thought you wouldn't come, I guess."

"Why not?" The lights caught the silver in the braid that lay over her shoulder, and Rio gave in to this first temptation. He reached out and picked up the heavy plait, his fingers lightly brushing over her bare skin.

"I'm not a wanted man, you know—at least not on *this* side of the river."

He raised her braid and rubbed it between his hands, the hair soft and fragrant beneath his touch. As much as it tempted him, the tight weaving vexed him. In addition, the style didn't match the gleam in her eyes, the way her mouth lifted seductively, the dip in the neckline of her blouse. With his customary swiftness, he flipped the clip off the end, then ran his fingers through the tangle, ignoring her exclamation of surprise.

"Mucho mejor," he murmured, almost to himself. "Much, much better."

The only other time he'd seen her hair down was the night he'd held a knife to her throat. Now, as his dark fingers twisted into the white blond strands, a shock as painful as the one he'd experienced that night rippled over him. Mercy Hamilton was the most beautiful woman he'd ever met. She was too good to be true—and he had absolutely no business doing what he was about to do.

Even as he had the thought, his hands tightened in the snarl of her hair, and she responded exactly as he knew she would. She moved closer to him and looked up expectantly, those blue eyes half-closed in the dim light from the square.

Desire shot through him like a triple jigger of Jose Cuervo. If he kissed her now, they'd never make it to the fiesta—hell, they might not even make it home. Involuntarily, his eyes cut to the cab of her pickup, then just as quickly darted away. Another woman, maybe, but not Mercy. She was too good for that.

Beneath his hands, in the colored lights, the silver in her hair turned to gold, and her ivory skin darkened to a dusky rose. She waited, her mouth slightly open, moist and ready for his, the shadow between her breasts as enticing as a siren's call. Rio told himself he should walk away. Right now. Pull his hands from her entrapping curls, turn on his heel and walk away. She was too good for everything. Too good for Ciudad, too good for the clinic, too good to be in this crummy little village going to a silly fiesta.

But most of all, she was too good for him.

He looked down into her eyes and even opened his mouth to tell her so, but she read his intent almost as if she'd read his mind. Her fingers wrapped tighter around his neck, and she pulled his lips to hers.

His body answered what his mind couldn't, and Rio's mouth came down on Mercy's. For one long moment, he tasted her lips, drinking from her as if he were a dying man. On her back, his hands spread flat. As the kiss deepened and she responded to him, Rio pulled her closer. Beneath his touch, she murmured and moved her arms to circle his waist. He could feel the press of her full breasts against his chest, and suddenly, he knew how the night would end. He didn't care, though.

Just for tonight . . . he would pretend.

They'd already passed the handmade puppets, the golden onyx stand, and the Catholic church women's stall, where they'd purchased steaming-hot tamales. Now Mercy watched Rio's broad back disappear into the crowd as he fought his way to the Corona bar. The night was warm, the food hot and the beer cold.

She fanned herself and waited. Compliments of the local funeral home, the stiff, dish-shaped piece of paper couldn't cool her, though. Nothing would, because the heat she was feeling had nothing to do with the weather and everything to do with Rio—the man whose very presence seemed to fill her with constant anxiety.

Until tonight, she'd never really seen him in a crowd, and his height surprised her once more. He towered over the people greeting him, his broad shoulders encased in a startlingly white *guayabera*. On anyone else, the loose-fitting shirt would have looked ordinary, but on Rio the effect was just the opposite. Embroidered in white thread, with the short sleeves emphasizing the diameter of his biceps, the casual cotton gave him a royal look, an authoritative aura, and she felt herself responding to it. The ragged, tight jeans and scuffed boots he wore with it didn't detract one bit.

Mercy's eyes dropped to his trim waist. The long tail of the shirt covered it now, but when she'd embraced him, she'd felt the hard, familiar outline of his sheathed knife at his belt. She shivered slightly in the damp night air. That knife symbolized everything about him that scared her—his offhand acceptance of violence, his harsh way of life, his way of earning a living....

She craned her neck, keeping him in view as he paid for their drinks, then headed back to their table. Before he took two steps toward her, however, he stopped abruptly, his pleasant smile changing into a black scowl. Even from where she waited, she could see his hands clench the bottles of beer, and for a moment, she was scared they might snap in two.

Her heart thudded against her chest. There was only one person who could bring that look into Rio's eyes—Greenwood.

She wrenched her gaze from Rio's face and searched the crowd, following the path his eyes had taken. It didn't take long to find Greenwood—he was the only man there who was as tall as Rio. Her mouth turned dry as she realized the lawman had seen Rio also.

For Mercy, the noise of the crowd faded. The only sound she could hear was that of her pulse. The pounding echoed the measured steps that Greenwood took as he walked toward Rio. She half rose from the bench where she'd been sitting, but Rio's eyes darted to hers, and he shook his head. With a puzzled look, Greenwood stopped and followed Rio's gaze. Mercy froze.

It was the first time she'd seen the older man without his mirrored sunglasses, and as his eyes scanned the crowd, she realized they were pale and cold. When they landed on her, goose bumps rose on her arms.

His gaze flicked back to Rio. Greenwood had made the connection, and Mercy felt her stomach plummet. For a moment, the three of them paused, trapped in a triangle of hatred, confusion and lies, the crowd swirling around them in unsuspecting gaiety. The music continued to blare, the partying didn't stop, but suddenly, the joy had been taken from the evening.

Greenwood took two steps closer to Rio, and Mercy held her breath as Rio's body visibly tensed. The thought entered her mind that she was grateful he was holding their drinks—he couldn't get to his knife. As quickly as the idea came, Mercy banished it. Rio wouldn't actually pull a weapon on a law official.

Would he?

She watched the two men exchange words, her fingers gripping each other so hard that the imprint of her nails became visible in the palms of her hands. In an instant, however, the confrontation was over. Greenwood shot her another look, then melted into the crowd. Rio stalked toward her, his face a stony mask of displeasure. The whole episode hadn't taken more than ten seconds, but Mercy was more than shaken. She leaned against the fence at her back, glad for its support, however unstable.

Rio reached her side and thrust one of the drinks toward her, his cold eyes chilling her in the gloom. "I guess you saw that?"

She nodded. "What did he want?"

"The usual—to harass me." Rio turned his head and searched the crowd, as if he could remove Greenwood by sheer force of will. "One of these days..."

The threat in his voice rippled over Mercy's spine, but she forced herself to ignore it. "He saw me, too, didn't he?"

Rio seemed to mentally shake himself, then he turned back to her. "Yes," he said briefly. "He wanted to know if we were together."

A knot formed in the back of Mercy's throat. "And what did you say?"

Rio took a long swallow of his beer, then stared at her defiantly. "This is Mexico, Mercy. He has no jurisdiction over here. No jurisdiction and no friends. He can't touch us here."

Mercy's fingers gripped the cold, clear bottle before her. Rio hadn't answered her question, and she had the feeling he wouldn't even if she pressed. Their eyes met, and he reached out to feather a finger over her cheek. "Forget him, *querida*. He's nothing—less than nothing. I don't want him to spoil the evening."

She nodded dumbly, but her heart turned heavy. Greenwood's appearance had reminded her of everything she wanted to forget. Just like Rio's knife...

"I saw Sister Rosa as I passed the nuns' booth." As if nothing had happened, Rio's voice was normal, its usual deep and caressing tones bringing Mercy back to awareness. "She threatened me if we didn't stop and buy something."

Forcing herself to put aside her troubling thoughts and match his casualness, Mercy nodded her head and spoke above the Tejano music blaring from a nearby stage. "They told me last week they had something special they wanted to show me."

"Let's go, then." Smiling easily, Greenwood's words obviously put aside if not forgotten, Rio took her elbow, ducking his head to her ear as they moved into the stream of people. "But I have a feeling this is going to cost me."

Amusement warmed his cool gray eyes, but underneath the smile, his usual intense concentration had turned up a notch, thanks to the sheriff. Even as Rio spoke to her and guided her through the crowd, he was poised and alert, an undercurrent of watchfulness running through him like the hum of an engine. It had been there before he'd seen Greenwood, but Mercy hadn't sensed it until now, as the power of it eased subtly into a higher gear. The realization, like everything else about Rio, both attracted and repelled her.

They reached the booth, and the nuns flocked around Rio as if Mercy were invisible. Obviously, some of them hadn't seen him in quite a while, and their delight in him forced thoughts of Greenwood into the background. Mercy shook her head in amazement and stood to one side. She almost felt like Alice in Wonderland with everything upside down. Who would have thought a convent of nuns would be so enchanted by a man who constantly broke the law? At first glance, it made no sense, but thinking about it, Mercy realized belatedly that it only confirmed what she'd begun to suspect— there was more to Rio, much, much more, than she'd first thought. The only question was, who was he, really?

Sister Rosa broke off first and came to Mercy, taking her by the arm. "I'm so glad you came," she said, her simple face breaking into a smile. "The sisters have been hard at work on something just for you. Don't let on that I told you, but look at the lace mantilla in the center of the table."

She dropped her grip on Mercy's arm and went around to the back of the table. A second later, Rio stepped up to Mercy's side and looked over her at the table of wares, his hands heavy on her shoulders. Before she could say a word, however, he reached from behind her and ran one finger over a stretch of delicate black lace in the middle of the table. In startling contrast, the delicate weaving stood out against the white and ivory linens as if it were calling to her.

"Is this what I think it is?" he said, his warm voice full of amazement. "I can't believe it." Almost reverently, he scooped up the fragile length of fabric and stared at it.

Shocked by the perfection of the workmanship in such an unexpected place, Mercy ran her own fingers over the lace. When she was a teenager, her parents had taken her to Belgium, where they'd toured the lace factories. Nothing she'd seen there, or anywhere, for that matter, could compare to the fine, tiny loops and stitches of this piece. The thread itself was so black it was almost blue, and from the silky texture, Mercy knew it alone had cost a fortune, not to mention the labor.

"It's gorgeous," she said. "Where did they get it, I wonder."

"They didn't *get* it anywhere." Rio's gray eyes fastened on hers. "The nuns made it," he said.

Mercy felt her eyes widen. "They made it? Here—in Ciudad?"

He nodded. "For many years, the lace of Ciudad Bravo was what kept the convent going, but that stopped when I was a child." He shook his head, the lace molding his fingers with fluidlike softness. "In fact..." His eyes narrowed as if in sudden pain, and for just a second, they turned a darker shade of charcoal. Scared, Mercy responded automatically, her hand going to his arm.

"What?" she said in alarm.

"My mother—she had a Bravo lace mantilla. She'd taken it off and had partially wrapped me in it when they found us both." His gray eyes regained their usual detached air. "I always wondered how a poor woman like her had managed to get one."

For Mercy, the lace in Rio's hands took on another meaning, and she reached out for it, prepared to return it to the table. The nuns might have meant well, but she wanted nothing that would bring such sad memories to Rio.

Just as her fingers took hold, however, his hand clenched around the needlework. "No," he said, shaking his head. "I'm going to buy this—for you."

Before she could protest, Rio had turned and was draping the length of black fabric over her hair. With a deft hand, he twisted it under her chin and let the ends flow over her shoulder and down her back.

Mercy had forgotten all about the nuns until she heard their clapping. They were standing behind the tiny table and admiring their handiwork, seeing it where they had made it to be. One of them handed her a mirror.

Mercy held up the oval of glass and felt shock ripple down her spine. The woman who looked back at her was not the real Mercy. Instead, this was the woman from her bedroom mirror, the one from another place, another time. And behind her, in the shadows, was a man with desire in his eyes.

If he had spoken out loud, Rio couldn't have communicated his feelings any clearer, and Mercy's breath suddenly caught in her throat. They were at that special juncture in a relationship, that turning point where every touch was a prelude, every look a promise. As Rio's eyes pierced hers, Mercy got a glimpse of how the night would end...and a sudden wash of urgency pooled deep within her.

Her fingers trembling, her stomach tightening, Mercy forced her gaze to return to her own reflection. The midnight lace fell around her face like a magic frame, the blond hair underneath it gleaming in the moonlight. The darkness of the material emphasized her paleness but made her eyes look twice as big and twice as blue.

The transformation disturbed her. She moved her hands toward it, as if to remove it, but Rio spoke from behind her. "Don't take it off." Their eyes met and locked. "I want to see you wear it."

He pulled out his wallet, but the nuns refused his money, and a second later, Rio and Mercy were walking away. Not, however, before she'd seen him slip a large bill into a donation jar that sat discreetly upon one edge of the table.

The crowds had gotten thicker, but for more than an hour, Mercy and Rio wound their way through the people, looking at the booths, enjoying the music. Mercy stayed on the lookout for Greenwood, but he'd obviously left. Finally, Rio led her to a quiet, secluded table. Under the dim colored lights, he pulled out her chair—a small backless bench, then leaned over till his face was level with hers.

With one hand, he gently lifted the lace by her cheek. "I can't tell you how gorgeous you look in that," he said. "When I first saw you tonight, I thought you were perfect, but I have to admit, the mantilla is the crowning touch."

Mercy felt herself blush. She wasn't accustomed to flattery, and the sincerity in Rio's voice told her he wasn't accustomed to giving it, either. "Thank you," she said.

He smiled, almost sadly, then spoke again, the cryptic words sending a foreboding shiver down Mercy's back. "No matter what happens," he said quietly, "I don't think I'll ever forget tonight."

Before she could ask what he meant, he rose and looked over his shoulder. "I'm going to get us something to eat. Don't leave."

She nodded once, then watched as he headed toward another stand, grateful for the chance to catch her breath. Seeing him, absorbing his reaction to the mantilla, having him touch her constantly, was beginning to tell on her. She felt as though she'd just done a ten-hour stretch in the operating room. She was exhausted and exhilarated, both at once.

Momentarily, she closed her eyes and took a deep breath. She knew what was coming. Knew that Rio would end up in her bed, knew that it would be a night she'd never forget, knew that she'd regret it in the morning. But most of all, she knew it was inevitable.

When she opened her eyes, Rio was standing at her side, two enormous platters in his hands. They were heaped so high with enchiladas, *chili con queso,* beans and rice that she forgot her trepidation of a moment before and began to laugh. "My God," she said, reaching for one of the plates, "how many people were you planning on feeding?"

He grinned, then sat down beside her, his back to the wall behind them. "I was hungry," he said. "And it's been years since I had a taste of home cooking like this."

Mercy's fork poised over her first bite of beans as his words sunk in. "I just realized something," she said in amazement. "I don't even know where you live."

Deliberately, he cut into the steaming enchilada. He kept his silence for a second too long, and Mercy began to feel uncomfortable for asking the simple question.

"Here and there," he said in a very offhanded way, shrugging his shoulders. "I keep apartments in several places, but I guess you could say Houston is home."

"Houston?" she repeated in amazement. "But that's hundreds of miles from here."

He reached for his beer, his fingers closing around the neck of the bottle. "I go where my work takes me," he answered, his light eyes flashing defiantly at her. Never taking his gaze from her, he drank deeply from the bottle, then placed it back on the table with a dull thud. "You should know that by now, Mercy."

The words held a touch of disregard, a trace of rebellion, that rippled over her like silk thrown across a table. "I know but I just never thought about it," she answered quickly. "You have to live somewhere when you're…in between jobs. I just wondered where that is."

"Have you ever been to Houston?" He asked the question while he rolled a tortilla. Mercy stared his dark, quick fingers. When he brought it to his mouth, her gaze followed, and she realized he was waiting for her to answer.

"I...I've never been there. No," she finally answered. The sight of his white, white teeth sinking into that flat piece of cornmeal somehow took her mind off the original question. She struggled to pay attention. "I had a friend who did part of his residency there, though. I think he said the hospital was named 'Ben' something or other."

"Ben Taub," Rio supplied. "It's one of the largest— has a great emergency room."

"You've been there?" she asked, remembering the scars she'd seen across his body.

He nodded in the dark and took another gulp of the beer. "Unfortunately, yes." Almost unconsciously, his fingers left the bottle and drifted to his left shoulder, where he absentmindedly stroked the muscle under his shirt. "I've been sewn up by the best," he said, his eyes suddenly turning hot as they took her in, "the best *and* the beautiful."

He held her gaze as long as she would allow, and like a wire alive with electricity, the look jolted her into awareness. When he took his hand and placed it on her arm, his fingers continued the shock. They were warm from touching his own skin. He squeezed her arm gently, then lifted his hand and lightly ran his knuckles over her skin. "I don't think I've ever really thanked you for taking care of me that night. Sister Rosa would scold me if she knew I'd forgotten my manners like that."

Mercy held her breath as his touch continued up her arm. It brushed up her forearm, then past her elbow to the side of her breast. The heat of his caress penetrated the thin cotton of her blouse, and she shivered. In reality, the touch barely registered, but desire had turned her nerve endings raw and exposed. When he finally stopped, his fingers rested lightly on the bare skin of her shoulder, where her blouse had slipped to one side. He stared at her and kneaded the muscle of her shoulder with fingers that were powerful but gentle. "You're awfully tense," he said softly. "Am I making you nervous?"

"No, not at all," she lied, her voice husky as she strained to sit still.

He moved closer to her and put his other hand on her left shoulder. Now he was completely behind her, sitting on the very edge of his own stool, a dark shadow between herself and the wall. A casual observer glancing her way might see only a single woman at a table, two plates, two bottles. Nothing more.

Mercy, however, could see *and* feel a lot more. Like two thighs in tight, torn denim—two thighs that stretched around the backless bench where she sat, straddling her. And two searing hands that now rested on both of her shoulders, their warm, probing fingers slipping under the loose neck of her blouse to stoke the fire building deep inside of her. And finally, a heated, sexy voice in her ear, warm breath caressing her cheek with barely checked promises.

"I'm glad you're not nervous, Mercy. I wouldn't want to think that I had caused this strain." As he spoke, his fingers worked against her shoulders. "You're so tight, Mercy," he whispered. "So tense. A beautiful woman like you shouldn't be this way."

His disembodied voice vibrated against her cheek. With each word that he spoke, Mercy felt a heavy undertow of desire break and pull against her. As his thumbs loosened her muscles, his other fingers splayed against her collarbone, and it was all that she could do to keep from grasping his hands and pressing them to where she really wanted to feel his touch. As it was, her own hands, which had been clutched tightly together in her lap, broke apart and clenched his knees. When he stroked her, her fingers tightened against him.

"That's good," he said, "*muy bueno*. You're getting the idea now." Above them, the silent moon wandered behind a cloud, and the night turned even dimmer. In the distance, Mercy could hear the band start a slow, sad ballad about a woman whose heart was breaking. Behind her, Rio inched closer, and suddenly it seemed as if the whole night existed only for them, as if they were the last two people in the entire universe.

The long length of his chest pressed against her back, and Mercy could have sworn that she felt his heart against her spine. It must have been her own pulse, however, as it beat an irregular pattern. Leisurely, his hands left her shoulders and drifted down over her arms, his mouth taking their place. Delicious trembles overtook her as he lightly nipped at the soft, exposed skin, kissing, then biting, sucking, then licking.

His fingers kept going until his hands were hot against her skirt. Slowly but relentlessly, they pulled the fabric up. The tablecloth hid what the darkness did not.

She murmured her protest, but before she could finish, it had died into a moan. His hands had found bare skin—this time her upper thighs—and she felt the flush of passion darken her face. Ineffectually, she spoke. "No, Rio, not—"

"No one can see us," he answered. "They don't even know we're here."

She let her head fall back against his chest, helpless to do anything but feel.

He dropped his lips and murmured against her skin, the words rumbling through his chest. "You taste like the moonlight. Like the stars and the sun and the sky."

His tongue slowly teased up the side of her neck, then outlined the edge of her ear. "Like honey and silver and . . . sex."

The darkness of their corner deepened as the last few lights dimmed and sputtered out. Mercy's spine curved into Rio's chest, and his hands drifted higher. Against her ear, he whispered. "And you feel like a dream I've always had but could never hope to live."

For endless minutes, like butterflies, his fingers feathered over her thighs, and he whispered into her ear, telling her what he wanted to do, teasing her until she could stand it no longer. Finally, she turned against his chest and faced him, her need for him an entity with power of its own.

"Come home with me," she said, her eyes moving over his dark face. "Come home and make love to me."

Chapter 9

The trip back to Mercy's cabin was a blur. Later, she remembered only snatches—giving Rio the keys to the old truck, stopping at the red light in town and kissing, then finally arriving at her cabin. When she was old and gray and memories were all she had to keep her warm, Mercy knew she'd never forget that one searing instant when they pulled into her driveway. It was a snapshot of impressions, a flash of heat and fire that would always stay with her.

Rio never let her feet touch the ground. He tore open the door of the truck, then pulled her into his arms. She wrapped her hands around his neck and buried her face against his chest as he carried her up the porch and through the doorway. She thought she might have been dreaming except she knew she wasn't. No dream had ever been this intense, this real, this hot.

She felt as though she had to slow down, to stop and think about what she was doing, but something inside her broke—a liquid heat, a fiery need, that she could neither deny nor hide. And Rio felt it, too. She sensed his urgency as clearly as she felt her own.

He carried her straight into her bedroom, where he laid her on the bed. Pale silver moonlight poured through her bedroom window and touched his face, and the sight of those cold eyes, now hot with emotion and desire, flamed the fires of her own hunger even higher. Despite this, he paused, and she could read in his face what it cost him to stop.

Her hands were gripping his arm, her cool, clean, loving hands, and Rio fought to maintain the control he'd been fighting for since the day he'd walked into her cabin. He flipped his wrist over and trapped her innocent fingers with his. Her eyes jerked back to his. "Is this really what you want?" he asked. "To bed a criminal? To make love to a *coyote?*"

She looked up at him. "I'm not making love to a *coyote*. I'm making love to *you*."

The words tore something loose in Rio's chest, knocked a small hole in the fence he kept around him. It had started falling at the fiesta, had cracked open a little further when he'd kissed her. Now it was threatening to tumble down completely, and he was scared. "But that's what *I* am," he persisted, some perverse part of him almost wishing she'd stop him. "Be sure, Mercy, because once I start, I will not stop."

"I *do* want you to stop—to stop *talking*," she answered, her own voice turning harsh, her fingers now gripping his. "I need you, Rio. Make love to me."

He stared at her a second longer, then pulled her roughly to him. When their lips met, they each knew the kiss they shared was a pact as much as a caress.

Mercy moaned against his mouth, then tilted her head back, her movement exposing the long ivory column of her throat. Rio's thumb rested in the hollow of it, and underneath his touch, her pulse throbbed. While he stared at her, her eyes closed, the dark-fringed lashes brushing down over their stormy depths.

The sight of those pale, blue-veined lids sparked Rio even more, and desperately he wanted to give her one last chance. "Open your eyes," he said harshly. "I want to know what you're thinking."

Instantly, she obeyed, but her words mocked his actions. "You can't tell what I'm thinking by looking at my eyes."

"Yes, I can," he answered in a serious voice, his thumb moving over her skin.

"Then tell me," she whispered. "What do you see?"

He looked into the azure depths. Just as she'd said, there was a raw, burning need within her, burning within those blue flames in an unmistakable heat. He would have known about it even if she hadn't admitted it, hadn't opened her eyes—he could feel it. It surrounded them in a smoky haze, so thick he could have cut it with his knife. The intensity fed the fire of his own need, and there was no way he could deny it any longer. "I see your passion," he finally said. "Your passion *and* mine."

Her lips parted, the tip of her tongue gliding over them, the sight killing him with desire. Their only point of contact was his hand on her throat, but that didn't matter to Rio. He was already more aroused then he'd ever been with any woman.

"Is that all you see?"

For some strange reason, he instantly thought of the last time he'd been in her bed. Wounded, angry, fearful—holding a knife to her throat. The situations were totally different, but Rio saw some spark in Mercy's eyes that had brought that memory to the forefront. For a second, he puzzled over it, then he tightened his fingers against her skin as he realized what it was. Her eyes opened wider against his clutch.

"No, that's not all," he answered. "I see your fear. I can taste it."

Imperceptibly, her breath caught, then she shook her head. "That's not true. You're seeing what you *think* is there."

"Prove me wrong," he said grimly.

She stared straight into his soul, then brought her mouth to his, her eyes still open as her lips crushed his. He knew she was lying—she *was* afraid of him, but suddenly, he didn't care anymore. A second later, she deepened the kiss, leaning in toward him, the soft pressure of her breasts against his chest sending an uninterrupted coil of sensation from his heart downward.

"How's that?" she asked, her eyes burning.

"It's a beginning," he said insolently. "But I'm still not sure."

She arched one blond eyebrow into a parody of disbelief. "What part of that didn't you understand?"

He shook his head. "You'll have to try it again." Pausing, he let his fingers slip lower, toward the shadow of her cleavage. "I always was a slow learner."

She lifted her free hand and rested it on his shoulder, picking up a curl of his hair and twining it once. As the swell of her breast warmed his finger, Rio sucked in his breath—it was *him* she had wrapped around her finger, not just his hair.

"That's not a problem," she answered in a husky whisper, leaning closer. "I always was a good teacher."

This time when they kissed, Rio captured her mouth and claimed it for his own, parting her lips with his tongue and tasting the sweetness she'd only teased him with before. He released her throat and slid his hand down her arching back, bringing her closer to him, the passion between them arcing like a shooting star. When he tore his mouth from her, his own pulse was pounding as though he'd just crawled under a fence and run for twenty miles, the devil behind him and in hot pursuit.

Their eyes met again, and he dropped all pretense. "I've wanted to do this since I saw you standing out there in the moonlight."

In the lost lightness of his eyes, Mercy saw what he was really saying and she nodded once.

He slid to the edge of the bed and stood, peeling off the white shirt as he rose, his slim waist now level with Mercy's eyes. The first few buttons of his jeans were already undone, and in that dark triangle of skin, a shadow of black curls tangled. Liquid desire slid into Mercy's lower body. "Take off my pants," he ordered.

She lifted her hands from the mattress and pressed them against his chest. His muscles were clearly defined, and as her fingers brushed over the scars, he never moved. Only when her lips found the rough white ridges did he moan and tangle his hands into her hair. Finally, her fingers curled over the edge of his jeans and pulled. His underwear came off, and as the pants slid over his narrow hips and down his muscled thighs, Mercy's breath caught in her throat, her hands falling away. He finished the task for her, kicking the jeans away, his eyes never leaving her face.

Even though she'd seen him nude before, she felt as though she were seeing a naked man for the first time.

Her lower lip caught between her teeth, Mercy reached out and touched him with one slim finger.

She started with the hard muscles of his chest, iron beneath her touch, then let her nail lightly graze each nipple before going lower. He shuddered slightly under her attentions, but stayed perfectly still otherwise, his hands gripping her shoulders, his eyes, with their pupils dilated, barely darker than the night surrounding the cabin.

When her hand paused above the thatch of black hair, he spoke, his voice hoarse with desire. "Stand up, Mercy. I want to see you, too."

She floated up from the bed, intensely aware again of the difference in their heights. As he reached down toward her, the contrast made her feel more of a woman than she ever had before. Tilting her head to look at him, Mercy lifted her hands to the drawstring of her blouse.

He reached out and stopped her. "No," he said softly, "I want to do it." Between his thumb and forefinger, he took the end of the ribbon and pulled. The blouse slipped down one shoulder.

He didn't take it off. A quiver of anticipation rippled down Mercy's back as he put his hands on her shoulders and turned her away from him. She didn't understand until she had turned completely, then their eyes locked in the mirror over her dresser. Excitement tensed and coiled within her like a six-foot rattlesnake, ready to strike. In the dim light of her bedroom lamp, her fevered eyes left his and followed his fingers as they slipped the blouse from her other shoulder.

An eternity passed in a heartbeat, then the blouse was lying in a puddle at her feet. She wore nothing underneath it. Quickly, her skirt followed.

When her nude body was finally revealed in the murky reflection, Rio's breath caught in his throat.

Light and dark, day and night, right and wrong, he thought with a painful catch in his throat.

Behind and above her, he towered, her head barely reaching his chin. His hair was straight and black, hers blond and softly tousled. Her blue eyes shimmered in the dusk; his gray ones shone in the dark. Where he angled, she curved; where she was soft, he was hard. But most startling of all were his sun-browned hands against her ivory shoulders.

Even in the dimly lit bedroom, where light and shadows were ill defined, the contrast rocked him to the bottom of his existence.

Unconsciously, Rio tightened his fingers on her shoulders, then loosened his grip and murmured his apologies when she flinched, his hands caressing and soothing the curve of her upper arm. Turning her in his arms, he looked down at her once more. "Are you sure about this?"

Her full lips curved upward. "I believe you asked me that earlier...and my answer hasn't changed." She reached up and curled her hands around his neck, bringing his lips down to hers.

A low moan built in the back of Rio's throat, and his hands went from her arms to the full softness of her breasts. Briefly, he allowed himself to cup their fullness, but the pleasure was too much too soon. He pulled back, and with his fingertips barely touching the sides of each one, he stroked their heavy weight. A second later, his thumb brushed over each nipple, sending them into peaks of sweet desire.

Mercy groaned into his open mouth, a verbal expression of her needs that threatened to pull Rio under. He wanted to take his time, to learn her secrets slowly, but that was harder to do with each passing moment. He tore his mouth from hers, and they tumbled to the bed.

Mercy landed on top.

When she rose up over him, she teased the tips of her nipples over his broad chest. Her hands followed, dancing over his muscles, through his hair and across his face, sending Rio mad with the delicate caresses. Through the thick cloud of his hunger, he refused to let her take over, however, and a second later, he rolled her to her back, stretching out along her side.

"This time," he growled, "is *my* time."

Her eyes darkened, twin lakes of passion. "*This* time," she agreed in a husky voice.

A black flash curled deep within Rio's mind, rising to the surface to mingle with the feel of her soft hands against his back and the clean scent of her perfume. The mixture was a heady cocktail, and it brought him to the edge of release.

He wanted to rise up, to part her thighs, to take her now, but *all* thought fled as she reached out and circled him with her hand, her fingers closing around him, the sweet, slow rhythm forcing his eyes to close and his breath to stop. "If you keep that up, this may be the *only* time."

"*That* is the first thing you've said tonight I don't believe," she whispered. "We've got all night—time for everyone." He smiled and bent to her once more, his lips claiming hers.

The skin of his hand was rough, the palm callused, as he captured her right breast once again. Mercy groaned into his mouth and curved into his touch. When his fingers left her breast and went lower, she trembled with expectation.

His touch was the essence of Rio—at once rough but gentle, slow yet quick, hot and cold. She parted her legs and gave herself up to his stroking caresses, shifting and moaning under his fingers. Never had a man learned her so quickly, so thoroughly, she thought in a daze.

Her eyes opened as he took his hand from her, then the bed shifted and he lifted his weight, settling between her thighs. Over his shoulder, Mercy saw the changing shadows in the mirror.

Her throat closed instantly from the passion that swelled within her. His dark, lean body was tucked between her legs as if it belonged there, his tight buttocks flexing as he balanced his weight on his elbows. He poised over her.

"Look at me," he commanded. "Look into my eyes."

Mercy turned her head to stare at the chill intensity of his gaze, and hot desire broke, spilling open within her. She sucked in her breath and lifted her legs, crossing her ankles over the narrowness of his hips.

"Take me now, Rio." Her words were a gasp and a plea. "Now."

His eyes heated into two burning coals, branding her with a look she knew she'd never forget. Never. A second later, he thrust inside of her.

She gasped, her nails raking his back, then arched higher to take him even deeper, her gaze never leaving his. "Is that what you want?" he said, his voice a sexy growl.

Every nerve of her body was screaming for movement, begging for the long, hot strokes she knew would be coming next. "More," she breathed almost incoherently.

"More?" he teased. "That's all I've got, *chica*. If you want more, you're going to have find a better man than me."

She shook her head, the rustle of her hair rising from the pillow. "No." The single word came from deep within her, from the same place she knew her need for him resided. "No one besides you," she whispered. "You're all I want."

His eyes narrowed with sudden vehemence, then within her, he tensed, his hips hot and heavy against her. "Good—because once this is finished, you're mine. *¿Comprende?* Mine."

She nodded once, the exquisite fullness of him more than she could stand. He read the acquiescence in her eyes—even though there'd been no resistance before— then granted her wish, rocking her with the absolute power she knew he'd been holding back.

A different woman entered Mercy's skin and took over—a wild woman with a level of utter savagery and desire that would have shocked Mercy had she been aware of the change. With every thrust of Rio's body, her mind contracted and her body responded.

Her fingers raked his shoulders and bit into them, caresses for tonight but bruises for tomorrow. Her ankles tightened over his buttocks, and she pulled herself even closer, begging him with her body for more, more.

He answered the only way he could, pressing his mouth against hers, his tongue moving in and out in matching rhythm. Mercy absorbed the driving pressure with everything she had, wishing there were some way she could get even closer, bring even more of him into her. Her hips rose to meet his, faster, faster.

Rio's eyes never left her face, never turned loose of her, and now, Mercy saw them narrow into two slits of driving arousal. Inside of her, a ring of passion widened, arcing out into circles of unbelievable pleasure.

She couldn't stand it a second longer. She closed her eyes and clung to him, his name leaving her tongue like a prayer, over and over, the sound slipping out the open window and into the black night.

One minute, he was asleep—the next, he was wide-awake.

Rio opened his eyes and lay perfectly still until he could orient himself. He was in Mercy's bed; by his side, she slept with open abandon, the sheet pulled down to her waist, one long white leg thrown carelessly above the covers.

He didn't know what had awakened him. Without moving, he listened, his eyes taking in the dusky room and then the woman at his side.

She'd surprised him, but then everything about Mercy surprised him.

He'd expected her to be a gentle lover, a woman who was accustomed to receiving more than giving, but she wasn't. She'd taken what he had to give, and then she'd turned around and given him more than he'd ever thought possible. She had a dark, sensual side to her that contrasted with her pale blond beauty. And he was more intrigued than ever by her.

A soft squeak broke the silence of the early morning, and Rio tensed again, realizing it was the sound that had woken him. Without disturbing Mercy, he slipped noiselessly from the bed and into the jeans he'd thrown down on the floor the night before. His fingers closed around the knife he'd placed on her bedside table, and he hugged the shadows of the room until he reached the window. When his eyes had adjusted to the early-morning light, he scanned the porch anxiously.

It was empty.

He peered through the lace of her curtains, studying the porch, taking in the clinic, watching down the road, but he spotted nothing. Even the river seemed to sleep, the tall grass beside it nodding in somnolence. Rio held his breath. He'd heard a noise—it had awakened him.

For a moment, the thought crossed his mind that Greenwood might have followed them home, but for what purpose Rio had no idea. Reason had no place in their strange relationship, however.

For a full five minutes, he waited beside the window, his only movement his fingers curling and uncurling around the knife, his breath shallow but slow. Finally, just as he started to take his first step toward the door, the squeak repeated itself, and Rio froze. A second later, his eye caught the slight movement at the end of the porch. It was Mercy's swing—catching the last of the early hour's breeze.

In a rush, he let out the breath he'd been holding, his eyes closing in thankfulness before they opened once more. He glanced toward the bed. Mercy slept on, her hair spread over her pillow like liquid silver, one hand clutching the sheet.

Instantly, he was torn. Part of him urged him back to her side; another part said no. He really wanted to climb into bed with her, to drink in the comfort she gave him, but another part of him kept his feet where they were.

As he stared at her, desire snaked around him, tempting him sorely. He needed the feel of her hair in his hands, the smell of her skin on his, the taste of her lips. At his side, however, his hands tensed, the hilt of the knife as cold and hard as his decision.

What they'd shared was not a mistake—in fact, it was the best thing Rio had done in years—but deep down inside, he knew it could never be repeated. She was a doctor, and he was—well, he wasn't what she thought he was, and that reality was something he didn't have the luxury to reveal at the moment. All he *did* know was that Mercy couldn't be his. Seeing Greenwood at the fiesta had served to emphasize that point, in more ways than Rio wanted to think about.

He slipped silently toward the bed, then halted, his outstretched hand inches from Mercy's face. He wanted to touch her one last time, to feel the velvet of her skin beneath his finger, but he stopped before the contact was made, the discipline of a lifetime denying him the pleasure he sought. It surprised him how much it hurt, though. He'd put that kind of pain behind him years ago, or so he'd thought.

With one long look of regret, Rio turned, picked up his shirt and boots, then slipped outside.

When she woke, he was gone.

She hadn't really expected him to be there, but seeing the empty indentation in the pillow made her heart trip anyway. In Mercy's world, men didn't slip in and out, like thieves in the night.

That's exactly what Rio was, though—a thief. He'd stolen into her life before she'd been able to protect herself, and now he'd gone a step further and taken her heart.

Naked under the sheets, Mercy flipped to her side in the rumpled bed and stared out the window of her bedroom, her hand stuck under her cheek. If her body wasn't so deliciously exhausted and her bed so tangled, she'd never have known he'd been there.

Outside, the morning sun was already beating down on the river, and from her vantage point, Mercy could see the diamonds of light sparkling and bouncing, as if chipped from its surface by the heat. Last night, the moonlight had done the same thing, but she'd barely noticed. She'd been too busy loving Rio.

Was what they'd shared really love, though, or something else? Something more primordial, more basic? Could she *love* a man like Rio? Someone who broke the law for a living, who disregarded the rules and made up his own as he went along?

Mercy flipped to her back and pulled a strand of hair from her eyes. Their lovemaking had been beyond anything she'd ever experienced, and only a fool would have tried to lie about it. Rio made love as he did everything else—with a smooth kind of abandon that sucked her into the center of his storm. For the hours they'd been together, Mercy had suspended everything, everything but her senses. But with the morning sun, she had to acknowledge the truth. She didn't trust him, she didn't like his job and she could never live with a man like Rio. A niggling question entered her mind and refused to give way, however.

Could she live without him?

When darkness fell, he returned.

Mercy stepped outside and found him sitting in her porch swing. She had no idea how long he'd been there.

Like a moth to a flame, she found herself silently at his side, and a second later, his lips were on hers. They didn't say a word, but communication was instant. In another second, they were in her bedroom.

The first time was for her—fast and hard and almost angry. She took his clothes from him, then pulled off her own as if they were burning her skin. In a flash of arms and legs and moon-flecked skin, they fell onto her bed, Mercy kissing him until she couldn't breathe, her hands sweeping over his body, feeling every scar, memorizing every slash. The speed of their lovemaking made it all the more intense, and Mercy felt as though she were skiing out of control, down the fastest mountain she'd ever found, with skis that flew above the ground.

The second time was for him—slow and smooth and steady—and in her saner moments, Mercy couldn't believe what was happening. He took her gently, as if he were the first. She closed her eyes and let him love her as if he were the last. The tender way he kissed her, the reverent touch of his hands, the sensitive attunement to her needs, drove her to the edge, then took her over.

Hours later, Mercy raised her head from Rio's shoulder and looked into his eyes. He'd been so still, she thought he was asleep, but the clear, chilling coolness of his gaze met hers straight on. "You're a beautiful woman," he said distinctly. "What in the hell are you doing down here, wasting your time in the Valley?"

The way he said the words, she knew he was voicing a question that had disturbed him for a long time. She smiled in the dim bedroom light. "Is that a variation on 'What's a nice girl like you doing in a place like this?'"

"Something like that." He eased up against the pillows and stuck his arms behind his head, his biceps turning into flat planes of muscle. "Why here?"

She pulled the sheet up to her breasts. "I come from a long line of doctors. It's a family tradition that you spend your first year out of medical school doing charity work. When I heard about the clinic in Ciudad, I knew I wanted to come here."

"Why? No one in their right mind would willingly live here."

"You do."

His eyes widened for just a second, then he laughed, a bitter sound. "It's my j—"

"Job," she finished. "I know, but you could do what you do somewhere else, couldn't you?" As distasteful as she found his work, Mercy also realized she knew very little about the mechanics of the situation. "Aren't there people all over who cross illegally?"

His face held a speculative look, as though he were trying to figure out why she was asking, then he apparently decided it was just curiosity. "I suppose so," he finally said, "but Ciudad holds a special interest for me." His voice turned harder and colder. "I guess you could say that nowhere else would serve my purpose at the moment."

Propping herself up with her elbow, Mercy turned on her side and stared at him. In the dim light, his profile was etched against the shadows, all hard lines and angles, planes without softness. Reaching out, she palmed his chest, then drifted her fingers lower, over the washboard surface of his stomach. "And what is your 'purpose,' Rio? Why do you really do what you do?"

He turned his head and studied her. "Do you really want to know, or is this pillow talk?"

"I want to know," she said slowly. "I . . . I don't understand it, and I have a hard time reconciling what you do with what you are."

"Can't they be two separate things?"

"No. I'm a doctor, and everything I do is colored by that. But you're like two different people—one who seems to care, and one who breaks the law."

His jaw tightened momentarily, and Mercy wondered if she'd gone too far. They'd never really discussed his "job," but things had changed. Their relationship was on a different plane now, and she wanted—needed—to know more.

He moved restlessly against the bed, a faint sign of unease. "I wish you wouldn't put it like that."

Mercy felt her eyes widen. "But that's what you do. You break the law."

"I stretch it."

Mercy sat up, pulling the sheet with her. "You bring people across the border, and they pay you. That's breaking the law."

"If I didn't do it, someone else would. At least with me, they're safe."

"Are they?"

His eyes cut to hers with a swiftness that took her breath. "What in hell does that mean?"

"You never told me who shot you, Rio. Paco never said who hurt him. And Sister Rosa said—" She broke off, knowing now that she'd gone too far.

"Said what?" His eyes were two diamonds, hard and cold, and when he repeated his words, they were the same. "Said what, Mercy?"

"Sister Rosa said that illegals had been coming to the convent in bad shape. Beat up, abused, hurt..."

"And you think I'm doing it?"

She held her breath. It was a tricky situation—she didn't really think he was capable of such behavior, not after he'd brought her Paco, not after he'd made love to her, but he *was* hiding something, and she had no idea what it was. She swallowed her indecision and spoke slowly, taking the middle road. "I...I'm not sure...I don't know what to think. But something tells me you're involved."

Lowering his eyes, he obviously tried to hide the flash of surprise that darkened their chilled depths, but Mercy had been waiting and watching for it.

He reached out and stroked his finger over her cheek, his voice a casual dismissal. "I didn't know you were clairvoyant, too. I thought you were just a doctor."

"Doctors *have* to read minds sometimes, if they're going to get the whole story."

His eyes met hers across the rumpled sheets. "Forget it, Mercy." The words were blunt, and his voice hard. "Put it out of your mind and forget it. I'm not going to tell you more."

Chapter 10

She couldn't forget it, though.

She couldn't forget the bleak look in his eyes, the tense way he held his shoulders, the tight lines around his mouth. Mercy had never known a man like Rio before—a man whose job it was to break the law—but something kept telling her there was more, a lot more, to him than she'd first thought.

The days passed in a haze of passion for her, though, and she ignored her worries—something she'd never been able to do before. He filled her nights with loving and her days with anticipation. Every minute they were apart, Mercy thought about him, and every minute they were together, she thought of nothing else. Even Greenwood faded into the background. When Rio suggested they go across the border for dinner one night, she readily agreed, feeling like a teenager on her very first date.

He picked her up at eight-thirty, and Mercy was glad when he walked onto her porch that she'd put on the nicest dress she'd brought—a light blue silk that matched her eyes. He'd dressed up also, replacing his usual jeans with neatly pressed gabardine trousers and a collarless white dress shirt. When she saw him, Mercy felt her heart turn over.

His eyes darkened with appreciation as he took her in. "I think we'll stay here," he said slowly, his voice a deep caress. "To hell with going out."

Mercy laughed, slightly embarrassed. They'd shared everything a couple could share inside the walls of her bedroom, but still Rio's overwhelming sensuality continually took her by surprise. But even more remarkable, to Mercy, at least, was her total and ready response to him . . . all of the time. She'd never met a man who could turn her on with a single heated stare. Rio didn't even have to touch her to make her ready for him. She smiled now and lifted a hand to her braid. "You promised me dinner and dancing," she teased, then paused. "But I guess that it could wait. . . ."

His steady stare warmed even more, but he shook his head slowly. "No," he answered, dragging out the reply. "I've always heard that anticipation is a powerful aphrodisiac. We'll test the theory." He bent down and brushed his lips against hers, his hands heavy on her shoulders. A second later, he lifted his mouth, his eyes locking on hers. "If you insist, however . . ."

Mercy laughed low in her throat. "No, no," she answered. "In the spirit of medical research, I think we should wait. I might just discover something they could name after me. Let's see, we could call it—"

"The Mercy factor," Rio supplied, giving her his arm and leading her down toward the truck. "You could even put it into a formula. The number of hours multiplied by the amount of desire equals . . . ?''

She grinned, then stepped into the truck and faced him. ''Equals the fact that we'd better leave now or I won't get my dinner and dancing.''

He answered her smile with one of his own, then went to the other side of the truck and climbed in behind the wheel. Twenty minutes later, they pulled into the crowded parking lot of what was obviously a popular restaurant. He cut off the engine and turned to her, his face losing some of the lightness their conversation had sparked.

''This isn't the Edwardsville Country Club, Mercy,'' he said seriously. ''I know you're used to better—''

Mercy lifted one finger and put it over his full lips, halting the flow of words. ''I don't care where we go,'' she answered softly. ''Just being together—that's enough.''

He arched one dark eyebrow. ''Are you sure?''

''Yes, I'm sure.'' She threw a glance toward the door. ''You come here all the time, don't you?''

''On occasion.''

''Then it's fine.''

He threw her a look that was half puzzled, half unsure, as if he'd never heard anyone voice that kind of confidence in him before, then he shrugged his shoulders and opened his door. A second later, he was helping her out of her side of the truck and up the steps to the restaurant door.

They held hands as they walked into the dimly lit room. As Mercy followed the maître d' around the small dance floor to a small table near the window, she felt Rio's warm touch in the center of her back. They'd never been out together, she realized belatedly, and in fact, besides the fiesta, this was the only other time they'd been in public at all. Heads turned as Rio pulled out her chair and she sat down, but Mercy didn't care. All that mattered to her right now was the tall, dark man facing her across the damask cloth, candlelight dancing over the angles of his handsome face.

He gave their drink orders to the waiter, then after the jacketed man left, Rio turned his eyes to her. Stretching his hand across the table, he covered her fingers with his. "Thank you for coming out with me tonight."

Mercy felt her eyes go wide in surprise. "You're thanking me? Where I come from, I should be the one thanking you."

He lifted one corner of his mouth in a sensual smile. "You'll thank me later," he said in a sexy growl.

"You're awfully sure of yourself," she teased.

"No," he answered slowly. "I'm sure of nothing. Nothing but you." His cool gray eyes searched her face as if he hadn't really seen her before. "And you always do the right thing, don't you? The proper, correct thing."

The waiter set two glasses on the table, poured the wine, then departed before Mercy spoke. Her fingers wrapped around the stem of the glass as she lifted her gaze to Rio's. "I was raised by two people who thought the 'right' thing was the most important thing. For all of my life, I've followed their lead."

"And now?" He raised his glass to his lips and drank deeply, never taking his eyes from her face.

She swallowed hard and wondered what her parents *would* think of Rio. It was a question she hadn't stopped to consider, but now that she did, she realized she didn't really care. That fact surprised her, and her face must have shown it.

"Have I done that?" he asked softly. "Have I made you forget about what's right and what's wrong?"

Mercy twirled the wineglass slowly, her eyes focusing on the crystal but her mind converging on her answer. "You've shown me life isn't as black-and-white as I've always assumed it was," she admitted, realizing the truth of her words as she spoke them. "I . . . I never thought I could fall for a man who breaks the law . . . but I have. I *really* have."

Rio's strong fingers covered hers, stopping their nervous movements. "Don't care for me, Mercy. I'm not worth it."

Her eyes flew up to meet his, and something inside of her broke, broke and shattered as if it were made of crystal like the goblet she continued to clutch. "It's too late," she whispered, then paused. "Much, much too late."

Rio didn't know what to do with Mercy's pronouncement. He knew what he *wanted* to do, but he also knew how impossible that was. At this point, he couldn't even acknowledge what her words even meant to him. She stared at him from across the table, and he knew she expected him to say something.

"You're a very beautiful woman," he said slowly. "And you can do a hell of a lot better than me, Mercy."

She shook her head soundlessly. "I don't think so."

Reluctantly, he pulled his hand from hers. "You deserve a husband, a family, a house in the country with three perfect children. For reasons that I can't explain right now, I can never give you those things." He reached for the wine bottle and refilled her glass, then his. "I'm the opposite of all that kind of life. I'm trouble and confusion, Mercy. Nothing more."

For a moment, her eyes flickered uncertainly. "I . . . I thought you felt something for me, Rio."

A part of his heart broke off at her words, and despite his intention not to respond, Rio couldn't help himself. He reached across the table and took her hands in his. "I do care for you, damn it," he growled. "But that doesn't change a thing. In my *profession,* I'll never be in one place, never be able to stay put. You still deserve better than that—and better than me."

"I don't want better." She paused, the blue light in her eyes almost glowing with the intensity of her feelings. "All I want is you."

The simple declaration reached down into Rio's soul and pulled out emotions that hadn't seen light in years. He fought the invitation of her words, battled with his desire to tell her the same. She didn't know what she was talking about—his secrets were many and dark. Something turned loose inside of him, though, and he gave in to his deepest yearnings. With a swift and graceful motion, he rose to his feet and pulled her with him to the dance floor. As always, he'd tell her with his body what he couldn't say with words.

Against his chest, Mercy laid her head and listened to his heartbeat, her arms circling his neck, the heat of his body warming her own. As she listened to that steady reassurance, she knew she'd never forget this one intense moment. The smell of his body, the feel of his hands, the sound of his breathing—they were all indelibly stamped on her memory like the outline of a new penny. Swaying to the music, she closed her eyes.

Rio's hands circled her waist, then slid around her back, his fingers splayed. Through the thin silk dress, Mercy could feel the heat of his touch. It reached deep inside of her and twisted something that hadn't existed before she'd met him—something that she knew would never be satisfied by the touch of another man.

He'd tried to ignore her words, but Mercy had seen in his eyes what he couldn't bring himself to say. She cursed whatever demons inside of him kept him from voicing his feelings, but she understood. Everything that Sister Rosa had told her was true, and the child he had been, made him the man he was. He couldn't give Mercy more than he already had. A small thrill went through her, though, as she remembered the look in his eyes. He *did* care for her—he might not be able to say the words, but he *did* care for her. She moved closer to him.

In response to her movement, he tightened his arms. Despite his size, he was the kind of man who had an innate grace no matter what he did, and Mercy wasn't surprised by his ability to dance. He followed the music perfectly, bending her body to his with an easy familiarity, his arms around her, the hard line of his right thigh insulated between hers. Guiding her deftly through the crowd, he made love to her as they danced, his breath warm against her hair, his frame pressed against hers. She clung to him.

For a handful of endless minutes, Mercy and Rio danced, swaying to the deep beat of the song, letting their bodies communicate as only lovers can. By the time the music stopped, they'd regained the equilibrium their conversation had disturbed.

Rio led her back to the table, pulled out her chair and bent over to kiss her lightly. Before he could straighten up and return to his own seat, however, a man approached their table. Mercy didn't see him until the last minute.

He was about Rio's height and build, and strangely enough, something about the way he held himself reminded Mercy even more of Rio. The resemblance stopped there, however. The stranger's eyes were black and unfathomable, his hair just as dark, except, she suddenly noticed with a shock, for one startlingly white streak across the front. He stopped at Rio's side and laid a casual hand on his arm. "Rio, *mi amigo,* what's happening?"

Rio stiffened instantly and whirled, obviously surprised by the man's appearance. "What in the hell are you doing here?" he said harshly. "I thought I told you not to—"

The man grinned and interrupted, an even row of white teeth showing behind his smile. "Who's the pretty *señorita?* You are going to introduce us, aren't you?"

Mercy watched Rio struggle to regain control of his expression, an undercurrent of tension rustling between the two men like wind before a storm. Finally, Rio looked down at her, his jaw tightening and releasing as though he'd forgotten she was even there. "This is Mercy Hamilton," he said tersely. "She's the doctor at the clinic in Ciudad." His eyes swept over Mercy with a message that clearly said *Don't ask any questions.* "This is Blanco Sanchez, Mercy."

The man took her fingers and bent over them, brushing the back of her hand with his lips. "How do you do?" he said with just the barest of accents. "It's a pleasure to finally meet you."

Mercy raised her eyebrows. "To *finally* meet me?"

"Your fame precedes you," he answered smoothly. "I'd heard a beautiful young woman was the new *doctora,* but I thought reports of your beauty to be exaggerated. Now I see they weren't magnified enough."

Mercy smiled politely at his overblown compliment, but at the same time, she gently pulled her hand from his grasp.

Scowling, Rio interrupted before the man could say more. "Did you want something, Blanco? Other than to bother me?"

The man raised one hand and dramatically laid it on his chest. "Bother you? *Amigo,* would I do something like that? No, no." He shook his head, the white streak gleaming strangely in the dim candlelight. "I merely saw you dancing and wanted to stop by and say hello." He turned back to Mercy and bowed slightly. "The pleasure was mine, Señorita Hamilton. I'll see if I cannot arrange to be ill in the near future so I will be in need of your services."

"I hope that won't be necessary," she answered.

"Then perhaps we'll meet another way," he said cryptically, his eyes turning to Rio's face. "In different circumstances." He dropped his voice, but Mercy could still hear him. "Why don't you walk with me back to my table?"

Rio nodded once, then gave Mercy a quick, hard look. "I'll be right back," he said, tense lines tightening around his mouth. "Don't leave."

She smiled and nodded, but as she watched the two men depart, a coldness replaced the former warmth of the evening. Blanco Sanchez was not just a friend. His eyes held the flat darkness of a man who didn't need people, except to use them. Mercy's stomach turned sour, her pleasure over the evening ruined. Nowhere they went, nothing they did, went untouched by Rio's life. Would it always be that way?

*   *   *

Mrs. Hernandez clutched her purse to her chest, the hem of the faded blue hospital gown she wore dragging the floor. Her black eyes darted from face to face, then she spotted Mercy and Mary. Mercy started forward through the press of the waiting room to meet the older woman, her heart turning over at the look of confusion and worry on her wrinkled face.

Last week, in an excited voice, Mary had called the clinic and told Mercy the plan had worked. She'd told her grandmother several times that she really wanted to see the big hospital, and after several discussions, her grandmother had finally acquiesced. They could go, and yes, as long as they were there, Mrs. Hernandez would see the other *doctoro*.

Mrs. Hernandez had insisted on one condition, though. Mercy was to accompany them. Touched by the woman's faith in her, for whatever reason, Mercy had immediately called for an appointment with Dr. Zilla, the cardiologist with whom she'd already consulted about the case. Luckily, the office had just received a cancellation for the next day. Mercy had taken it instantly and, early that morning, she'd picked up Mary and her grandmother and headed out.

During the three-hour trip, they'd stopped six times. For water. For the bathroom. Once to look at a patch of wildflowers wilting beside the road. Mercy had endured each delaying tactic with patient understanding. She didn't care how long it took to get there—as long as the elderly woman got the care she needed.

Reaching Mrs. Hernandez's side, Mercy put her arm about the woman's hunched shoulders, squeezing them with what she hoped felt like reassurance. "It won't be too long now," she said. "Dr. Zilla said he'd get right to us."

Mrs. Hernandez nodded uncertainly, then shot off a string of Spanish. Mercy caught enough to know she was asking what the heart specialist was going to be doing.

"He's going to listen to your heart and lungs—just like I did—with a stethoscope. Then he'll need some blood and urine samples. He'll finish up with a chest X ray and an electrocardiogram."

The older woman's eyes grew huge at the seven-syllable word, and Mercy hastened to explain the test. "It won't hurt," she said, after giving a brief synopsis of the procedure, "and it will let us know exactly what your heart is doing." She smiled her support as Mrs. Hernandez's mouth puckered into a moue of skepticism, then gently directed her toward one of the chairs lining the room.

The three of them sat down, and Mercy picked up a magazine. It immediately fell open to an article describing the perfect lipstick, but the words went unread. Instead, Mercy thought of the same thing she'd been thinking about for the past few weeks every time her mind went idle. The upheaval going on in her own life. Things were so crazy with Rio. She couldn't stop thinking about him and their days together, but at the same time, she worried constantly about what kind of future the relationship had...or didn't have.

A few short minutes later, Mrs. Hernandez's name was called, and Mercy jumped up, grateful for the interruption in her pointless speculations. With Mary in tow and Mrs. Hernandez's elbow firmly in her hand, Mercy guided them into one of the examining rooms.

Dr. Zilla, a short, efficient man with graying hair, took immediate and complete control, his Spanish a blur of words even faster than Mrs. Hernandez's. Before they knew what was happening, Mercy and Mary found themselves back in the waiting room, Mrs. Hernandez hanging on Dr. Zilla's arm with her eyes turned adoringly toward him. She barely seemed to know her support team had been banished.

The next four hours crawled by, and for once, Mercy got a taste of what she'd heard her own patients complain about countless times in the past. Thoughts of Rio crowded everything else out of her mind, then finally, a beaming Mrs. Hernandez came to the door and informed Mary and Mercy that "Dr. Z." would see them now.

The consultation was brief and to the point. "She's definitely experiencing some arrhythmia, probably due to the onset of congestive heart failure." Dr. Zilla looked at Mary over the chart he had in his hands. Her young face wore a confused expression, and with an apologetic glance in Mercy's direction, he adjusted his explanation to reflect layman's terms. "Your grandmother is in her eighties. Her ticker's tired."

Mary twisted a tissue between her fingers. "Is…is she going to die?"

"It's a serious condition, but if you watch her diet and make sure she takes her medication, I think she's got plenty of time left." He handed a sheaf of papers to the young girl. "This is a low-salt diet I like to see my patients use. She can't have any alcohol, either, and if she lost a few pounds, it certainly wouldn't hurt."

Accepting the papers, Mary nodded and sniffed. Dr. Zilla turned to Mercy. "The blood and urine work is still pending, but I'll be in touch with you some time later this week. I think she'll be fine, but I'll want to discuss her meds with you after I see the numbers."

"Of course." Mercy smiled and extended her hand. "And thanks again for taking us so quickly."

"No problem," he said easily. "I've been wanting to meet you anyway. I think you're doing good work out there. We need more people like you—people who are willing to live in the rough places and help the ones who can't get in." He smiled, and his whole face transformed into an expression of warm approval and admiration. "Keep it up, Doctor."

All the way home, the three of them smiled.

A week later, Mercy closed the door of the clinic behind her, then stepped into the fading light of the sun as it dropped onto the horizon. It had been a terribly busy day, with a seemingly never-ending supply of patients. From broken legs to poison ivy to a case of false labor that hadn't looked too false for a while—they were all coming to her now. Mrs. Hernandez had passed the word. Mercy could perform miracles.

She smiled as she paused, her right hand on the muscles of her neck, kneading them without thought as she let the hot, humid air wash over her. She *was* thrilled by the work, and everything she did in the clinic was as rewarding as she'd ever hoped it could be. In addition, Dr. Zilla's words from last week still warmed Mercy every time she thought of them. *This* was exactly why she'd wanted to become a doctor—exactly.

If only her personal life was as smooth.

Ten days had passed since she and Rio had gone out to eat, and he hadn't come by once. She'd been busy, of course, with the clinic and with the extra concern over Mrs. Hernandez, but when she wasn't occupied with work, Mercy thought constantly of him.

She reached her back porch, but her legs refused to carry her any farther. Sinking into the wooden swing, she let her head tilt back to the top slat.

Without her being able to stop it, a mental image formed in her mind of their last time together. The sad song that had filled the restaurant, the heavy warmth of Rio's body against hers, the way he'd placed his fingers across her back—the sensations all replayed themselves like a never-ending movie. She forced herself to relax, commanded her muscles to stretch and forget, but no matter what she did, her body remembered what her mind wanted to put aside.

She let her eyes open slowly. The sun had sunk, leaving behind a gold-tinged strip of peach that hung above the river like an unfurled ribbon. Staring at it, Mercy let the thoughts that had been plaguing her all week long come into their full realization.

She *had* to be honest with herself.

She was falling in love with Rio, and it was time to acknowledge that fact.

At first, he'd been excitement—forbidden excitement, but now he was something else. He was a man she cared about, a man she didn't want to hurt. She loved him.

She wanted him in her life and in her bed . . . and not because of who he was or wasn't, but because of who *she* became when she was around him. He made her into the woman she'd seen in her bedroom mirror—the woman who existed within her but whom she'd never had the courage before to acknowledge. She was the flip side of Mercy, the side opposite the girl who made all A's, the woman who graduated tops in medical school, the person who only knew the straight and narrow. And now that that side of Mercy had been released, she knew it would never go back into the box—and in truth, she didn't want it to.

The night absorbed Rio's shadow as he slipped under the cover of Mercy's porch and edged toward her bedroom window. For hours he'd been watching and waiting, down by the river, but the man he looked for had never shown up. Blanco's information had been wrong, obviously. For anyone else, this frustration might have been unbearable, but Rio had simply shrugged his shoulders and eased toward Mercy's house. He'd been waiting for years—a few more weeks wouldn't matter. Not at this point—not when he was this close to his prey...

He rounded the corner of her porch and saw that her bedroom window was dark. While he'd been at the river, he'd seen her come up from the clinic, watched her sit in the swing, then followed her with his eyes as she'd disappeared into the cabin. He'd had a lot of time to think about what was happening to them, and he'd come to one very important decision.

He absolutely could not continue to see Mercy.

The scene in the restaurant had proved that to him. She was starting to care too much, and he didn't deserve it. She had no idea who he was, where he came from, what he really did. He had bad blood, very bad, and he wasn't going to take what she offered. Even if life were simple and he had a nine-to-five job, her love was too precious to be squandered on the likes of him.

With that very thought ringing in his head, however, Rio's feet led the way to her house. Now he stood in the dim veil of her porch, his heart pounding as though he'd just swum the length of the Rio Grande. Despite his best intentions, despite his careful consideration, despite everything, Rio couldn't fight his feelings for her. They sang in his blood like a wild addiction, demanding to be recognized, commanding him to her side. He was helpless to do anything else, and that loss of control frightened him more than anything.

With soundless steps, Rio slipped up to her open bedroom window. The slight breeze from the river had picked up the curtains with invisible fingers, and now they were pulling the lace into her room. Behind their filmy cover, he could see Mercy in her bed, one leg thrown over the covers, one ivory hand falling gracefully toward the floor.

She looked so innocent, so seductive, that his body responded immediately. Before he knew what he was doing, his hands were on the sill. Even as he cursed her apparent carelessness at leaving the window open, he forced it up another notch, then silently folded his long frame and slipped inside.

Rio was quiet—in his business you were either quiet or dead—and Mercy continued to sleep as he reached her bedside and stared down at her. Something twisted inside of him as he watched the even rise and fall of her chest, something screamed out at him and told him how unsuited they were, one to another. On the other side of that scream, however, a siren's call sounded, too. Sounded and pulled him closer...

He dropped to one knee and allowed himself to touch her—just one soft caress against her silken cheek. Automatically, in her sleep, she turned against his hand and placed her lips in his palm, kissing the hard, roughened center. A second later, she pulled it to her and tucked it under her cheek, murmuring in pleasure.

Rio's heart cracked open a little wider, and he cursed silently. He'd done a terrible thing by making her love him, and when she learned the truth—who he really was and what he really did—she'd never forgive him his lies. And he would never forgive himself, either.

For the first time in his life, he considered abandoning his efforts. In his next breath, however, he knew he couldn't. Like a hound getting close to the fox, he was beginning to smell the end. Now was not the time to quit, no matter how hard it was, no matter whom he hurt in the process.

The woman who held his hand—and his heart—couldn't stop him. He wouldn't allow it, and reluctantly, Rio tried to ease away. As much as he wanted to climb into her bed and press her to him, he knew it would be another mistake, another crime. It wasn't one he'd commit.

As he disentangled his fingers from hers, though, Mercy's eyes fluttered open, their crystalline depths going from confusion to awareness to pleasure. She smiled sleepily, then reached up and cradled his stubble-covered face in the palm of her hand.

"I thought I was dreaming," she said, her voice a husky seduction. "But it's really you, isn't it?"

Rio nodded, refusing to trust his own voice. If he spoke now, he might tell her how he really felt, name the tenderness that swelled inside of him for her, acknowledge his caring. He might tell her that he loved her....

She lifted her other hand, and it joined her first one, which had now wound around his neck. Exerting a gentle pressure, she inexorably pulled him toward her. As though reading his mind, she spoke. "Love me, Rio," she said, her eyes piercing his in the darkness. "Please—love me."

She gave voice to the plea that was in his own heart, and with an anguished groan, Rio kissed her, his hands cradling her head. He wanted to exist nowhere else but in her arms, and for one long minute, he pretended that he could.

Her fingers threaded into his long hair, the urgency in her touch communicating itself with startling clarity. He tried to resist, but he couldn't, and when her mouth parted under his, Rio gave way to the temptation, driving his tongue between her lips and into her smooth wetness. Into his open mouth, she moaned, then pulled him closer, her hands dropping to his back, then to his biceps. He clenched her naked shoulders, the skin beneath his touch so hot, he realized with a start that she burned with a need as great as his own.

With an effort greater than any he'd ever experienced, Rio forced himself to pull back. She protested, her hands tight against his shoulders, her short nails biting into his skin. "Don't leave me, Rio," she said, her chest rising with her quickened breath. "Please, whatever demons you have, let them rest tonight and stay with me."

He shook his head, his long hair brushing across her bare breasts. "Why do you want me, Mercy? After everything I've shown you, the things you know about me? How can you still want me?"

She stared into his face, her fingers clutching his arms. "I love you *because* of those things—*because* you can still love and care and exist in the very face of that kind of life." Her blond hair shimmered in the pale light as she sat up straighter, pulling the sheet up around her. "I had everything, Rio, absolutely *everything*, that I ever wanted. You had nothing, but in spite of that, you still care—just like I do. You care about people, you care what happens to them, you care—whether or not you can admit it, you care. That's why you do what you do."

Her eyes, those startling blue eyes that seemed as if a light glowed behind them, grabbed his and refused to let go. "That tells me something, Rio. It tells me you're more than you admit to—and *that's* what I love."

The last word she spoke seemed to echo in the silence of the still, small room, and Rio realized he'd been holding his breath. He let it out in a rush to speak in a tortured voice. "This isn't love, Mercy. It *can't* be love."

Through the open window, a night bird's song pierced the silence, but Mercy's eyes never left his face. "You can call it whatever you want to," she said. Her hand clutched his shoulder, and he felt the touch twist inside of him with blinding resolution. It was as if she'd held a hot poker to his skin and branded him. "Name it what you will. But don't deny it."

In the silver light from the window, Mercy watched the play of emotions cross Rio's face. She knew she'd spoken the truth, and nothing he did or didn't do now would make any difference. For one long minute, she was sure he would stand and leave, rise, like dark smoke from a chimney, and disappear out her window as silently as he'd come. She braced herself, but he didn't move. He sat as still as if carved from a piece of Texas granite, the only movement in the room his hair as the hot breeze picked it up, then sent it fluttering across his shoulders.

"You're absolutely right," he finally said. His voice was a weary acknowledgment, like that of a drunk who was reaching for the bottle but cursing himself while he did. "But what in the hell are we going to do about it?"

Mercy released the breath she'd been holding, then extended her arms, the sheet dropping to her waist. Rio's eyes went down with it, then back up to her face. "We'll figure that out," she said evenly, "later."

He hesitated for only a heartbeat, then he groaned and pulled her into his arms, crushing her against his chest, his hands caressing her bare back with wild desperation. When his lips found hers, he demanded that she part them, and with willing agreement, she did. He took possession of her mouth and claimed it for his own, his tongue weaving over her lips, then plunging inside.

Rio's hands were everywhere at once, in her hair, at her throat, over her breasts. His touch demanded as much as it gave, and in an instant, she found herself responding, tearing at his clothes as if she were a madwoman. Never breaking the seal of their kiss, he struggled out of his shirt, then tore himself from her to rip off his pants. A second later, he was beside her, his lean form a dark outline in the paleness of the sheets.

He never stopped moving, his hands roaming over her body, forcing her to respond and arch against him. His mouth followed his touch, over her face, down her neck, to her breasts, where he cupped their fullness, then brought his lips to each nipple, pulling it into erect awareness of his attentions. She gasped and pushed against him, her own hands clawing at his back, urging him on, her eyes closed as if to block out everything else.

Time and place turned into dimensions that held no interest. Nothing could have stopped them now. They were completely oblivious to the rest of the world, and their entire existence narrowed to the double bed. What Mercy asked for, Rio gave. What Rio needed, Mercy provided. They required nothing beyond themselves.

The urgency built within Mercy, built like a summer storm that had been brewing and forming for days, and when she knew she could hold it back no longer, she urged Rio on top of her, his heavy thighs wedging between her legs with a demand she eagerly met. He poised over her, the heat from his slick body a mirrored temperature of her own.

"Look at me," he commanded. "I want to see you."

Instantly, she opened her eyes, and her vision was filled with the clear gray coolness of his own. Even in the depths of Rio's passion, the chilling color of his eyes did not change. The expression on his face told her, however, what those cold eyes wouldn't.

He swallowed, the column of his muscular neck moving with the effort. "Tell me now," he said, poised between her legs, his hips taut with effort. "Tell me that you want me."

Her heart broke at the harsh denial in his voice. Even at this moment, he expected her to recant, to tell him it had all been a horrible mistake. Instead, she did the only thing possible. She wrapped her legs around him and lifted her hips to meet him, forcing him to plunge inside of her. He tensed, almost fighting her, then with a groan, he gave in. With a pounding intensity that made her mad with desire, he drove against her—over and over and over.

For Mercy, at that moment, life ceased to exist. She dropped into a place where the only sensation was Rio's hard length inside of her, rocking her back and forth. She knew nothing but that fullness, that feeling, that only a woman knows when the man she loves is within her. She reveled in it, she absorbed it and then she gave in to it, the rhythm of his body demanding that she release everything to him.

She drew him closer, and their bodies fused into a single expression of desire, united by their growing emotion and awareness of each other.

Rio finally collapsed against her, then rolled to one side, his chest rising and falling with the effort of their

lovemaking as he pulled her to his side. She buried her
face into the crook of his neck and took a deep breath,
willing her heart to slow, her pulse to stop racing. Finally, at length, the beat took on a more normal rhythm.
She curled against him and absorbed his heat, needing
nothing more, allowing nothing less. She trusted him
with her body. She trusted him with her heart.

Did his secrets really matter?

Chapter 11

When she heard the clock strike seven, Mercy woke. Rio was still beside her.

For a moment, she didn't move. Instead, she stared at him, savoring the luxury of observing him without those gray eyes watching her.

He was stretched out on the bed, his lean form too long for the mattress, the sheets tangled around his legs. A ray of sunshine striped his bare chest, and in the light, his smooth muscles gleamed like burnished copper. A stubble, even darker than it had been last night, shadowed his cheeks and gave him a rough, dangerous look.

Mercy held her breath. It wasn't just a look; it was reality. Rio *was* a dangerous man. He'd proved that the night they'd met and every time they'd been together since. But somewhere between then and now, she'd learned that underneath that patina, he cared. In fact, he cared *too* much.

As if he'd sensed her thoughts, he frowned, his expression going into lines of quiet intensity. With his next breath, he turned his head against the pillow and reached out for her. When his fingers found Mercy's hair, they tangled in it, then tightened as if he wanted to bind her closer to him. He didn't relax, not even in sleep, she realized with her heart in her throat. What kind of life did you lead if you had to guard against loss while you slept?

Without warning, Rio opened his eyes. In the cool gray depths, there was instant vigilance, so intense, so extraordinary, that it stole her breath. He didn't move a muscle.

"You're awake," he said, his voice husky and low.

"So are you," she answered with fascination. "I've never seen anyone simply open their eyes and be that aware. One minute you were asleep, and the next awake. That's amazing."

He blinked then and slowly raised his arms up over his head. Grabbing the top of her headboard, he stretched his arms out, the ropy muscles rising into sharp relief. "It's not amazing," he said. "It's called survival."

Seduced by the strength in his arms and chest, Mercy watched as he clasped his hands together, then stretched once more. His words finally soaked in. "Survival?"

"When you grow up in an orphanage, you learn to wake up fast. If you don't, you might not get any breakfast."

Mercy rolled to her side and propped up her head with one hand, pulling the sheet up around her. "Was it hard? Growing up there, I mean?"

He shrugged his shoulders, his face knotting into his familiar closed expression. He answered, albeit reluctantly, "I'm sure there are tougher ways, but I don't know them."

"Sister Rosa doesn't strike me as being that much of a curmudgeon."

He frowned slightly, as though remembering something from a long time ago. "She isn't, but the mother superior was. She ran that place with an iron fist. Every kid there was scared to death of her."

"And that's why you go sit by her side now that she's dying. Because she was a mean old lady you hated."

Rio's eyes jerked to her face. "Who told you that I do that?"

"Sister Rosa."

He lifted his dark eyebrows. "She tells my secrets. I'll have to go over there and straighten her out."

"I don't think anyone could 'straighten out' Sister Rosa. Not even you."

He smiled briefly, then leaned against the headboard, his hands tucked behind his head. "You're probably right," he admitted. "She would be a formidable adversary."

"That's why you're hiding Paco there, isn't it? Because you know she'll protect him."

Rio looked down at her, surprise darkening his face. He started to speak, then just shook his head. He wouldn't answer her question, but the gleam in his eye told her all she needed to know. She took a deep breath of relief, then refocused. "Was Sister Rosa the one who encouraged you to leave Ciudad?"

His eyebrows arched. "What didn't she tell you?"

Mercy grinned. "Someone helped you get out of here. It must have been her."

"It wasn't Sister Rosa," he finally admitted. "It was the mother superior. She went to the University of Texas before joining the order. When I graduated from high school, she was determined that I go to college, too." He looked out the window, his eyes unfocused. "She got me a scholarship from the diocese, held a bake sale to buy me an old truck, then sponsored a raffle to get me some new clothes and my books." He picked up his knife from the nightstand beside the bed and absentmindedly tested the blade. "I owe her," he said in a faraway voice. "I owe that whole convent whatever they ask."

For some reason—the inflection of his voice, the unconscious pain in his face—Mercy thought of Sister Rosa's tale of the injured illegals who had been coming to the convent. A knot closed around Mercy's heart. Rio had something to do with that, something that wasn't good, and in that one quick moment, Mercy realized it. Just as she'd realized Blanco Sanchez was probably involved. When she'd met him at the restaurant, she'd known he had something to do with Rio's work, but she hadn't wanted to ask. She'd ignored it just as she'd ignored everything else lately. The time had come, though, the time to start asking the questions she should have been asking all along. Without conscious thought, she'd been puzzling over the missing pieces of Rio's life, and now they were starting to fall into place.

"You owe them," she repeated his words in a deceptively soft voice, almost as if she were talking to herself. "You owe them, and it has something to do with the people who've been assaulted coming across the river. I wonder—does Blanco Sanchez owe them, too?"

Her question immediately brought Rio out of his trance, and he flashed her a look of complete and total surprise. More than any words he could have spoken, his expression managed to confirm what Mercy had just suspected. Obviously realizing what he'd done, he threw off the sheets without saying a word, then abruptly swung his feet to the floor of the bedroom and stood.

The broad expanse of his naked shoulders and back was as straight and rigid as a bar of steel.

In the living room, the clock ticked off the minutes, but the sound was swallowed as the refrigerator kicked in, its hum filling the void. Mercy wished she could put her heart into a void also—a place where it wouldn't hurt and ache for the man who stood before her, the man whose own heart seemed to hold nothing but secrets and pain.

He picked up his jeans, thrusting his legs into them. Leaving them unbuttoned, he finally turned to face her, his expression unrelenting. "Stay out of it, Mercy." He reached toward the nearby table and picked up his knife, the ice in his voice matching his freezing eyes. "You should never have gotten involved—not with the nuns, not with Sanchez and certainly not with me." He shook his head, his dark hair brushing his shoulders, his voice taut with self-disgust. "It was a mistake for me to ever let this go this far." He paused, his gaze raking over her painful intensity. There was anguish behind his words, suffering that he felt as surely as she did.

Mercy stared at him, willing the tears in her eyes not to fall. "I'm already involved. I got involved the night you and I met and you held a knife to my throat. I got involved when you brought Paco here, and I lied to Greenwood for you." She paused, then spoke again, her voice strangling. "I got involved when we went to bed together."

He stood before her like a stone soldier, never blinking, never moving. If she hadn't known better, she would have thought he couldn't even hear her. Her voice wavered even more, but she ignored it. "In fact, I'm not just 'involved,' Rio. I love you."

His facade cracked. Anyone else might not have seen it, but Mercy did. For just a second, he wavered, an obvious war taking place behind the cool gray of his tortured eyes. Mercy watched him and cursed herself. She hadn't meant to say the words, but they'd escaped, and she couldn't take them back now. What did it matter, anyway? They were the truth.

Rio's lips—the lips that had met hers a hundred times—pursed into a straight, unrelenting line. "You *can't* love me, Mercy. I'm . . . I'm not what you think I am."

"You don't know what I think," she cried. "And if you did, you might be surprised." He continued to stare at her coldly, and unable to stop, Mercy spoke again, almost desperate this time. "Why can't you trust me, for God's sake?"

He looked at her for a long, slow moment, then he spoke. "I am *not* who or what you think I am. That is all I can tell you. To say more would jeopardize people's lives, including your own. I refuse to do that." His hand tightened on the hilt of the knife, and his expression softened imperceptibly. "You're a wonderful woman, Mercy, and I . . . I think more of you than I ever thought possible. A long time ago, I decided I couldn't have a normal life, couldn't love, couldn't feel, but you've proved that wrong." He swallowed hard, the effort of his control almost too much for Mercy to watch. Finally, he spoke again, and this time his voice had regained its tone of steel. "I'm sorry, though. I just can't tell you more."

For days afterward, Mercy relived the conversation, trying to wring from it any more bits of information that she might have missed. No matter what she did, however, nothing else came to light. She couldn't ask Rio any more, either. He'd made that more than clear.

Every night he came to her.

Every night they made love.

But every morning he was gone.

He wasn't going to give her another chance to look inside his soul, and slowly she began to realize that. It was difficult, though, one of the most difficult things she'd ever done, to not ask him the questions that rang in her head like so many bells: What was he doing for the nuns? Why had they asked him to help them? What was the connection with the injured illegals? What part did Blanco play, and even more importantly, what part did Greenwood play?

By the time she made her biweekly visit to the convent, Mercy was about to go mad with the puzzle her life had become. Seeing Rio at the mother superior's side did nothing to help.

"I didn't know you were coming here today," she said softly.

Deep in thought, he startled slightly. It had been a long time since anyone had managed to get that close to him without his knowledge. With a weary hand, he rubbed his eyes. For the past few months, the days had been too long and the nights too short. He dropped his fingers and stared at the woman he'd come to love.

He'd loved her since the first moment he'd seen her, standing in the moonlight that hot summer night, staring down at the river. If he'd had any sense at all, he would have crawled off into the desert and tended his own wounds then—it would have been less painful than what he was going through now. And losing her was going to be even more agony.

It would happen, too. As surely as the sun would rise tomorrow, she would leave him the minute she found out.

He'd tried to prepare himself for that eventuality by distancing himself from her, but every time he pulled back, she inched forward, pulling him closer to her. She refused to realize that he wasn't good enough for her, and without telling her the truth of his existence, he knew she'd never give up. And at this point, he just couldn't do it.

Her blue eyes caressed him for a moment as though she could see the torture he was going through, then they shifted to the frail woman in the bed. Bending over, Mercy gently lifted a lock of pale gray hair from the mother superior's forehead. "And how are you doing today?" she questioned softly.

Putting aside his useless thoughts, Rio looked at the elderly nun. It was hard to reconcile the body in the bed, wasted by illness, with the vibrancy of the forceful woman she'd once been. He squeezed her fingers gently, and her eyes fluttered open. Mercy's eyes darted to his in obvious surprise.

"Does she always respond to you?"

Rio shrugged his shoulders. "Not all the time—she knows I'm here, though."

Mercy nodded thoughtfully, her gaze going back to the sickly nun. "Are you in any pain, Mother?"

A fragile smile lifted the nun's lips, and she moved her head against the pillow, so slightly that Rio would have missed the movement from anyone else. "No," she whispered. Her watery eyes swung from Mercy's face to Rio's. "Have you told her?" she said cryptically.

Her implication was obvious—to Rio. His gut tightened immediately. He'd asked Sister Rosa not to tell the mother superior what was happening—she didn't need to be troubled by the outside world now—but the good sister had obviously disagreed. "She enjoys hearing about you," Sister Rosa had said. "She *wants* to know, and you know how she is—if she asks, I have to answer."

As if she could read the struggle going on inside him, the nun struggled to speak once more. "Rio, you must tell her... father... important." The nun's fingers, as slender and frail as the reeds by the river, clutched at his hand. "I... I insist...." Her voice trailed off, and her eyelids fluttered down. She'd obviously exhausted every ounce of her effort in saying even those few words.

Mercy flashed Rio another look, then began to tuck the sheets around the slight form of the nun. "You need to rest, Mother," she said softly. "You should conserve your energy."

One more time, the mother superior's eyes struggled open. She ignored Mercy's words, choosing instead to pin Rio with a steady but weak gaze. She tried to speak but couldn't, and Rio felt tears spring into his eyes. She didn't have to talk, though, because Rio knew exactly what she was communicating. He met her eyes, then nodded once. With a sweet smile, she allowed her eyes to close.

Rio stood. Across the bed, Mercy stared at him, her obvious questions turning her blue eyes dark with curiosity. Their gazes locked, and for one long second, Rio was torn. He loved her, he wanted to trust her... but it would be pointless, especially when she found out the truth. In the next heartbeat, he turned and left. He would give the dying woman his last breath if it would help her... but he couldn't tell Mercy his secret.

* * *

The dark expanse of the river wrapped around the dozen men like a blanket, hot and suffocating. The heat was so intense that even the water did nothing to help—it was as warm as the air. In the sluggish night, they moved slowly, but their eyes darted.

Rio was the first to cross, and as his feet dug into the opposite bank, he felt a rush of pure adrenaline. He'd been waiting for weeks, but tonight was the night . . . he knew it . . . he tasted it. He turned his head and watched the others scramble up the small incline behind him. They'd been a good group, had done exactly as he'd told them to, and the action was about to begin. Greenwood didn't have a chance.

An ironic smile lifted one corner of Rio's mouth as his eyes caught a flash of white. Blanco. He was predictable as a rattlesnake, but tonight, even he had chosen to show up. Almost as much as Rio, he wanted a taste of the sheriff's blood. *Almost,* Rio thought to himself, *almost but not quite.*

The hate that corroded Rio's heart had been there ever since he could remember, starting with the schoolyard taunts that still rang in his ears. He hadn't understood at first, wasn't even sure the other kids knew what the word meant, either. To them, *bastard* was simply another name they could call someone. When Sister Rosa had gently explained, however, Rio had understood . . . understood and hated. No, no one could hate Greenwood as much as he did. No one had the reason Rio did.

The man with the white streak in his hair obviously sensed Rio's stare, and he lifted his head, the movement pulling Rio back into the present. The night was dark, with a moon that came and went, but nothing could have hidden the flash of Blanco's smile. He lifted his thumbs up in a sign that everything was all right.

Rio's stomach clenched at the sign. Things were okay now... but would they stay that way? With Blanco around, you could never tell. Rio put his mistrust behind him—there was nothing else he *could* do—and lifted his hand, pointing toward the tall grass. Blanco nodded once, then turned and spoke to the ragged group of men behind him. In an instant, they'd fanned out, a thin line of hope, wet and nervous. Several matches flared as cigarettes were lit, and Rio grinned to himself. Blanco knew what he was doing, that was for sure.

For several minutes they waited, talking softly among themselves, anxious laughter sometimes breaking the uneasy silence. As he crouched in the grass, waiting like a dark, sleek panther on the front edge of the river, Rio glanced toward Mercy's cabin. Her lights were off. What was she doing? If she looked out, could she see them?

His stomach tightened at the thought. She was too smart; she'd realized he wouldn't answer any more of her questions, so she'd simply begun to put it all together—without his help. She'd made that much clear when she'd figured out where he'd taken Paco. The thought shot through his mind that he probably should have told her the whole truth from the very beginning, that he should have let her know exactly who and what he was, but in the next instant, he knew he couldn't. Not until Greenwood was dealt with...

Suddenly, Rio's eyes were jerked to the highway by a moving set of headlights, growing larger as they approached. Someone was coming. His head twisted toward the group of men, but he didn't have to tell them. They'd seen the lights also, and a vigilant expectancy rose from them, like a mist off the river. Instantly, Rio's heart began to pump in earnest. The outline of the Bronco was clearly visible, and there was no mistaking the tall silhouette sitting behind the wheel. Even in the dark, Rio could recognize Greenwood—just as he'd seen him a thousand times in his dreams.

The truck slowed as it approached the riverbank, and from his vantage point, Rio could see that the sheriff had his window rolled down. In an arc from the steering wheel to the outside of the car door, the red glow of a cigarette ember moved, like a miniature shooting star. Greenwood was adjusting the spotlight attached to his vehicle.

A rush of energy, druglike in its intensity, jettisoned into Rio's veins with shocking speed. He glanced toward Blanco. In the dark, all he could see was the white streak move—he'd seen Greenwood's motion, too, and he knew, as well as Rio, what was about to happen.

Rio melted back into the grass, his breath ragged and torn as he sought the refuge of the greenery. A second later, it happened. Pure white light burst into the clearing with cutting clarity, outlining every man in stark detail. They threw up their hands and started instantly jabbering in Spanish, their fear, Rio knew, not counterfeit. Simultaneously, Greenwood threw open his car door and started to yell, his deep Texas drawl snaking across the space with venomous orders to stay still.

He was alone, for once, his deputy nowhere to be seen, and Rio let his eyes briefly close in relief. It would make the whole operation go that much smoother. When Rio's eyes opened again, Greenwood was out of the truck, his weapon in his hand, his voice booming as the men milled in mock confusion, one or two of them actually darting into the night. One ran past Rio, and he recognized the slim form, giving the man the high sign as he dashed past. He nodded, then ignored Rio, continuing on, his spring gaining speed as he cleared the range of Greenwood's pistol.

Rio turned his attention back to the center of the clearing, his pulse pounding in his ears so loudly he thought it might give him away. Greenwood was waving the gun and ordering them all to lie down. Rio's jaw tightened as he watched the remaining men, Blanco included, stretch out in the dusty night.

Slowly, Greenwood walked along the outer ring of men, his weapon drawn, his invectives continuing. Anger and prejudice bubbled in him like poison, spewing over the men at his feet. Rio inched closer to the circle of men. This was what he'd been waiting for, been hoping for, and the hand that gripped his knife didn't shake.

Finally, Greenwood stopped beside Blanco, and Rio grew still also. "Roll over," the uniformed man ordered, with a vicious kick to Blanco's side. "You! Right now!"

Rio winced in sympathy, but Blanco remained still. He was baiting Greenwood, drawing him out, and even though Blanco enjoyed that kind of thing, Rio couldn't help but hold his breath. How far would Blanco go? To almost any length, Rio realized as Greenwood drew back his pointed boot once more and Blanco rolled over in the dirt, his hands splayed.

"What's the problem, *amigo?*" He grinned as though he'd just heard a good joke. "We're just taking a little walk."

"Yeah," Greenwood growled. "A little walk across the river, eh?" He prodded Blanco with the tip of his boot. "And what's that around your waist? You always take a load of dope and five friends with you when you take a walk?"

Rio watched Blanco widen his eyes. "Dope?" He shook his head vigorously. "No, no. No drugs—not me."

"Then what is that?" Greenwood pointed his gun toward Blanco's waist. "A girdle?" He chuckled in appreciation of his own joke, looking around as if the others should laugh also. They glared at him stonily.

Blanco furrowed his brow. "It's...it's nothing, *señor*. Nothing important."

Without warning, Greenwood pulled back his foot and delivered a vicious kick to Blanco's side. As Blanco grabbed his ribs and rolled over, Rio's fingers clenched on his knife. God, how he wished he could just stand up and let it fly! His teeth ground with the effort of staying still.

"Get up, you lazy wet," Greenwood said with an icy calmness. "And take off that shirt. I know you've got drugs in there, and I intend on relieving you of your burden."

With a groan, Blanco stood uncertainly, his fingers fumbling with the buttons on his shirt. Blanco was trying to give him plenty of time, Rio realized, and he put it to good use, coming nearer the circle until he was almost directly in front of them both but still hidden by the darkness. Two seconds later, Blanco tore off the Velcro-snapped wallet that had been around his waist, and despite his obvious pain, he threw it at Greenwood's feet with a cagey smile.

"There you are, my friend," Blanco said in a deadly smooth voice. "Take whatever you want."

For a second, Rio thought Blanco had gone too far, pushed Greenwood past the limit, but Rio misjudged the sheriff's greed. The man bent over and snatched up the belt, his fingers tearing into the money that Rio had put there himself.

"Very good. It *is* money, not dope," Greenwood said, his head nodding. "For once, I found a greaser who wasn't lying." Rio watched Blanco's face tense and grow pale at the insult, and his heart clutched. If Blanco let Greenwood get to him, the whole operation would go up in flames.

Blanco had his right arm around his waist, holding the side where Greenwood had kicked him. His fingers tightened until even Rio could see the white of his knuckles. In the black of the night, his eyes glittered dangerously. "The truth?" he repeated in a deadly calm voice. "Is that all you want, *señor?* How about this? You're a rotten, stinking son of a bitch, and your time is coming to an end. You've just screwed your last *wet.*"

Rio shut his eyes and wished he could close his ears. Why in heaven's name was Blanco doing this? He was going to pay for it with his life.

Greenwood raised his head slowly from the wallet of money. In Blanco's eyes, Rio could see a reflection of hatred—his own, Greenwood's, Rio's—who knew? All he *did* know was that the time had come. Greenwood had taken the money, Rio had seen him do it, justice was about to be served. Without thinking further, he stepped forward into the circle of light. Startled, Greenwood jerked his eyes from Blanco to Rio. A second later, the sheriff fired.

She was standing on the porch when she heard the shot.

Mercy froze, the fingers she had wrapped around a coffee mug squeezing the china so hard it should have shattered.

It didn't. But her heart did.

She knew instinctively what the sound of the gun meant. She knew it involved Rio, and she knew it involved Greenwood.

In an instant, she put down her coffee mug on the railing of the porch, turned and ran inside. She had to contain her panic, had to keep it in control, or she would never manage to get to the river. Over and over, she told herself she was a doctor, trained to handle emergencies, but her heart didn't hear the admonition. It hurtled itself against her chest in what almost seemed like an angry attempt to leave without her. On legs that barely held her up, she rushed to her closet for the small black bag her father had given her when she'd graduated from medical school. Inside were the barest of necessities . . . not enough to keep the man she loved alive.

With that one thought, her false composure collapsed. She grabbed the bag with a single helpless cry and dashed out the door, stumbling in the darkness in her haste. She had no idea what waited for her at the river, but she knew whatever it was, it wasn't good.

In the past few weeks, especially since she'd seen him at the mother superior's bedside, Rio had been a storm, building daily, and she'd been hopeless to do anything but watch. The gunshot signified that the tempest had finally broken. The damage was about to begin.

Her sandals slipped over the dusty ground, providing no traction, but she continued at a breakneck speed, small bushes and rough terrain ignored. Her bag bounced against her side, and with each hit, Mercy issued a prayer. *Let me be wrong, dear God. Please don't let it be him, please. Don't let me find him bleeding or...*

By the time she reached the tall grass near the riverside, her vision had finally adjusted to the darkness. Still she saw nothing until a flash of movement caught her eye. With it, she heard the first of the voices. They were angry and raised in violence. With a catch in her throat, she recognized Rio's deep timbre. Her knees turned to water. At least he was still alive.

Her breath died in her throat, but she forged ahead, mindless of any danger to herself. Using only the sound of the voices to guide her, Mercy stumbled toward the river.

As long as she lived, she'd never forget the moment she came upon them.

Like a piercing arrow, Rio's eyes immediately locked on hers, his knife never wavering from Greenwood's neck. "What in the hell are you doing here?"

Mercy froze in stunned silence. Even her blood seemed to stop after it drained from her face, leaving her cold and senseless. Rio and Greenwood were poised in a violent embrace. A third man lay at their feet. As Mercy's eyes swept over him, they registered the blood on his shirt, the agony in his posture, the groan coming from his lips. She couldn't see the wound itself, but she saw a flash of white in the darkness of his hair, and with a shock she realized who he was—Blanco Sanchez.

She lifted her face once more to Rio and Greenwood. For the first time, she saw the blood on Rio's shirt. Was it his...or someone else's? Her heart tumbled into action, bringing her back to life with a jolt. "Are...are you hurt?"

Rio's eyes blinked suddenly, but before he could answer, Greenwood laughed. "He's all right, Doctor. Don't you know it's hard to kill a snake?"

In the dim light of the dying moon, Mercy flicked her eyes between the two men. The point of Rio's knife was digging into Greenwood's throat, not cutting him but close. The cold steel gleamed darkly with an obscene stain... and the hand that held it was bloody, too. Her concern turned to confusion. Who was hurt? Who'd drawn the first blood?

Rio spoke, his voice as cold as his face. "Get out of here, Mercy. Right now. Turn around and go back to your house."

"I heard the gunshot, Rio. I'm—"

The man at Rio's feet moaned, then rolled over slightly. She took one step forward, toward Blanco, but Rio's voice paralyzed her. "Leave him alone, Mercy. He doesn't need your help."

Before she could answer, Greenwood grunted with pain, and Mercy realized with a start that his sleeve was bloody, too. A long vertical slice up the uniform's fabric was all she needed to see to know what had happened. "You cut him!" she gasped, her eyes huge with disbelief. "Rio—he's a policeman!"

"He's scum, Mercy, and he deserves to die." Rio jerked his head toward the man in the dirt. "Greenwood just shot Blanco—that's what you heard. He was shaking him down, trying to get his money." The face that she'd caressed with love and gentleness now turned into a mask of hate that chilled her. "That's what he does, you see. He finds poor peasants who don't have crap, and then he uses his uniform and his power to scare then half to death. The ones who don't have the good sense to comply get a worse fate." His arm tightened across Greenwood's neck. "Unfortunately, I'm not the judge and jury, or he'd die the kind of death he deserves. I'm only the—"

"Don't listen to him, Dr. Hamilton." Greenwood's ragged voice cut into Rio's voice. "*He* sliced Blanco—I saw it—I was here trying to help and..."

Confusion swamped Mercy like a tidal wave, leaving in its wake tatters of reality. She started to back up, to put some distance between herself and the deceptiveness that was swirling around her. There were other voices behind her, a group of men, but she didn't know who they were, and she couldn't tear her eyes from the man she loved...the man who'd clearly gotten in over his head.

Greenwood spoke again. "If you turn right now and run away from here, you might just get away, Dr. Hamilton. You might make it to your cabin, where you can pick up your phone and call my office." His voice had regained some strength, and it was level and steady—not the voice you'd expect from a man with a knife at his throat.

Stumbling to a stop, Mercy flicked her eyes to Rio's, but he only stared at her in stony silence. Greenwood spoke again. "He's a ruthless killer, and he's been lying to you since the day he showed up at your house."

Mercy felt her eyes go wide, and Greenwood laughed—a short bark with no humor. "Yeah, I knew he'd been there, but I couldn't prove it. Why do you think I was telling everyone to stay away from the clinic? I was trying to get you out of there. Now he's lying again. *He's* the one who's been shaking down the wetbacks for months now, taking their money, beating them up. I've been on his trail, I know. He's preying on innocent people. He seeks out weak ones, just like he sniffed out you—"

Mercy stuttered, her voice revealing her growing bewilderment. "I...I don't—"

"I understand," he said silkily, still in control. "Believe me, Dr. Hamilton, I understand. A woman like you—all alone—helpless." He moved slightly in Rio's grip and tried to look at him. "He's slick, and he took advantage of you . . . told you some tales, I'd imagine. You can still get out of this mess, though. You can go get me help. I'll make sure you're rewarded. . . ."

Mercy's forehead wrinkled in uncertainty. He was offering her a way out, an excuse, in exchange for helping him. Her eyes begging Rio to deny Greenwood's words, she looked at the man she loved. The wall he kept around him, however, was beyond penetration. He'd said all he was going to say.

"Decent men don't get their way with knives." Ignoring the blade at his throat, Greenwood spoke again, his badge winking in the moonlight that had suddenly broken through the clouds. "I *know* what kind of man Rio Barrigan is. I've seen him grow up, I've seen him turn bad." He closed his eyes as though he wanted to block out the images, then opened them again. For the first time, Mercy realized with a start, she was really seeing his eyes, not his sunglasses, and they were light gray. Incongruously something about them seemed familiar, almost reassuring. "You can help me."

A thread of doubt wound itself around Mercy's heart. Almost everything Greenwood was saying was true. Rio *was* ruthless, he *was a coyote, his childhood had* been terrible. It was completely understandable that he'd become the man he was.

But she loved him.

She looked at Rio again. "What's going on here, Rio?" Her voice was low, soft and questioning as their eyes locked.

As with every other question she'd posed to him, Mercy didn't expect him to answer. This time, though, he did.

"I work for the United States government, Mercy. I'm a special agent with the Immigration and Naturalization Services."

The world tipped and skewed sideways, his words going with it, sliding into a hole that he'd dug himself. Mercy gaped at him, her mind picking up the pieces and snapping them into the puzzle with wild abandon. It could explain so many things—his secrecy, his coming and going, the contradiction of his care versus his "profession." Still it seemed too much for her to comprehend. "A special agent?" she repeated in a dazed voice.

Greenwood's laugh broke the silence. "That's ridiculous, Doctor. You don't actually believe that, do you?" Greenwood nodded toward Blanco. "They were fighting, and I came up on them. Fired my gun, tried to stop them, but this maniac came after me with his knife. He's no more an agent of the government than the man on the moon." He jerked forward, but the tip of Rio's knife held him back—held him back so well that a dark spot of red welled up at its point. "What kind of special agent would do this?" he cried. "There's procedures, there's rules to the game. He's a vicious animal, not a special agent!"

Mesmerized, Mercy stared at the single drop of blood as it slid down Greenwood's neck and onto Rio's fingers, connecting them in a bizarre link that she knew she'd never forget—just as she wouldn't forget the look of blazing hatred that knotted Rio's face every time he'd mentioned Greenwood's name in the past. With a start, she realized Rio was speaking to her.

"Greenwood is behind the shakedowns, Mercy. I've been down here trying to catch him. He'd already shot Blanco when I ambushed him—he was getting away—I had to stop him." His voice took on a desperate quality, something she'd never heard before. "Don't you see? I had to pose as a *coyote* to get him. I couldn't tell you. I couldn't tell anyone."

In a daze, she asked, "And the men you brought across? Are they pawns in this cat-and-mouse game?"

"They're *federales*—Mexican policemen. They wanted to help catch Greenwood as much as we did. They're calling in for reinforcements now. They'll be here any minute. Don't you hear them behind you?"

Greenwood barked out a harsh laugh. "My God, Barrigan! You've thought of everything, haven't you? And you even got lucky in the process!" His eyes turned toward Mercy, and in the moonlight, they almost seemed sympathetic. "You've been taken for a ride, little lady, in more ways than one."

Slowly, Mercy felt her heart crack. It was a tiny fissure, then the separation grew wider and wider, the pain so intense she thought she might actually faint from the agony. She stepped closer to the two men and looked Rio straight in the eyes, knowing her confusion and indecision darkened their depths.

She loved Rio, loved him desperately, but she'd always known he had secrets. Deep, dark, dangerous secrets. Secrets that could kill.

Rio stared at her, and in that second, he read her thoughts as unmistakably as though she'd spoken them. He'd done it in the past and he was doing it now.

She didn't completely believe Greenwood, but she doubted Rio. And that was all he needed to know.

He closed his eyes against the anguish, his heart ripping out of his chest with searing wretchedness.

He'd tried to tell himself she was different—that she would believe him, that she did love him. He'd been fooling himself all along, trying to have her *and* finish off Greenwood.

He'd been wrong.

Behind him, he heard the distant scream of racing tires, then seconds later, dust rose around them in a choking cloud. The vehicle's engine cut, and excited voices, mostly in Spanish, rose in animated confusion. Rio gave Mercy one last look, then, never breaking his stare, he dropped the knife from Greenwood's throat and pushed the older man toward the spotlights suddenly blazing from the truck.

For years, Rio had worked toward this moment, consciously and *unconsciously*. In his dreams, he'd imagined it. In his nightmares, he'd bungled it. Now he didn't even care. He'd gotten everything he wanted, and he'd sacrificed everything that mattered. He'd won—and he'd lost.

Mercy's face drained of blood, turning into a white oval of shock and disbelief, her eyes two dark spots of chaos. They jerked from Rio to his side, where uniformed men rushed up and handcuffed Greenwood before leading him toward the dark green INS truck. At the same time, two medics appeared beside Blanco and began to tend to him. Rio forced his gaze back to hers. He'd wanted to love her, but he'd been wrong. As the situation became clearer, she reached out toward him . . . but it was too late.

Her voice cracked, and so did his heart. "I . . . I'm sorry, Rio. I . . . I saw the blood on your knife . . . I . . . I thought—"

"I know what you thought," Rio said harshly, his voice a pain-filled slash across the darkness. "You thought *exactly* what I knew you would."

He turned and disappeared into the dark.

Chapter 12

Mercy's pain had stages.

The first one was shock.

Completely numb and paralyzed with confusion, she allowed one of the "illegals," a man who, in reality, worked for the Mexican government, to escort her home. In silent disapproval, he walked by her side to her porch, then disappeared back toward the river without saying a word. Mercy stared after him dumbly, unable to ask questions, unwilling to face reality.

The second stage was rage. For days after the event, she angrily paced her porch. With each step, she cursed Rio Barrigan. He'd lied to her, he'd used her, he'd taken advantage of her. She repeated this mantra over and over, her head screaming with invectives against the absent man she thought she'd loved.

When she used up every drop of righteous wrath she

had, the next step came. It was grief, and in it, she floundered, a drowning woman without a life jacket.

She cried so much that her eyes were almost swollen shut. When she would finally manage to stop sobbing and make it out to the clinic, she'd only last for an hour or so, and then the sorrow would return, leaving silent tracks of tears running down her cheeks.

By the end of the second week, Mercy was a wreck—a total, absolute wreck.

Friday night found her sitting on the front porch. Actually, she thought with blank distraction, it was Saturday morning—3:00 a.m. on Saturday morning. The darkest hour, the time when nothing seems possible, when everything hurts the most. Her hands twisted in the black lace mantilla that Rio had bought her, its soft folds wrapping around her fingers like gauze. The beautiful bandage didn't insulate her from the pain, however. Her eyes were dry now—she'd already cried every tear she had—and they stared out over the dusty landscape, the bleak horizon mirroring the desolation in her heart.

Rio was gone.

In his place, there was a single image, one that had haunted her throughout the past two weeks. She couldn't get out of her mind the impression of his face when she'd had that one flash of doubt. He'd read the emotion before she even consciously conceived it, before she was even aware of it herself. The misgiving had come, then fled, an ephemeral question more than a thought, really, but that didn't matter, a fact that Mercy realized now. Rio had seen it, had understood her suspicion, and that was all he cared about. Her hands went into fists, and they beat her knees with useless frustration, the dull thud swallowed up in the moonless night.

She couldn't make sense of her own actions. She'd tried during these horrible weeks, but nothing had worked. She told herself that it was her upbringing. She'd been raised to see law officials as good, honest people, people she could trust and depend upon, people she should respect over everyone else.

She told herself it'd been shock—the shock of seeing Rio hold the knife to Greenwood's throat, the certainty that he'd already slashed him.

She shook her head with disgust and stood, the forgotten veil dropping to her feet. Watching it glide down like a lacy shadow, Mercy felt her heart plummet with it. Rio was gone. Did it really matter now why she'd done what she'd done? It all boiled down to one thing. She'd made a mistake—the biggest mistake of her life—and nothing she did was going to change it.

Rio was gone.

Her throat tight with misery and unshed tears, she bent over and picked up the mantilla. Rising once more, she turned and shuffled back to her screen door. Her fingers curled around the rusty handle, but before she could pull the door open, she looked over her shoulder, once again, into the hot, humid night. Her eyes searched the tall grass by the river, then moved toward the arroyo near the back. Empty black stillness returned her gaze. Nothing moved.

Rio was gone.

The first hint of autumn tinged the air. Mercy stood near the back of the crowd, feeling strangely out of place as the nuns silently told their beloved mother superior goodbye. She'd died, at last, in her sleep, slipping her earthly ties with dignity.

One by one, the women eased toward the simple coffin, the breeze stirring the branches of the water oak above their covered heads. Some put their hands briefly on the top of the wooden casket as though reluctant to turn loose, but most of them bowed their heads for a second, crossed themselves, then slipped quietly away. Mercy watched, awed by the calm on their faces. They'd loved her, but they knew her time to move on had come.

Mercy wished for a measure of their serenity. She still mourned.

Rio had been gone exactly one month.

As much as she'd hated to admit it, Mercy thought the funeral might bring him back, but the only man at the service had been the traveling priest. Her sore heart had cracked a little more, but she'd hardly felt the pain. She was almost inured to it now.

The last of the nuns walked up to the coffin, and a second later, Mercy turned away. She was pulled from her own grief by the look on Sister Rosa's face. Without thinking, she automatically went to the older woman and placed her hand on her arm.

The nun's face was lined with bereavement, and silently the two women embraced.

"I'm glad you came," she said after they broke apart. "You were the only person who knew how brave she was those last few months."

Mercy spoke softly, dappled sunlight dancing over them. "She *was* brave." Her eyes left the grave site and focused on the river just beyond. "A lot braver than a lot of people I know."

Sister Rosa stared at her quietly, then the tables turned. She put her hand on Mercy's arm, the bereaved now comforting the lost. When she spoke, her voice was a subtle reprimand. "You've got to stop beating up on yourself, Mercy. You made the only decision you could with the information you had."

Mercy turned back to the nun, but the black-and-white figure seemed to waver in her tear-filled eyes. Mercy hadn't realized she was so transparent. "I should have believed him," she whispered. "I... I loved him, but I didn't trust him."

Silently, the nun nodded and draped her arm around Mercy's shoulders, guiding her toward a low bench facing the water. She didn't speak, but her quiet understanding took over, and suddenly Mercy wished her tears were as noiseless—but they weren't. By the time they'd reached the serenity of the garden seat, her crying wouldn't stop, and her racking sobs broke the peaceful setting.

The nun had worn her old-fashioned habit today out of respect for the occasion, and as she held Mercy, great wings of black enfolded her in a gentle, forgiving hug. Sister Rosa said nothing. All she did was hold Mercy and pat her back, her hand occasionally stroking the length of braid that cascaded between Mercy's shoulders.

Mercy had thought she had no more tears left, but she'd been mistaken, as she had been about so many things. A fresh attack robbed her of her breath, and for a second, she could do nothing but snuffle against the starched fabric of Sister Rosa's veil. The nun tightened her arms and murmured words of comfort. Finally, finally, the tears dissolved into hiccups, the hiccups into sighs and the sighs into a hard lump that lodged against the back of Mercy's throat. It stayed there and burned with disappointment and overwhelming desolation.

Sister Rosa eased back and produced a lacy handkerchief from the folds of her habit, her expression drawn in sympathy. Hiding her face in its cotton freshness, Mercy took the square of fabric gratefully. She felt awful crying like this, especially in light of the nun's own grief. When she said so, Sister Rosa waved aside the comment.

"The mother superior's pain is over." She stared hard at Mercy's face. "Yours isn't." She paused, then spoke again. "Do you want to talk about it?"

"I . . . I'm not sure I can."

"I'm not sure you can't."

Mercy's eyes brimmed again, but the tears stayed there, shimmering in their fullness. "I don't know what to do." Mercy swallowed, the ache in her throat almost as painful as the one in her heart. "I let him down terribly, Sister Rosa. I . . . I didn't mean to, but everything was so confusing, so scary." She kept on, knowing what she was saying probably made no sense to the other woman, but the words had a mind of their own, spilling from her without direction. "Greenwood was there, and he sounded so convincing. Rio tried to explain that he worked for the INS, but it sounded so bizarre, so far-fetched, that I couldn't make sense of it. Before I could say anything, he'd assumed the worst. He's done that in the past—he reads my eyes and then . . ."

The nun nodded thoughtfully. "I know," she said simply. "Rio told me."

Hope exploded in Mercy's chest. Could it be? "When?"

"He told me right after it happened," the nun answered quietly. "The minute Greenwood was locked up, Rio came here."

Disappointment cut through Mercy with a sharpness rivaling that of Rio's knife. A tiny part of her had hoped he'd just been there, just come by. She was wishing for a dream, though. He wasn't here. He'd left. And he wasn't returning.

Sister Rosa looked at Mercy as though judging her, then she spoke. "Rio came back to Ciudad because we asked him to, Mercy." She adjusted the folds of her habit with a calm, soothing manner. Mercy watched her, her heart turning over. "He didn't want to return, but we— the nuns—called him and told him how bad things were. The illegals were coming into the convent, hurt and wounded. We knew he worked for the INS and knew there was no one else who would help us."

"You knew he worked for the INS?" The answer was obvious, but Mercy couldn't keep the incredulous question from popping out.

"Oh, yes. He's always stayed in touch with us. He'd never come home before, though."

"Until you asked him?"

"We *are* his only family, you know." Her voice held a gentle criticism as though Mercy should understand that fact already. Before Mercy could reply, the nun's face hardened into lines of deeper condemnation. "Well, actually, that's not entirely true, though God knows we all wish it were."

Uneasiness rippled over Mercy like the leading edges of a thunderstorm. "I thought Rio was an orphan. He told me his mother died, that he had no other family."

Sister Rosa nodded once, curtly. "That's partially true—his mother is dead. Unfortunately, however, his father isn't."

The bizarre words coming from the nun's prim lips hit Mercy—the first drops of the downpour. "You *know* who his father is?"

The starched veil moved once. "Yes," she said tightly. "And I wish to God I didn't." Her fingers tightened on the crease, turning it into sudden wrinkles. "And I *know* Rio wishes the same thing."

Mercy could no longer contain herself. "Well, who is it?"

The sister paused for only a moment, then she spit the name out as though it tasted bad. "Rick Greenwood."

Mercy blinked, the sheer senselessness of that reality one she couldn't absorb. "The sheriff?"

The nun nodded.

Mercy gripped the edge of the bench as her mouth fell open in total disbelief. "No," she said, her voice reflecting her horror. "That's not . . . it can't be. . . ."

"Yes, it *is* the truth, my dear." Sister Rosa's face reflected the disgust and aversion that was breaking over Mercy. "I know it's hard to believe. Greenwood is so horrible."

Mercy dropped her face into her hands and shook her head, the horror of the whole situation coming down over her. With a start, she realized why Greenwood's eyes had seemed familiar. She'd seen them lying across the pillow from her—in Rio's face!

She moaned. God! How could it have felt to arrest his own father? She didn't know which was worse—his past or his present. With a sob, she decided on his past. How could it have felt to grow up like that, to know our father hated you—hated you enough to try to kill you? To know that you had no one but yourself to depend on, no one but yourself to trust?

The word resounded in her head like thunder. *Trust.* The one thing she hadn't been able to give him...the one thing he needed the most.

She raised her stricken face to the sister's. "I didn't know...."

The nun reached over and squeezed Mercy's hand. "He didn't *want* you to know. If he had, he would have told you."

"But he *should* have told me," Mercy cried. "If I'd known, if I'd—"

Sister Rosa shook her head. "He couldn't tell you, Mercy. He couldn't tell you because it would have jeopardized the situation even more. If he'd told you he was an agent, if he'd told you about his father, it would have put everyone in danger, not just himself." She paused, her face tense with the effort that Mercy understand. "Rio would sacrifice anything—everything—before he'd hurt anyone during an operation like this. *That's* why you were kept in the dark."

Mercy felt her face crumple. "But if I'd known..."

"You would have done something different, I know, but what's done is done. You can't go back and change it now." The nun looked out over the garden, her face mirroring Mercy's pain. It was obvious how much she cared for Rio, too. "It's over," she said softly. "Let it go."

Rio let go of the branch of the weeping willow tree and stepped back from its swinging leaves. He'd heard enough.

He hadn't meant to eavesdrop, but when he'd seen Mercy standing in the dappled light of the cemetery, the sun glinting diamonds off her hair, he'd been shocked into stillness. The past few months had been torture for him—pure and simple torture—and to suddenly see her like this, talking to Sister Rosa, listening with those big blue eyes, well, the sight had damn near killed him.

He'd stayed, though. Stayed for the funeral, out of sight and out of earshot...until now. The mother superior had always told him he shouldn't eavesdrop, that he'd only hear ill of himself. Well, he'd heard the truth this time—something he'd been trying to avoid for years. And it hurt worse than a lie would. Hurt as bad as it had the first time he'd heard it.

He turned and strode away. Following the path behind the cemetery, he came out of the shade and headed for the river. Five minutes later, he reached the sluggish brown waters.

How had he fallen in love? So fast? So completely?

He sat down beside the slow-moving stream and picked up a handful of rocks. Staring at their wavering image, Rio blinked rapidly. How could you love someone and lose her—all in the space of a few seconds? He'd pondered the same question over and over in the weeks past, but he'd never come up with an answer.

His fingers tightened over the pebbles, their sharp edges biting into his palm. He *did* love her. He'd never told her, never even told *himself* until this very moment. Seeing her back there in the garden had been the trigger, though, and hearing Sister Rosa lay out his past like so many blocks of black-and-white tile had jolted him. Suddenly, he could deny it no longer. He loved Mercy Hamilton as he'd never loved anyone else in his life. She was good, and beautiful, and honest, and forthright, and he loved her.

In fact, he *loved* her as much as he had *hated* Greenwood.

The thought startled him, and for a moment, Rio couldn't catch his breath. *Had* hated him. Past tense.

His breath hooked in his throat for a moment, then he pulled in deep drafts of air like a drowning man. Was it possible? Was his hatred for the man gone? Had the control he'd held over Rio's life disappeared?

The night the operation had gone down, he'd felt nothing but betrayal. Mercy's inability to trust him had outweighed everything else, and the moment he'd awaited for so long had dissolved in the acid wash of disappointment. Even the next day, when he'd *personally* locked Greenwood into the county jail, Rio had felt empty of all emotion. They weren't a father and son. That was a reality so bizarre Rio had denied it since childhood, so locking the sheriff up had been like jailing any other petty criminal—a job, nothing more. The sense of accomplishment, the sense of relief, the sense of revenge he'd long savored—none of it had been there.

He hadn't realized until now how empty that feeling really was. Hatred for his father had occupied a tremendous space in his heart, and now that location had been excised. There was nothing left. Nothing left but hollowness.

He could leave it empty or he could fill it. Fill it with love.

Love for Mercy.

His fingers clenched the rocks with renewed confusion. With love came trust. Mercy hadn't trusted him before. Would she now? As soon as he had the thought, he knew the answer. If he'd told her the truth to begin with, had given her a *reason* to trust him, she would have. She'd told Sister Rosa that, and he believed her. The question was—was he ready for it? Could he give love, as well as receive it? Give it as freely as the mother superior had given it to an orphaned infant over thirty years ago?

Suddenly, he opened his hand and threw the rocks as hard as he could, relishing the physical release. Arcing in the bright sunlight, they curved toward the water, then splashed down, their rippling circles swallowed a second later by the torpid currents.

There was only one way to find out.

She was standing in the middle of the yard, staring toward the river. From his vantage point in the high grass, Rio took in her figure with greedy eyes.

A wash of moonlight covered her, highlighting her silvery hair and throwing shadows against the curves of her body. The night was hot, very hot, as though fall had changed its mind and retreated. As he watched, she lifted her hands. He knew before she'd raised them to her shoulders what she was going to do. It was a gesture he'd seen a thousand times, but it never failed to grab him. As though performing a choreographed dance, she completed the move, lifting her heavy hair off her shoulders and piling it on her head with her fingers. Rio wished he were the breeze as it kissed her neck. A second later, she dropped the heavy mass, sighed audibly, then turned and headed for the cabin.

Rio didn't hesitate.

In a flash, he was behind her, one hand on her arm, another at her neck. She gasped and swirled around, her perfume enveloping him in a forbidden haze as he locked his arms around her. For one blind moment, she panicked and fought, her fists against his chest, her breath coming in short, sweep gasps.

"Mercy, it's me," he said, her clenched hands hard against his chest. "It's Rio."

She continued to resist, her body tense in opposition to his, the curves he knew and loved molding against him as she hit ineffectually at his chest. He cried out her name again, then released her body and grabbed her wrists, pinning them high above her head. For a moment longer, she twisted and fought, trying to get loose, then finally, gulping for breath, she stopped her struggle and fell against him. Her chest heaving, she lifted her tear-streaked face to his.

They looked into each other's eyes—blue to gray, hot to cold, female to male—and a length of silent communication passed between them.

Rio acknowledged his mistakes.

Mercy admitted her doubts.

They stayed that way for another heartbeat, long enough to declare one more message—a message of love—then Mercy fell against his chest with a strangled sob.

Her arms pulled around his neck as she buried her face in the comfort of his embrace. Nothing mattered anymore.

Nothing.

Rio murmured words of love and understanding, his lips dropping fevered kisses on her hair, her eyelids, her cheeks. She clung to him and he to her.

Countless moments passed as they soundlessly made their pledges, then reluctantly, Rio pulled back and looked into her eyes, her face cradled in his hands.

"I'm sorry, Mercy. I'm sorry I didn't tell you the truth—"

She reached up and stopped his words, her finger soft against his lips. "I understand," she said instantly. "You couldn't."

He swallowed against the sudden lump in his throat, then bent his mouth to hers. The kiss was long and deep and said much more than any words. When she finally pulled away, he felt immediately bereft.

"You had no way of knowing what was going on," he said, looking into her eyes, "and you believed exactly what I'd led you into believing. I should have been surprised if you'd reacted any other way." He let his hand cup her face. "You deserved the truth, and because I didn't trust you, I gave you nothing but lies. Can you ever forgive me?"

"I'm the one who should be asking *your* forgiveness, Rio. That night..." She stopped, searching for the right words, a play of emotions crossing her face before she finally spoke again. "I...I didn't think Greenwood was telling the whole truth, but I didn't know what *to* believe. Things were so confused, so crazy. I saw the gun, I saw your knife. I didn't know what to think."

"Greenwood's a con man, and he had a uniform to back him up. Anyone would have believed him, and besides, I gave you no reason to trust me. There was a smoking gun, and unless you knew the whole story, you couldn't have understood." His hands slid to her arms, her velvet skin warm and inviting beneath his touch. "I...I thought he was going to kill Blanco. If I hadn't thrown my knife, Greenwood's aim would have been perfect, and Blanco would have been dead instead of suffering from some broken ribs and a bullet graze. I couldn't have let that happen."

"Who is Blanco?" she asked softly. "When I saw him in the restaurant, I thought you two were adversaries, but obviously, he was helping you that night. Now it sounds like he's more than just a friend."

Rio looked toward the river. "I guess you could say he's both. We go back a very long way—to the orphanage, in fact. For a while, we were like brothers. Blanco was the only kid there who seemed to understand me, but . . . along the way, we parted somehow." He turned and looked at her, wanting to hide from the truth, but knowing he no longer could. "When I chose the law on the U.S. side of the river, he chose the Mexican side. He walks too close to the line, but I couldn't let Greenwood kill him." He paused. "I hope you understand that, Mercy."

"I do now. I understand a lot that I didn't then." Her eyes darkened. "But you should have told me Greenwood was your father, Rio. I would have understood."

Against her arms, Rio's fingers tightened. "I couldn't," he answered simply. "As long as I've known, I couldn't even admit the relationship to myself, much less to you. I was afraid it would be one more strike against me." He searched her face, trying to judge her reaction. "He's a horrible man, Mercy. All his life, he's been wreaking havoc—this isn't something new, you know."

She nodded. "Sister Rosa told me about the incident when you were just a kid."

"He hated me from the beginning, and I'll always believe he had something to do with my mother's death. Why I survived the night she died, I'll never know." He shrugged his shoulders. "He's made a life out of taking advantage of everyone he could. How could I ask you to love me? With a father like that?"

She shook her head, the movement tossing her hair. "I love *you*, Rio. Do you think I really care who your father is?" She didn't wait for his answer before continuing to speak. "You don't know *my* parents. Does it matter?"

He smiled slowly, allowing his heart to lift the tiniest bit. "No." He drew the word out as though savoring the realization. "It doesn't matter—not one damn bit. The only important thing is you, you and our love."

"That's right," she said instantly, her hands warm against his chest. "And I *do* love you."

His words were husky as he gathered her into his arms and pressed his face against her fragrant hair. "I love you, too," he said, his heart swelling with emotion.

For one long moment, they let their lips and hands express it more, then a dove broke the silence, crying out from the banks of the Rio Grande. Rio pulled back at the sound and looked down into Mercy's eyes. "I've been asked to run for sheriff. What do you think?"

"Sheriff? Here?" Her eyes widened in surprise. "In *this* county?"

He threw his head back and laughed. "Is the idea that outrageous to you?"

"Well, it *is* quite a switch, you have to admit," she said. "For the past four months, I've wondered how I could fall in love with a man who broke the law for a living. Then I find out he's not *really* a criminal . . . and *now* you hit me up with this!"

"Does that mean you don't approve?"

She knit her fingers behind his neck and grinned. "If I loved you when you were a crook, I guess I could love you as a lawman."

"It would be a different kind of life," he warned. "Long hours, bad pay, dangerous work. We'd be stuck here in Ciudad for a while."

"I think I could handle it," she said. "And in case you've forgotten, I signed a contract to stay here for at least a year. Ciudad is stuck with *me.*"

"What if I ran for the position but didn't win?"

"*You* lose?" She smiled again. "I seriously doubt Sister Rosa would allow that to happen. She'd have everyone of those sisters out campaigning for you." Mercy shook her head, her blond curls moving in the breeze. "I'll support you in whatever you want to do, Rio."

He looked off into the distance for a moment and struggled to maintain his composure. No one had ever expressed that kind of trust in him. Her words made him feel anything was possible. He took a deep breath, then let his gaze return to her face.

"If you agree, then I think I'd like to try," he said quietly. "The people here need help. They need someone who can restore their faith in the system, and they need someone who understands their situation. Only someone who's been on their side of the fence for a while could do that."

"You'd bring more than that to Ciudad, Rio, and you know it. You understand their situation, yes, but you care," Mercy said, her voice tight with conviction. "You care about the people, and that's the most important thing."

He locked his gaze with hers. "What I care for most," he said quietly, "is you. Always remember that, Mercy.

You are the most important thing in the world to me. No matter what happens, no matter where we go—I'll always love you.''

Her blue eyes filled with tears, and she nodded once. ''I love you, too.''

With one accord, Mercy and Rio turned their heads toward the river, their long shadows rippling against the shallow current. What had separated them before called them together now, and in silent agreement, they twined their arms about each other and moved toward the water.

They kept going until they stood in the center of the river, the water parting and continuing around them. Like all the problems they'd faced and conquered, the river split, then melted back to one—as they had and always would. With a silent pledge of love, their eyes met and locked, then under the stars of the west Texas night, they kissed.

*   *   *   *   *

The first book in the exciting new
Fortune's Children series is

HIRED HUSBAND

by *New York Times* bestselling writer
Rebecca Brandewyne

Beginning in July 1996
Only from Silhouette Books

Here's an exciting sneak preview....

Minneapolis, Minnesota

As Caroline Fortune wheeled her dark blue Volvo into the underground parking lot of the towering, glass-and-steel structure that housed the global headquarters of Fortune Cosmetics, she glanced anxiously at her gold Piaget wristwatch. An accident on the snowy freeway had caused rush-hour traffic to be a nightmare this morning. As a result, she was running late for her 9:00 a.m. meeting—and if there was one thing her grandmother, Kate Winfield Fortune, simply couldn't abide, it was slack, unprofessional behavior on the job. And lateness was the sign of a sloppy, disorganized schedule.

Involuntarily, Caroline shuddered at the thought of her grandmother's infamous wrath being unleashed upon her. The stern rebuke would be precise, apropos, scathing and delivered with coolly raised, condemnatory eyebrows and in icy tones of haughty grandeur that had in the past reduced many an executive—even the male ones—at Fortune Cosmetics not only to obsequious apologies, but even to tears. Caroline had seen it happen on more than one occasion, although, much to her gratitude and relief, she herself was seldom a target of her grandmother's anger. And she wouldn't be this morning, either, not if she could help it. That would be a disastrous way to start out the new year.

Grabbing her Louis Vuitton totebag and her black leather portfolio from the front passenger seat, Caroline stepped gracefully from the Volvo and slammed the door. The heels of her Maud Frizon pumps clicked briskly on the concrete floor as she hurried toward the bank of elevators that would take her up into the skyscraper owned by her family. As the elevator doors slid open, she rushed down the long, plushly carpeted corridors of one of the hushed upper floors toward the conference room.

By now Caroline had her portfolio open and was leafing through it as she hastened along, reviewing her notes she had prepared for her presentation. So she didn't see Dr. Nicolai Valkov until she literally ran right into him. Like her, he had his head bent over his own portfolio, not watching where he was going. As the two of them collided, both their portfolios and the papers inside went flying. At the unexpected impact, Caroline lost her balance, stumbled, and would have fallen had not Nick's strong, sure hands abruptly shot out, grabbing hold of her and pulling her to him to steady her. She gasped, startled and stricken, as she came up hard against his broad chest, lean hips and corded thighs, her face just inches from his own—as though they were lovers about to kiss.

Caroline had never been so close to Nick Valkov before, and, in that instant, she was acutely aware of him—not just as a fellow employee of Fortune Cosmetics but also as a man. Of how tall and ruggedly handsome he was, dressed in an elegant, pin-striped black suit cut in the European fashion, a crisp white shirt, a foulard tie and a pair of Cole Haan loafers. Of how dark his thick, glossy hair and his deep-set eyes framed by raven-wing brows were—so dark that they were almost black, despite the bright, fluorescent lights that blazed overhead. Of the whiteness of his straight teeth against his bronzed skin as a brazen, mocking grin slowly curved his wide, sensual mouth.

"Actually, I *was* hoping for a sweet roll this morning—but I daresay you would prove even tastier, Ms. Fortune," Nick drawled impertinently, his low, silky voice tinged with a faint accent born of the fact that Russian, not English, was his native language.

At his words, Caroline flushed painfully, embarrassed and annoyed. If there was one person she always attempted to avoid at Fortune Cosmetics, it was Nick Valkov. Following the breakup of the Soviet Union, he had emigrated to the United States, where her grandmother had hired him to direct the company's research and development department. Since that time, Nick had constantly demonstrated marked, traditional, Old World tendencies that had led Caroline to believe he not only had no use for equal rights but also would actually have been more than happy to turn back the clock several centuries where females were concerned. She thought his remark was typical of his attitude toward women: insolent, arrogant and domineering. Really, the man was simply insufferable!

Caroline couldn't imagine what had ever prompted her grandmother to hire him—and at a highly generous salary, too—except that Nick Valkov was considered one of the foremost chemists anywhere on the planet. Deep down inside Caroline knew that no matter how he behaved, Fortune Cosmetics was extremely lucky to have him. Still, that didn't give him the right to manhandle and insult her!

"I assure you that you would find me more bitter than a cup of the strongest black coffee, Dr. Valkov," she insisted, attempting without success to free her trembling body from his steely grip, while he continued to hold her so near that she could feel his heart beating steadily in his chest—and knew he must be equally able to feel the erratic hammering of her own.

"Oh, I'm willing to wager there's more sugar and cream to you than you let on, Ms. Fortune." To her utter mortification and outrage, she felt one of Nick's hands slide insidiously up her back and nape to her luxuriant mass of sable hair, done up in a stylish French twist.

"You know so much about fashion," he murmured, eyeing her assessingly, pointedly ignoring her indignation and efforts to escape from him. "So why do you always wear your hair like this...so tightly wrapped and severe? I've never seen it down. Still, that's the way it needs to be worn, you know...soft, loose, tangled about your face. As it is, your hair fairly cries out for a man to take the pins from it, so he can see how long it is. Does it fall past your shoulders?" He quirked one eyebrow inquisitively, a mocking half smile still twisting his lips, letting her know he was enjoying her obvious discomfiture. "You aren't going to tell me, are you? What a pity. Because my guess is that it does—and I'd like to know if I'm right. And these glasses." He indicated the large, square, tortoiseshell frames perched on her slender, classic nose. "I think you use them to hide behind more than you do to see. I'll bet you don't actually even need them at all."

Caroline felt the blush that had yet to leave her cheeks deepen, its heat seeming to spread throughout her entire quivering body. Damn the man! Why must he be so infuriatingly perceptive?

Because everything that Nick suspected was true.

* * * * *

To read more, don't miss
HIRED HUSBAND
by Rebecca Brandewyne,
Book One in the new
FORTUNE'S CHILDREN series,
beginning this month and available only from
Silhouette Books!

FORTUNE'S Children™

New York Times Bestselling Author

REBECCA BRANDEWYNE

Launches a new twelve-book series—FORTUNE'S CHILDREN
beginning in July 1996 with Book One

Hired Husband

Caroline Fortune knew her marriage to Nick Valkov was in
name only. She would help save the family business, Nick
would get a green card, and a paper marriage would suit both
of them. Until Caroline could no longer deny the feelings Nick
stirred in her and the practical union turned passionate.

MEET THE FORTUNES—a family whose legacy is greater than
riches. Because where there's a will...there's a wedding!

Look for Book Two, *The Millionaire and the Cowgirl*,
by Lisa Jackson. Available in August 1996 wherever Silhouette
books are sold.

Look us up on-line at: http://www.romance.net

FC-1

MILLION DOLLAR SWEEPSTAKES

SWP-M96

You're About to Become a *Privileged Woman*

Reap the rewards of fabulous free gifts and benefits with proofs-of-purchase from Silhouette and Harlequin books

Pages & Privileges™

It's our way of thanking you for buying our books at your favorite retail stores.

PROOF OF PURCHASE
Offer expires October 31, 1996

SIM-PP155

Pages & Privileges™

**Harlequin and Silhouette—
the most privileged readers in the world!**

For more information about Harlequin and Silhouette's PAGES & PRIVILEGES program call the Pages & Privileges Benefits Desk: 1-503-794-2499

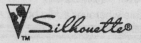

Silhouette®

SIM-PP155